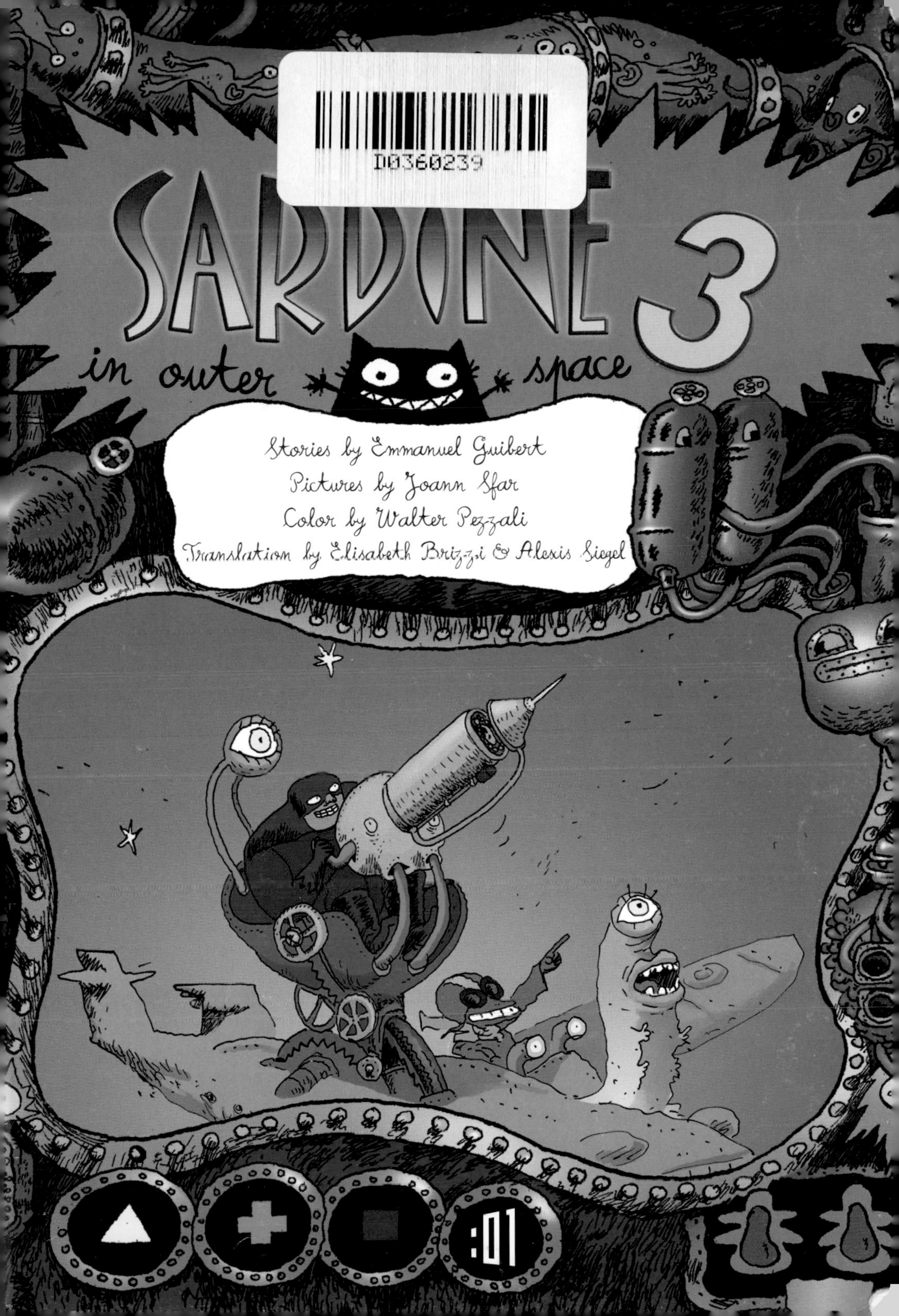
SARDINE 3
in outer space
Stories by Emmanuel Guibert
Pictures by Joann Sfar
Color by Walter Pezzali
Translation by Elisabeth Brizzi & Alexis Siegel
:01

Contents

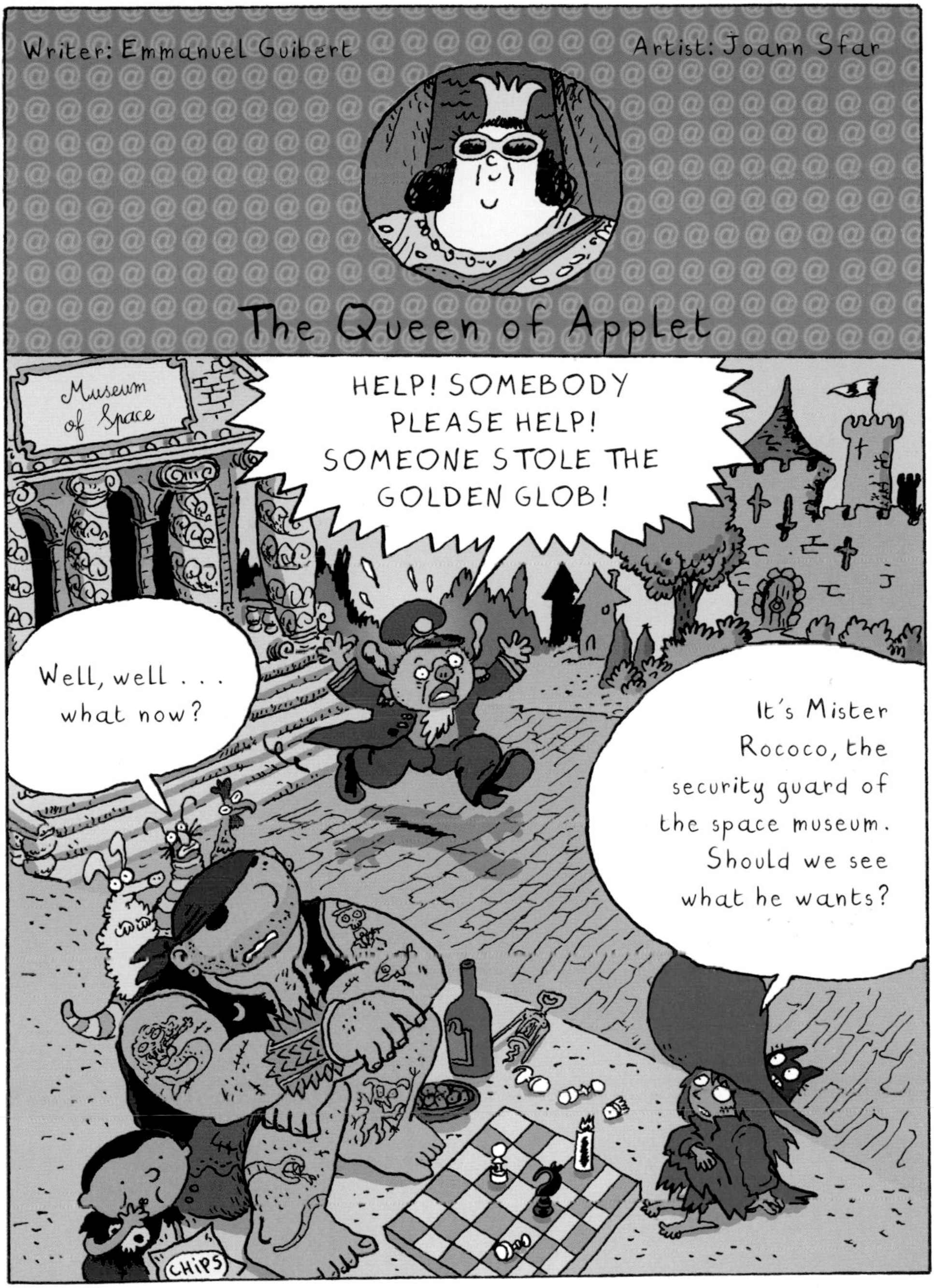

Writer: Emmanuel Guibert
Artist: Joann Sfar
The Queen of Applet
Museum of Space
HELP! SOMEBODY PLEASE HELP! SOMEONE STOLE THE GOLDEN GLOB!
Well, well . . . what now?
It's Mister Rococo, the security guard of the space museum. Should we see what he wants?
CHIPS

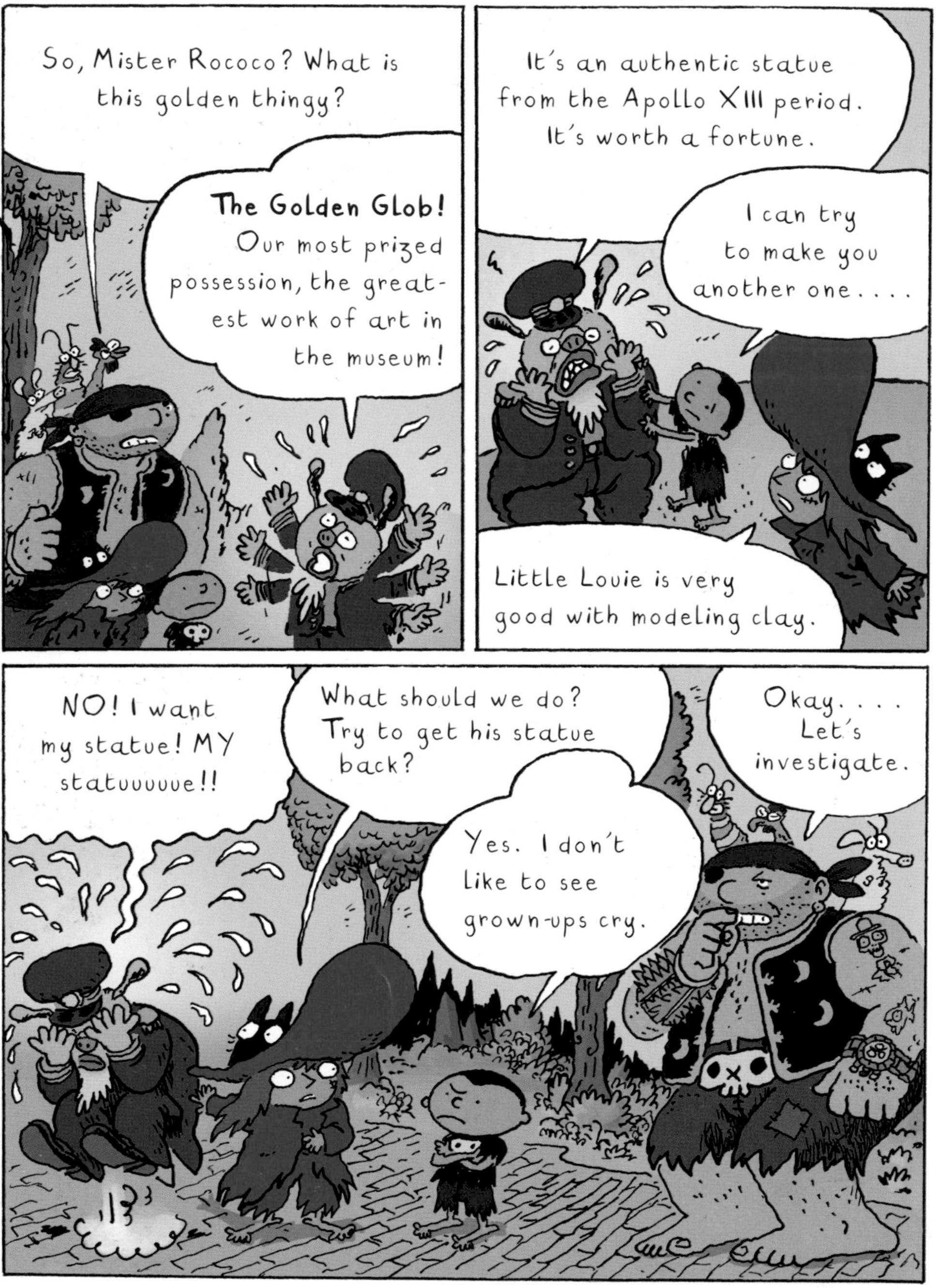
So, Mister Rococo? What is this golden thingy?
The Golden Glob! Our most prized possession, the greatest work of art in the museum!
It's an authentic statue from the Apollo XIII period. It's worth a fortune.
I can try to make you another one....
Little Louie is very good with modeling clay.
NO! I want my statue! MY statuuuuue!!
What should we do? Try to get his statue back?
Yes. I don't like to see grown-ups cry.
Okay.... Let's investigate.

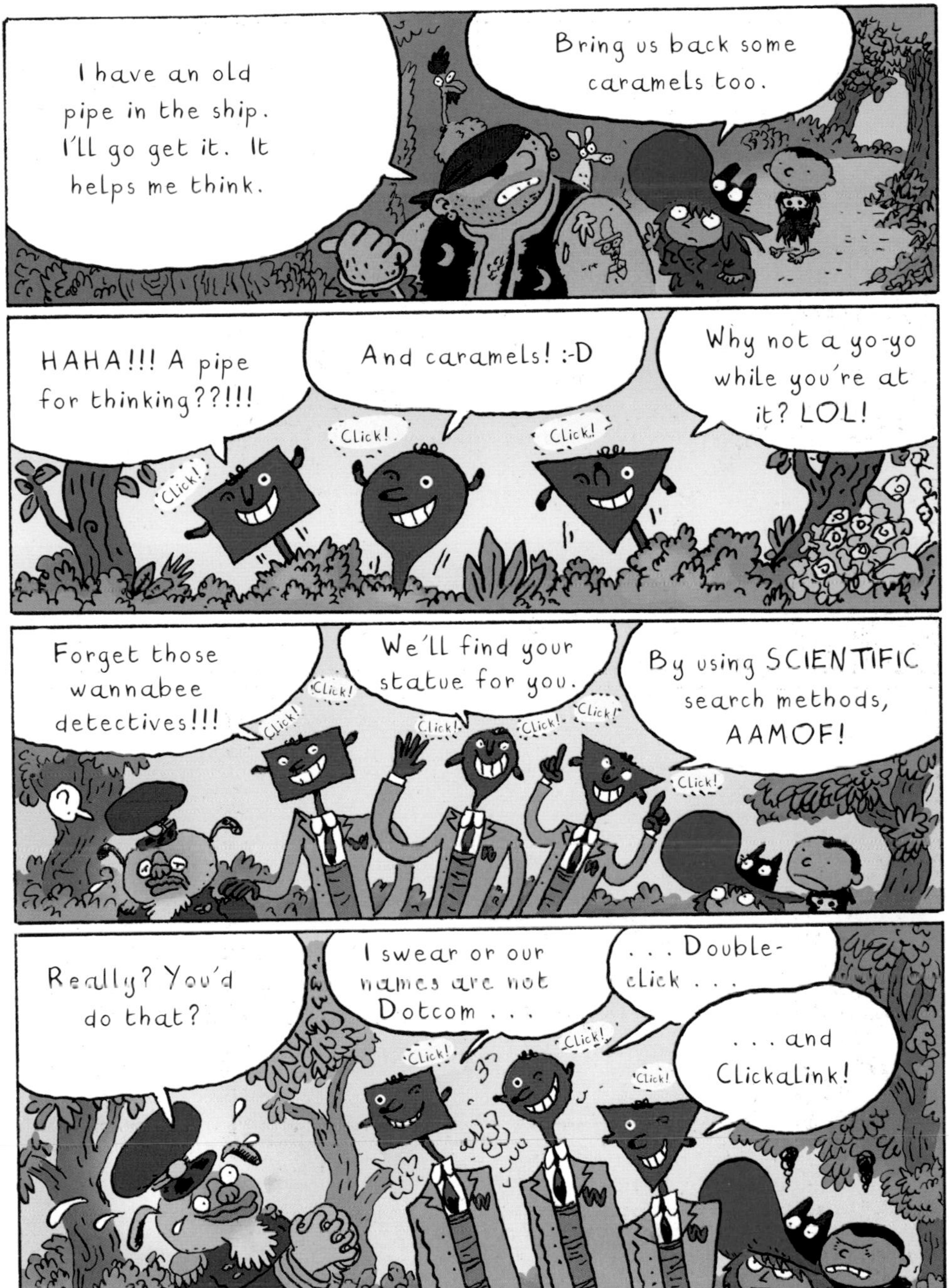

I have an old pipe in the ship. I'll go get it. It helps me think.
Bring us back some caramels too.
HAHA!!! A pipe for thinking??!!!
Click!
And caramels! :-D
Click!
Click!
Why not a yo-yo while you're at it? LOL!
Forget those wannabee detectives!!!
Click!
Click!
We'll find your statue for you.
Click!
Click!
Click!
By using SCIENTIFIC search methods, AAMOF!
Click!
Really? You'd do that?
I swear or our names are not Dotcom . . .
Click!
Click!
. . . Double-click . . .
Click!
. . . and Clickalink!

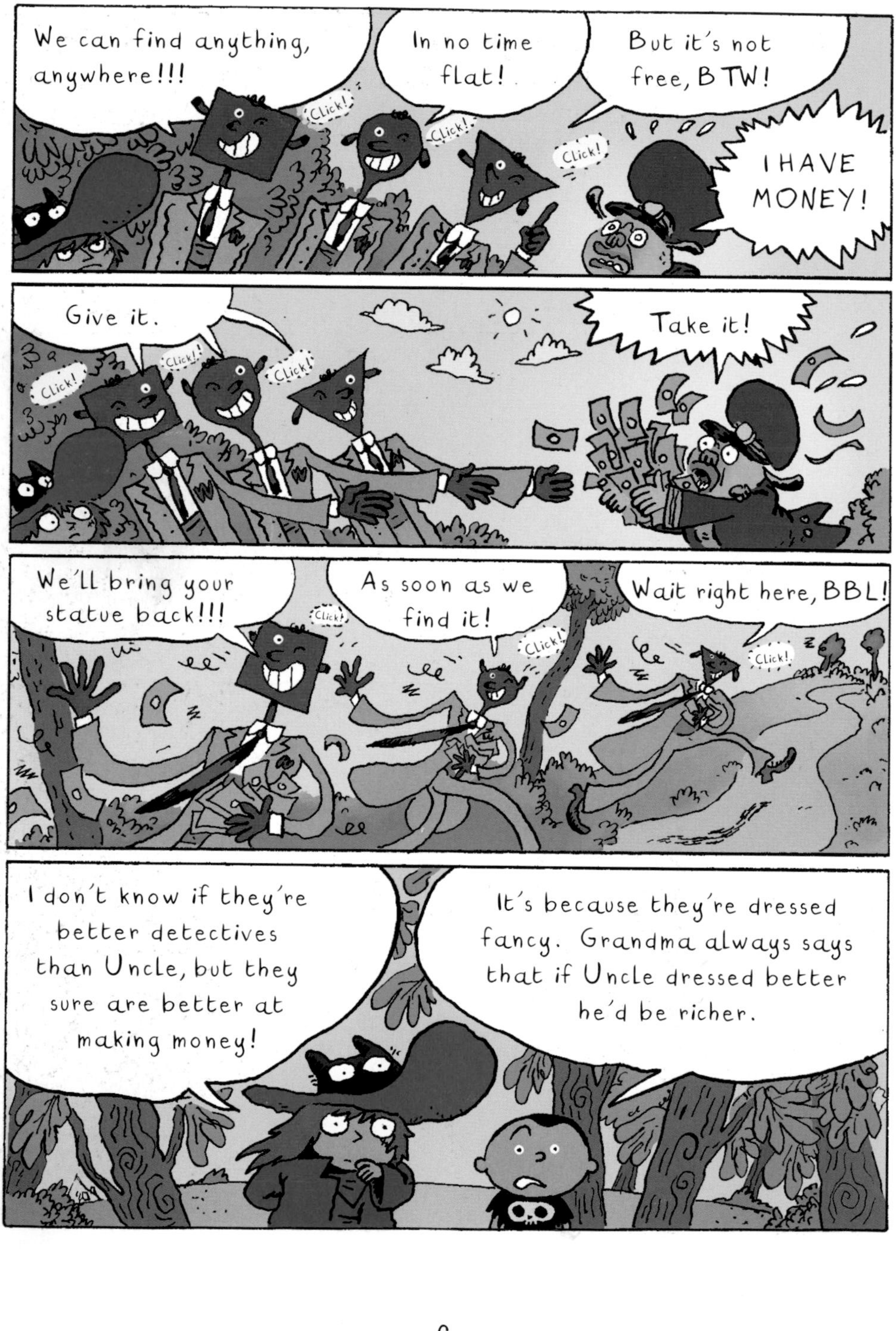
We can find anything, anywhere!!!
In no time flat!
But it's not free, BTW!
I HAVE MONEY!
Give it.
Take it!
We'll bring your statue back!!!
As soon as we find it!
Wait right here, BBL!
I don't know if they're better detectives than Uncle, but they sure are better at making money!
It's because they're dressed fancy. Grandma always says that if Uncle dressed better he'd be richer.

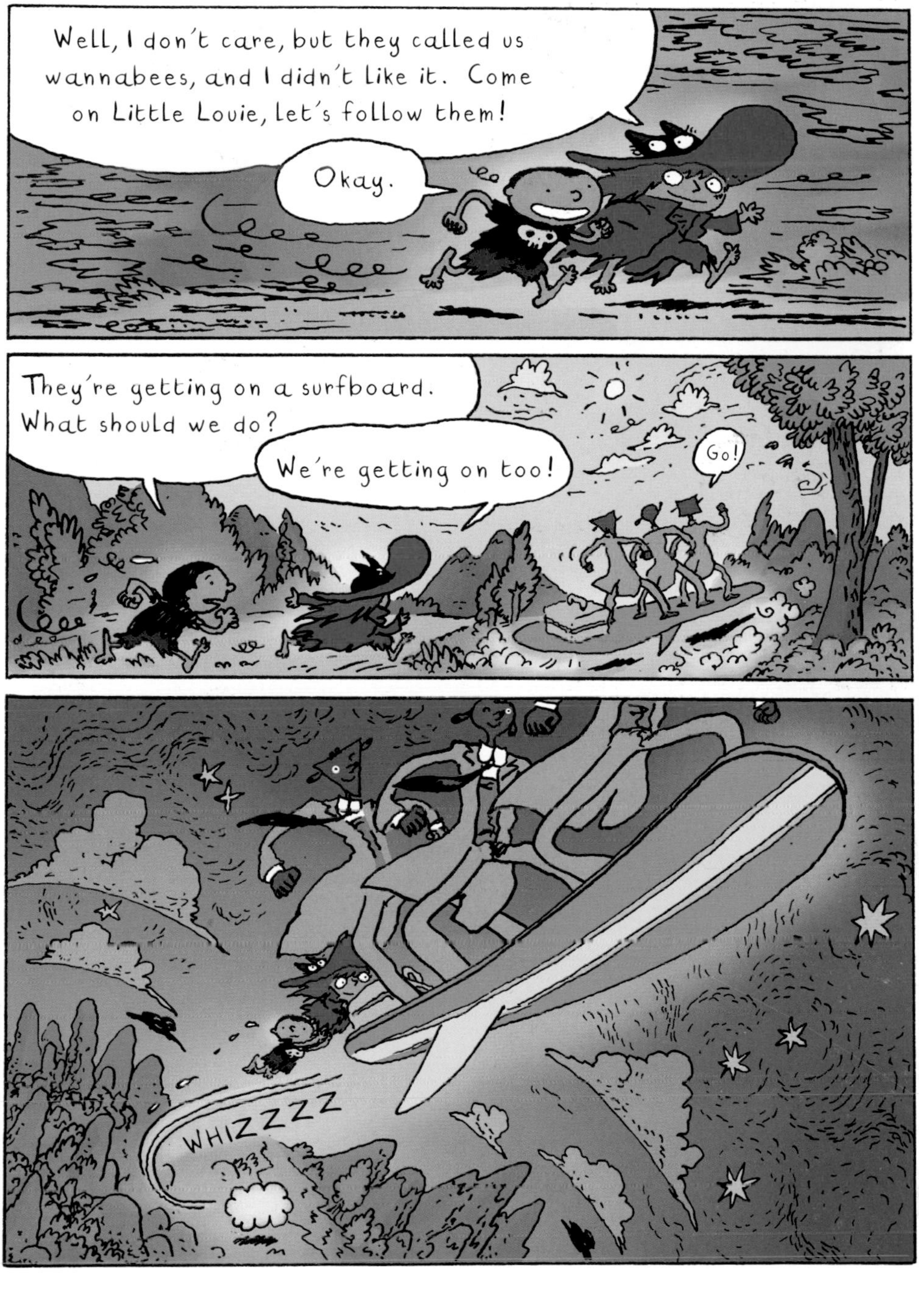
Well, I don't care, but they called us wannabees, and I didn't like it. Come on Little Louie, let's follow them!
Okay.
They're getting on a surfboard. What should we do?
We're getting on too!
Go!
WHIZZZZ

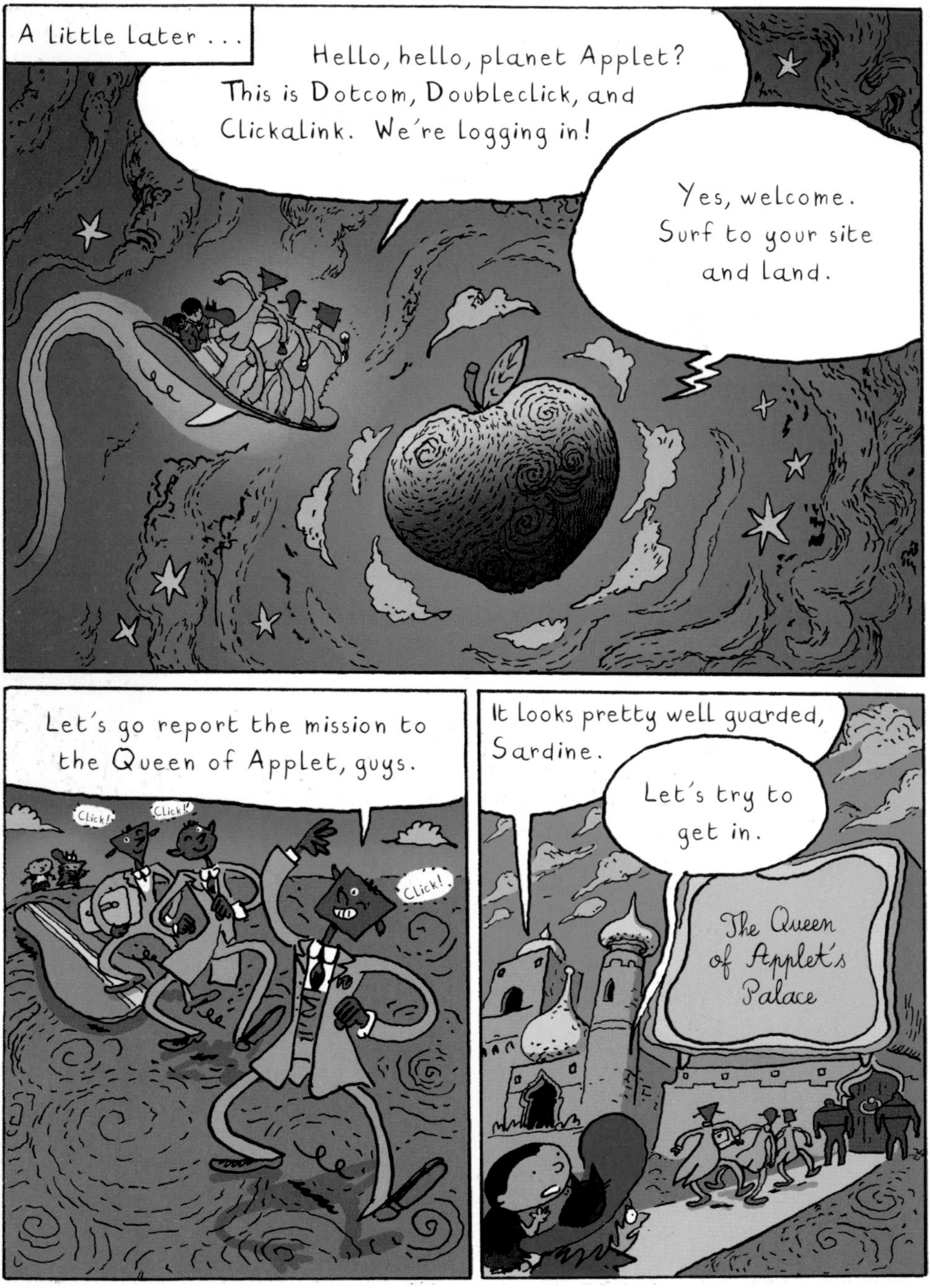
A little later . . .
Hello, hello, planet Applet? This is Dotcom, Doubleclick, and Clickalink. We're logging in!
Yes, welcome. Surf to your site and land.
Let's go report the mission to the Queen of Applet, guys.
Click!
Click!
Click!
It looks pretty well guarded, Sardine.
Let's try to get in.
The Queen of Applet's Palace

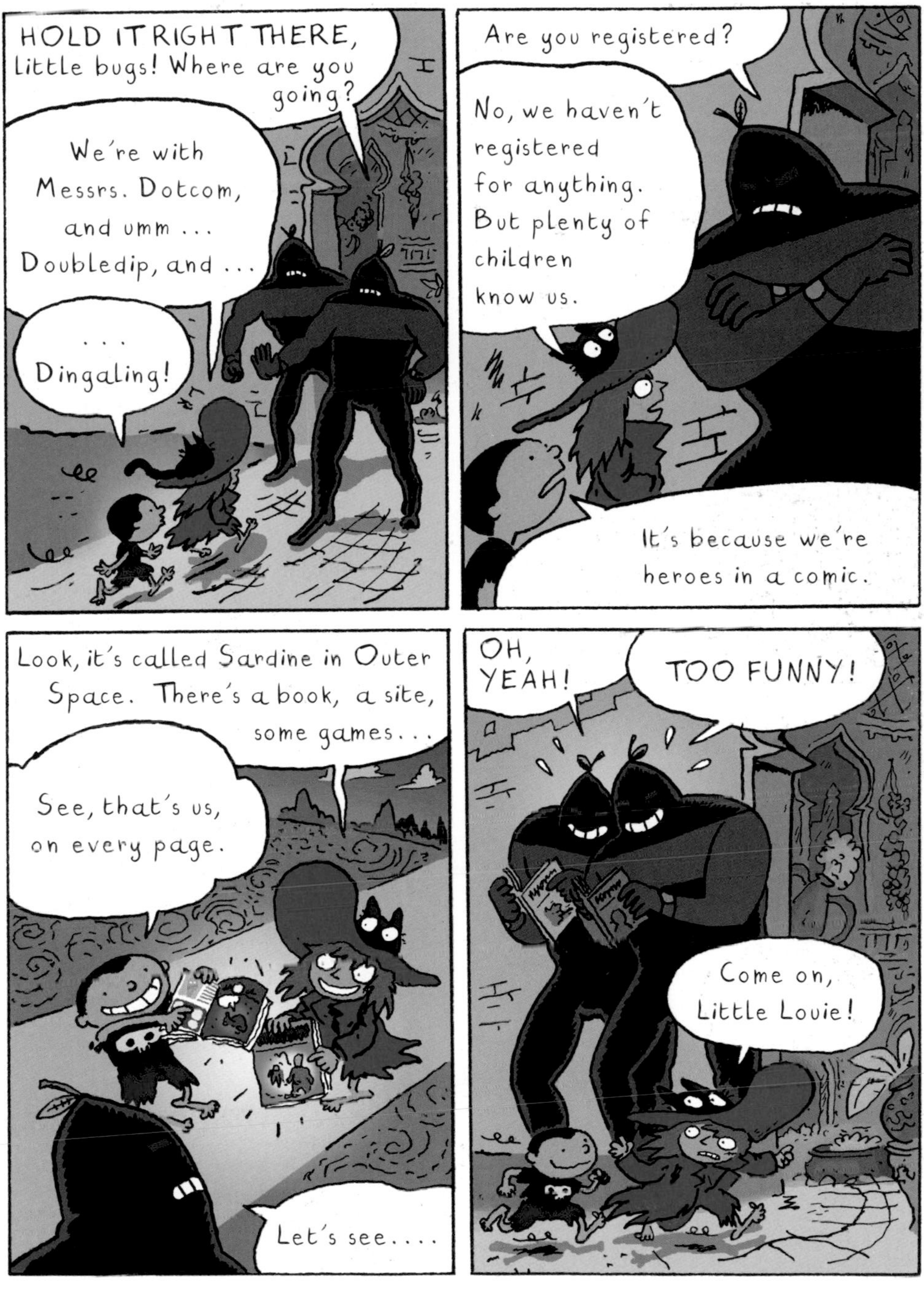

HOLD IT RIGHT THERE, Little bugs! Where are you going?
We're with Messrs. Dotcom, and umm ... Doubledip, and ...
... Dingaling!
Are you registered?
No, we haven't registered for anything. But plenty of children know us.
It's because we're heroes in a comic.
Look, it's called Sardine in Outer Space. There's a book, a site, some games...
See, that's us, on every page.
Let's see....
OH, YEAH!
TOO FUNNY!
Come on, Little Louie!

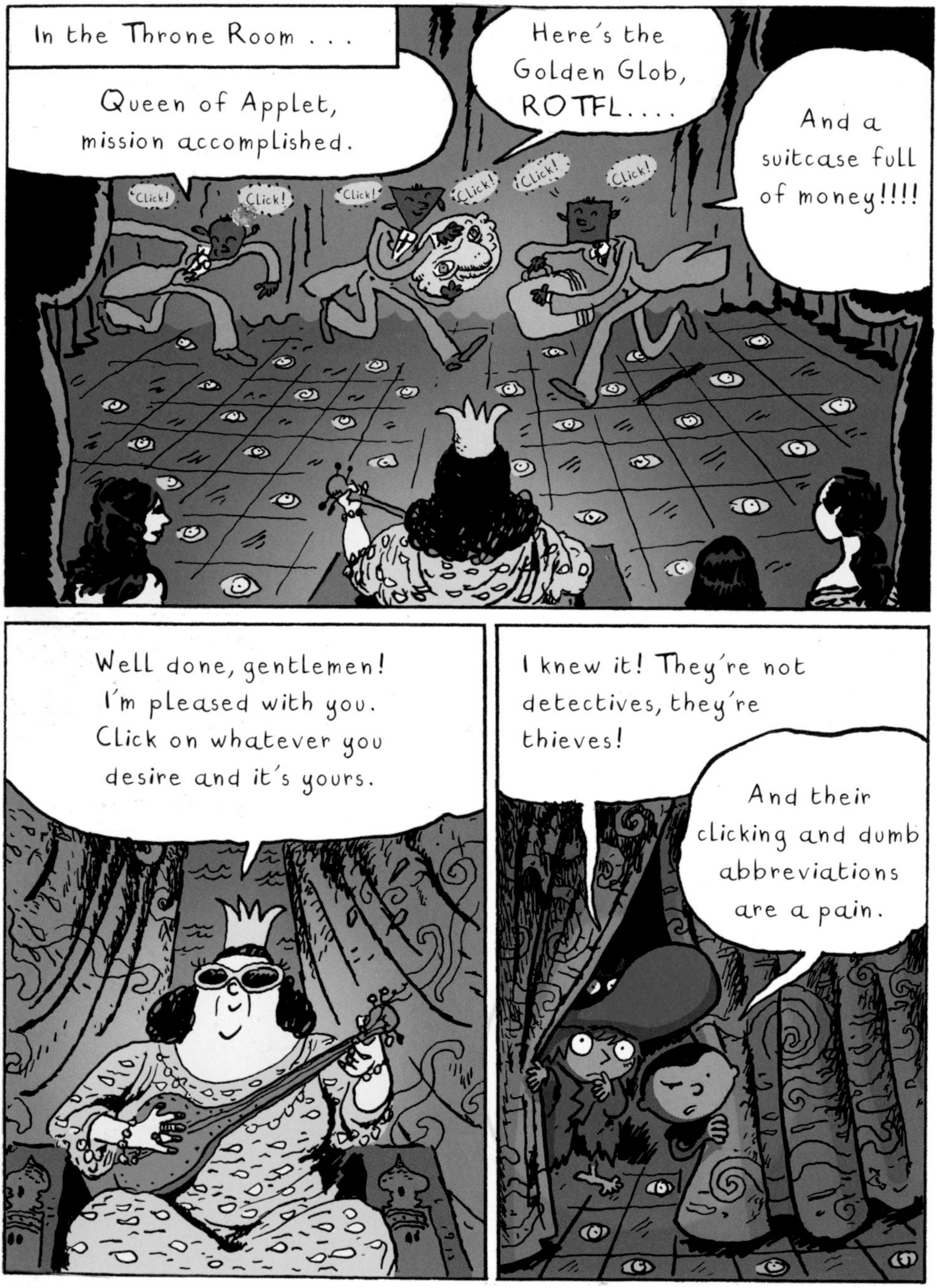
In the Throne Room . . .
Queen of Applet, mission accomplished.
Click!
Click!
Click!
Click!
Click!
Click!
Here's the Golden Glob, ROTFL. . . .
And a suitcase full of money!!!!
Well done, gentlemen! I'm pleased with you. Click on whatever you desire and it's yours.
I knew it! They're not detectives, they're thieves!
And their clicking and dumb abbreviations are a pain.

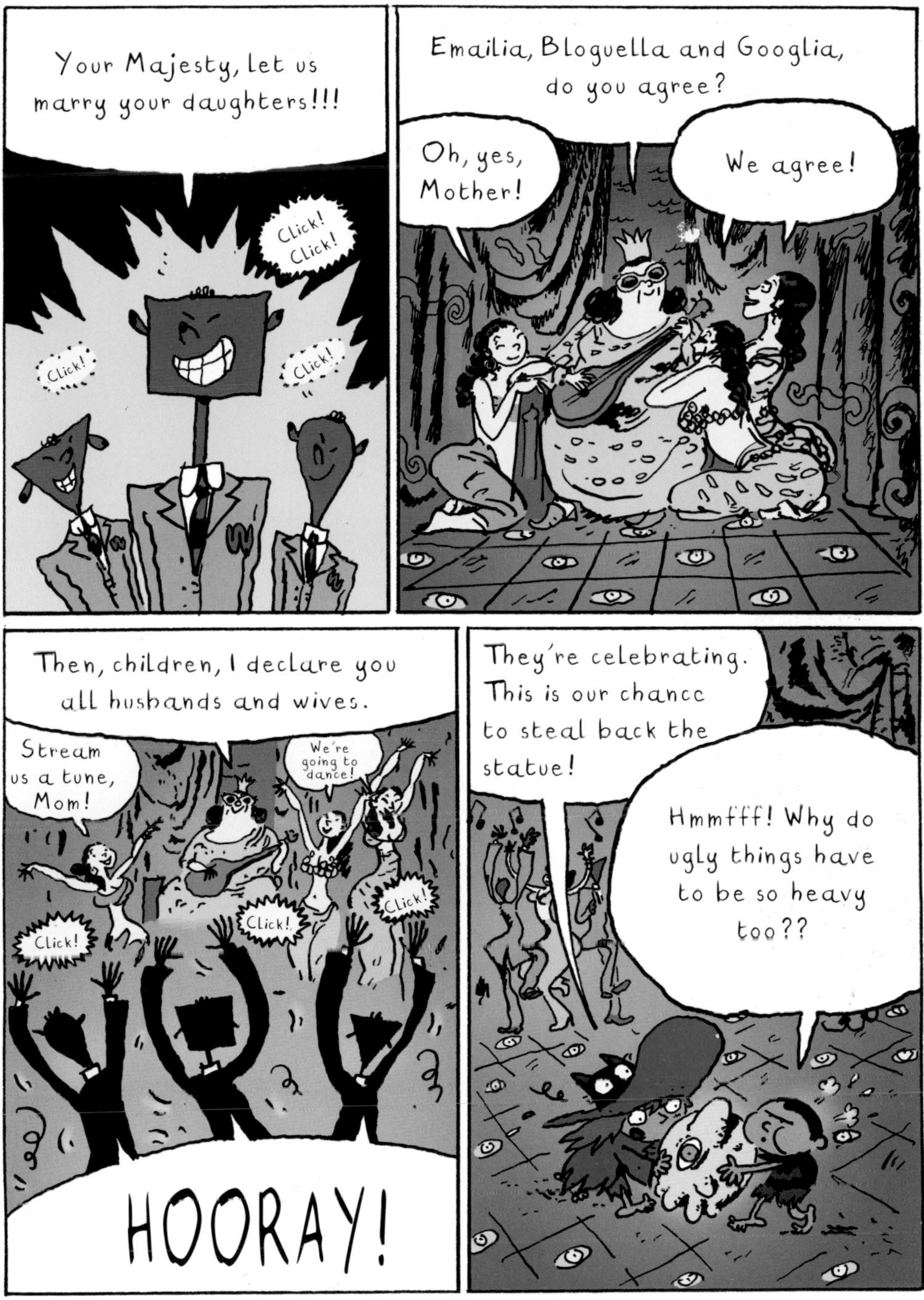
Your Majesty, let us marry your daughters!!!
Click! Click!
Click!
Click!
Emailia, Bloguella and Googlia, do you agree?
Oh, yes, Mother!
We agree!
Then, children, I declare you all husbands and wives.
Stream us a tune, Mom!
We're going to dance!
Click!
Click!
Click!
HOORAY!
They're celebrating. This is our chance to steal back the statue!
Hmmfff! Why do ugly things have to be so heavy too??

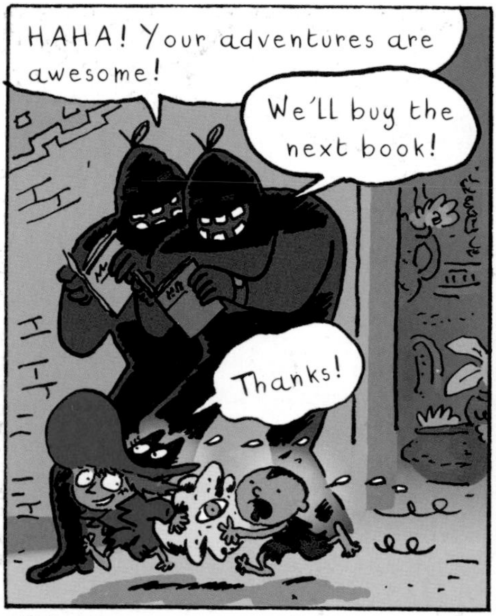
HAHA! Your adventures are awesome!
We'll buy the next book!
Thanks!

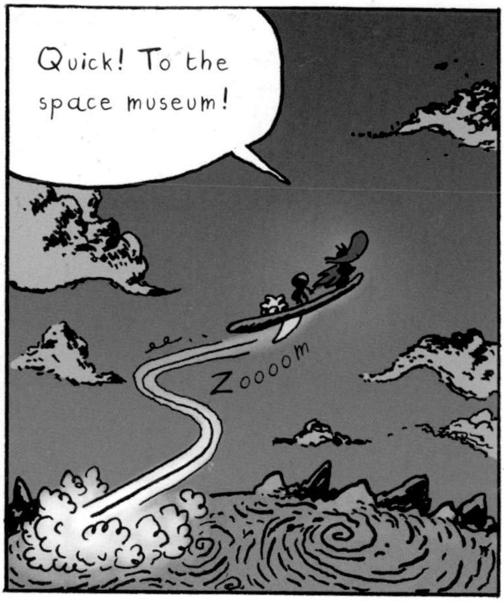
Quick! To the space museum!
Zooooom

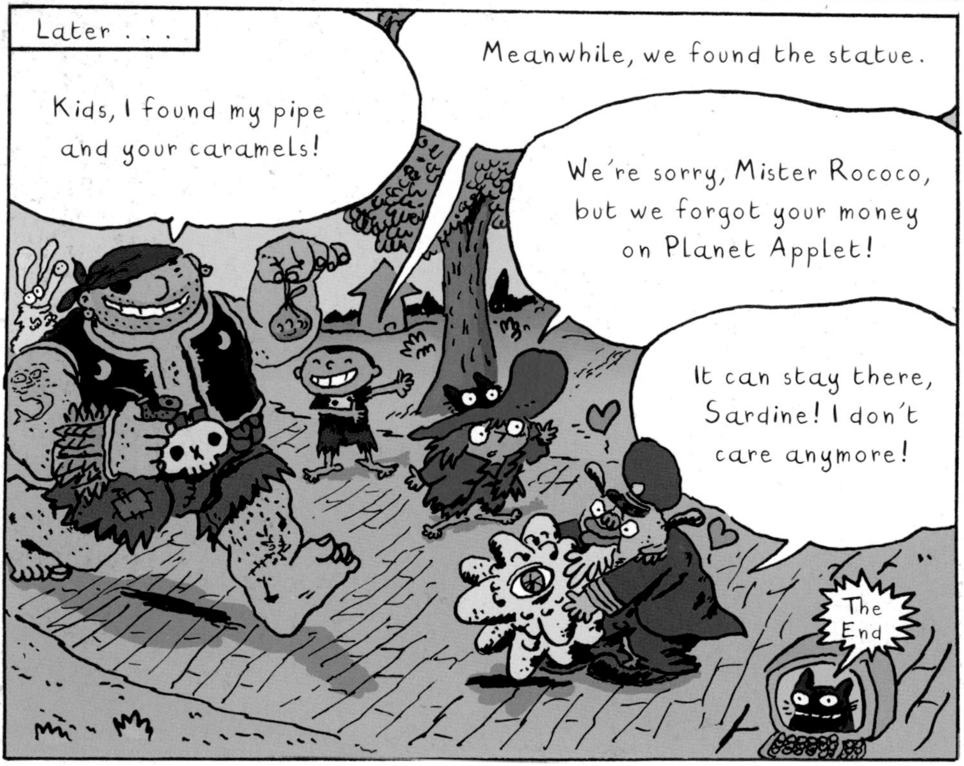
Later . . .
Kids, I found my pipe and your caramels!
Meanwhile, we found the statue.
We're sorry, Mister Rococo, but we forgot your money on Planet Applet!
It can stay there, Sardine! I don't care anymore!
The End

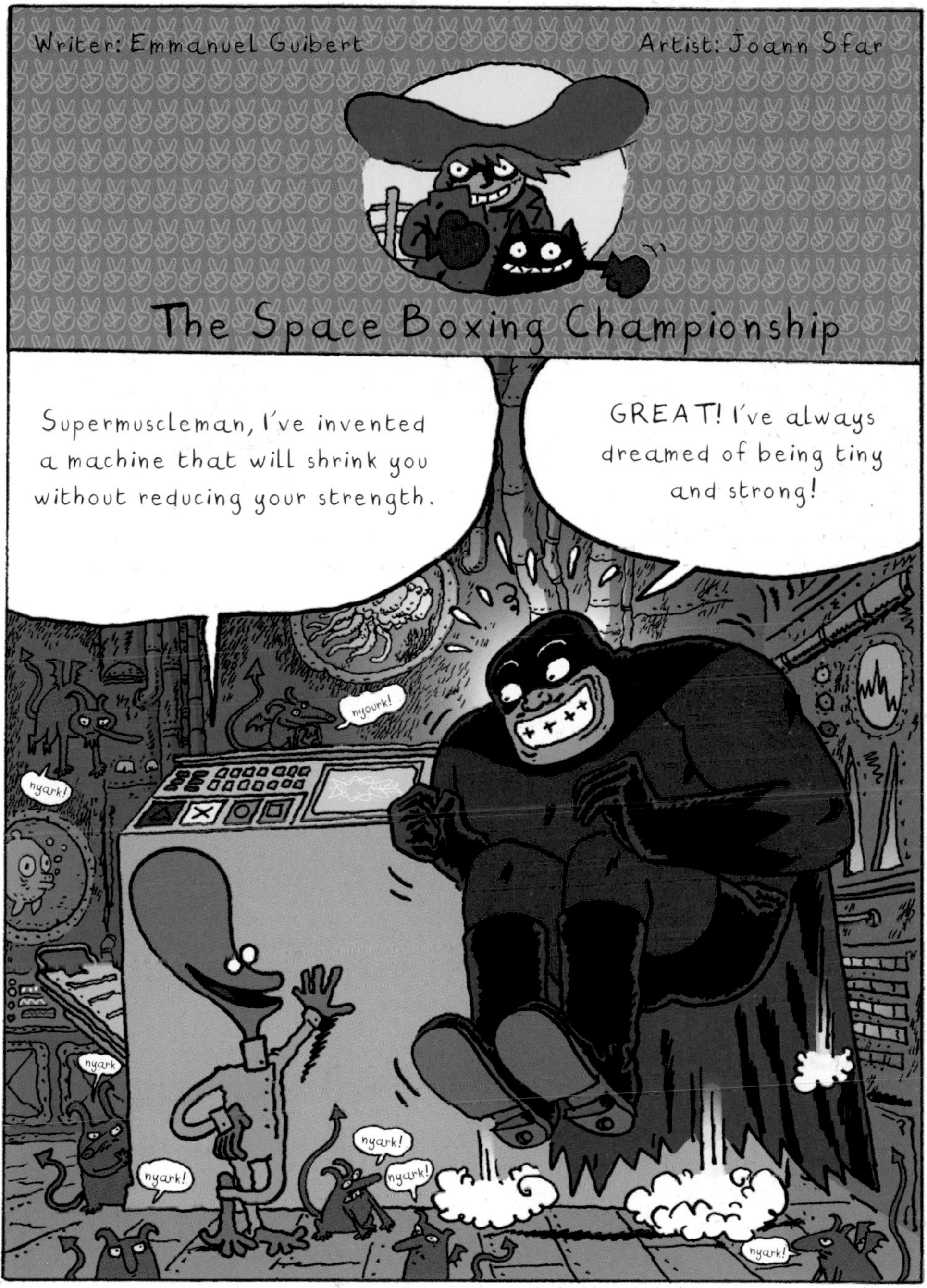
Writer: Emmanuel Guibert
Artist: Joann Sfar
The Space Boxing Championship
Supermuscleman, I've invented a machine that will shrink you without reducing your strength.
GREAT! I've always dreamed of being tiny and strong!
nyourk!
nyark!
nyark
nyark!
nyark!
nyark!
nyark!

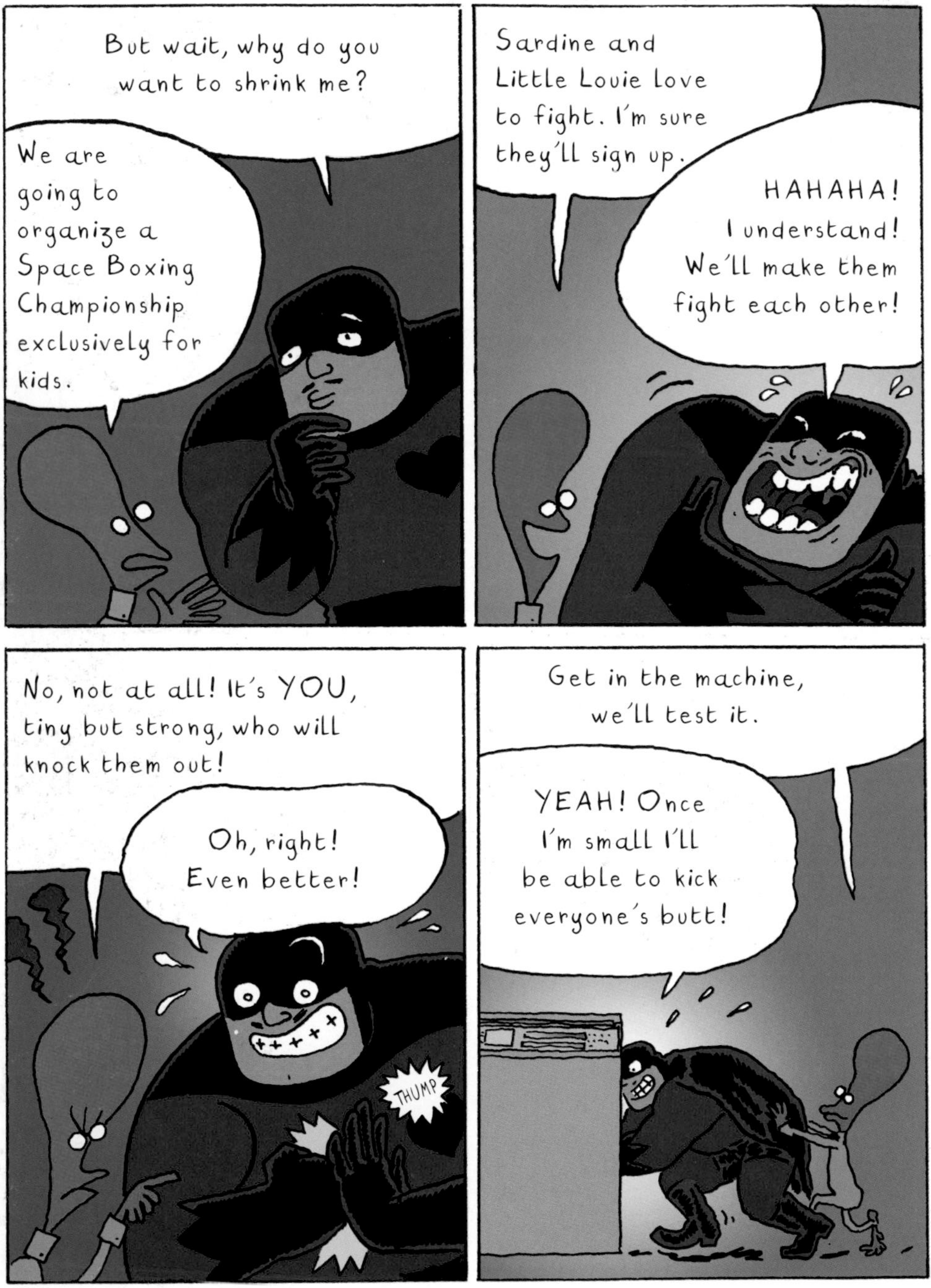
But wait, why do you want to shrink me?
We are going to organize a Space Boxing Championship exclusively for kids.
Sardine and Little Louie love to fight. I'm sure they'll sign up.
HAHAHA! I understand! We'll make them fight each other!
No, not at all! It's YOU, tiny but strong, who will knock them out!
Oh, right! Even better!
THUMP
Get in the machine, we'll test it.
YEAH! Once I'm small I'll be able to kick everyone's butt!

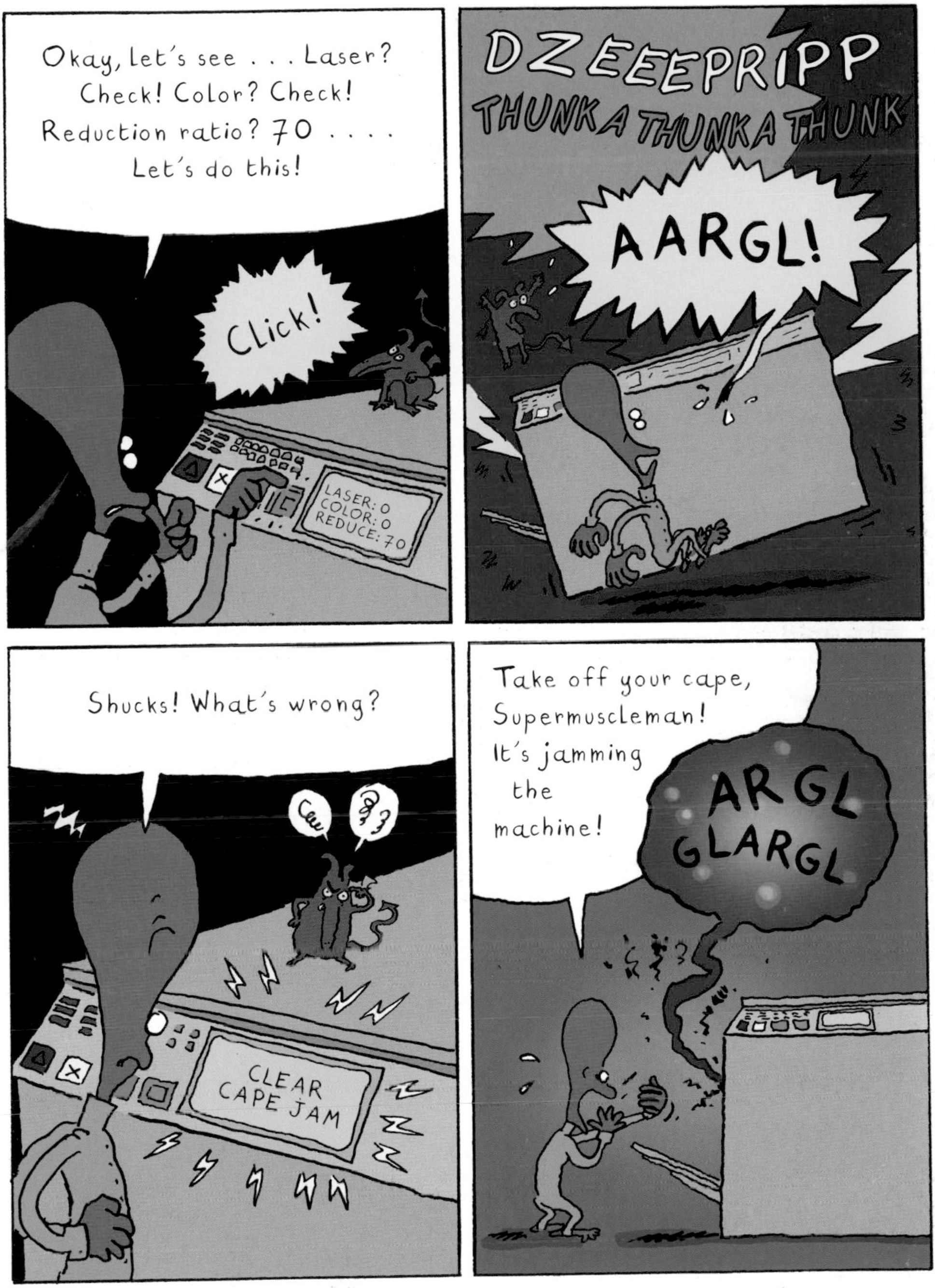

Okay, let's see . . . Laser? Check! Color? Check! Reduction ratio? 70 . . . . Let's do this!
Click!
LASER: 0
COLOR: 0
REDUCE: 70
DZEEEEPRIPP
THUNKA THUNKA THUNK
AARGL!
Shucks! What's wrong?
CLEAR CAPE JAM
Take off your cape, Supermuscleman! It's jamming the machine!
ARGL GLARGL

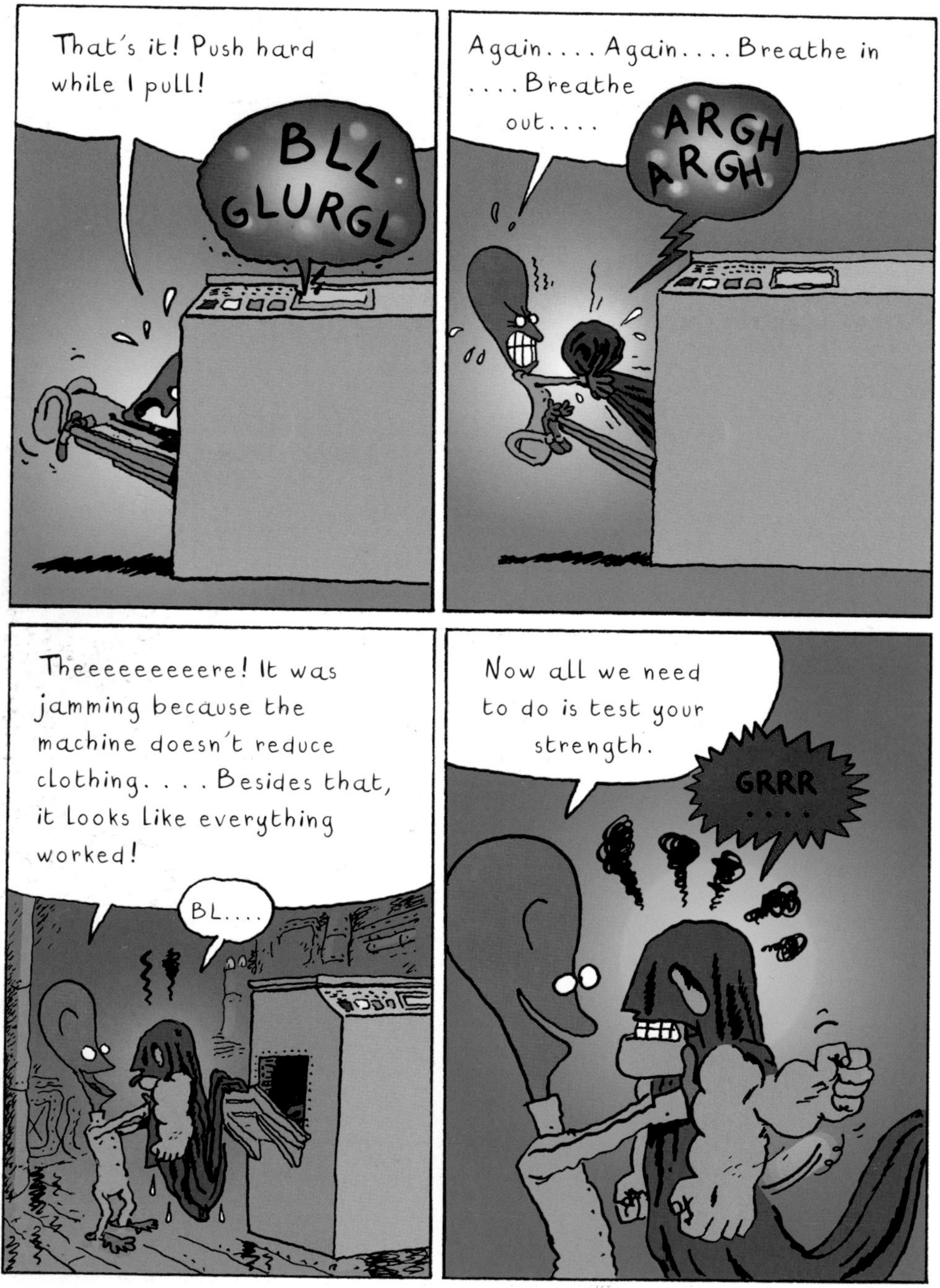
That's it! Push hard while I pull!
BLL GLURGL
Again.... Again.... Breathe in .... Breathe out....
ARGH ARGH
Theeeeeeeeere! It was jamming because the machine doesn't reduce clothing. . . . Besides that, it looks like everything worked!
BL....
Now all we need to do is test your strength.
GRRR ....

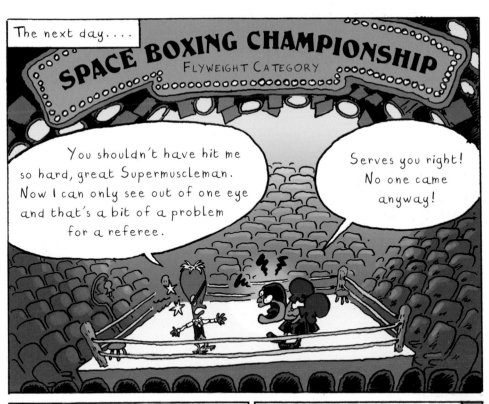

The next day....

SPACE BOXING CHAMPIONSHIP
FLYWEIGHT CATEGORY

You shouldn't have hit me so hard, great Supermuscleman. Now I can only see out of one eye and that's a bit of a problem for a referee.

Serves you right! No one came anyway!

No kids showed up! It's a total failure!

I don't understand ...maybe their moms and dads wouldn't let them....

Umm.... Excuse us, is this the boxing day care?

17

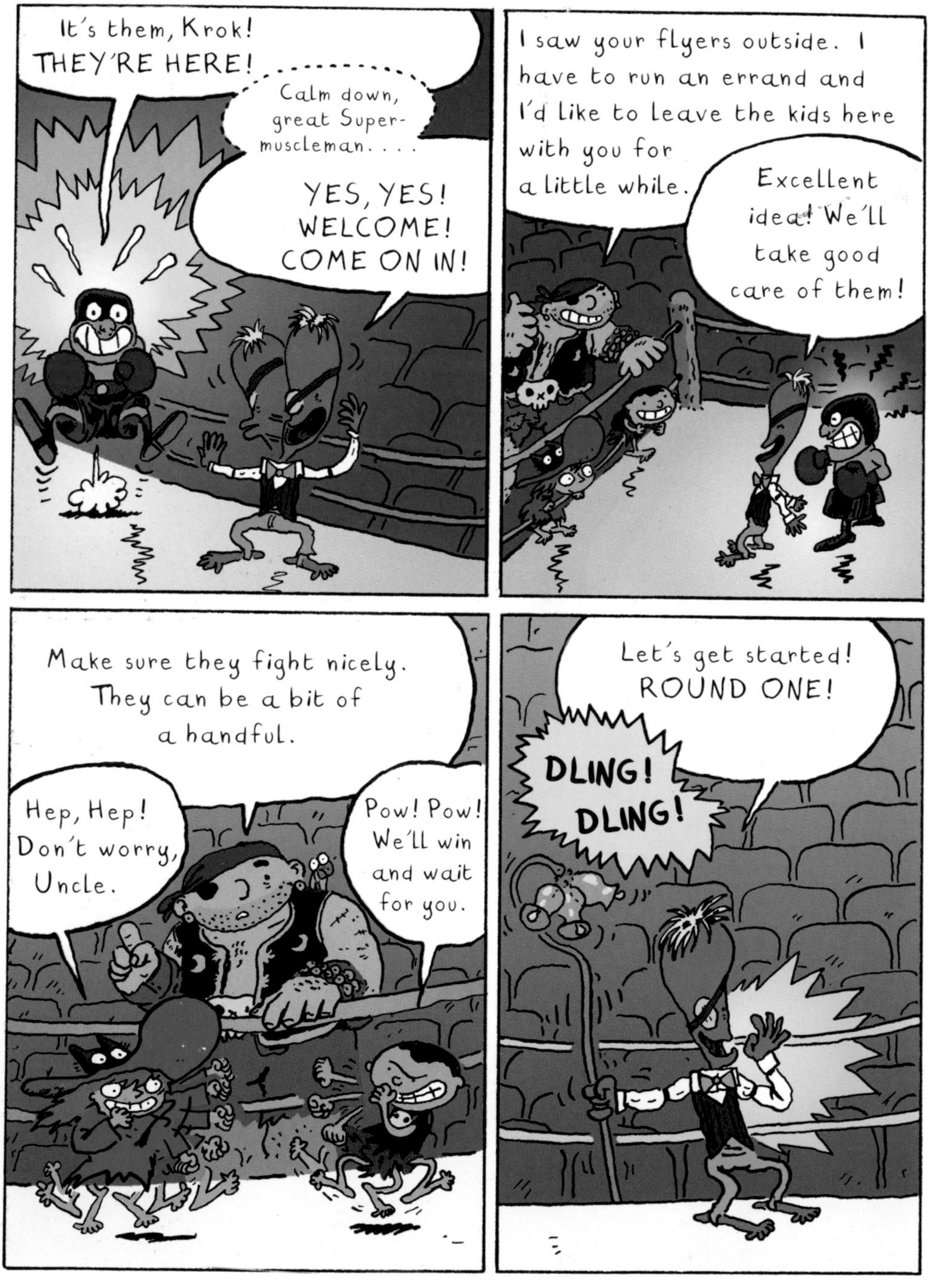
It's them, Krok! THEY'RE HERE!
Calm down, great Super-muscleman. . . .
YES, YES! WELCOME! COME ON IN!
I saw your flyers outside. I have to run an errand and I'd like to leave the kids here with you for a little while.
Excellent idea! We'll take good care of them!
Make sure they fight nicely. They can be a bit of a handful.
Hep, Hep! Don't worry, Uncle.
Pow! Pow! We'll win and wait for you.
Let's get started! ROUND ONE!
DLING! DLING!

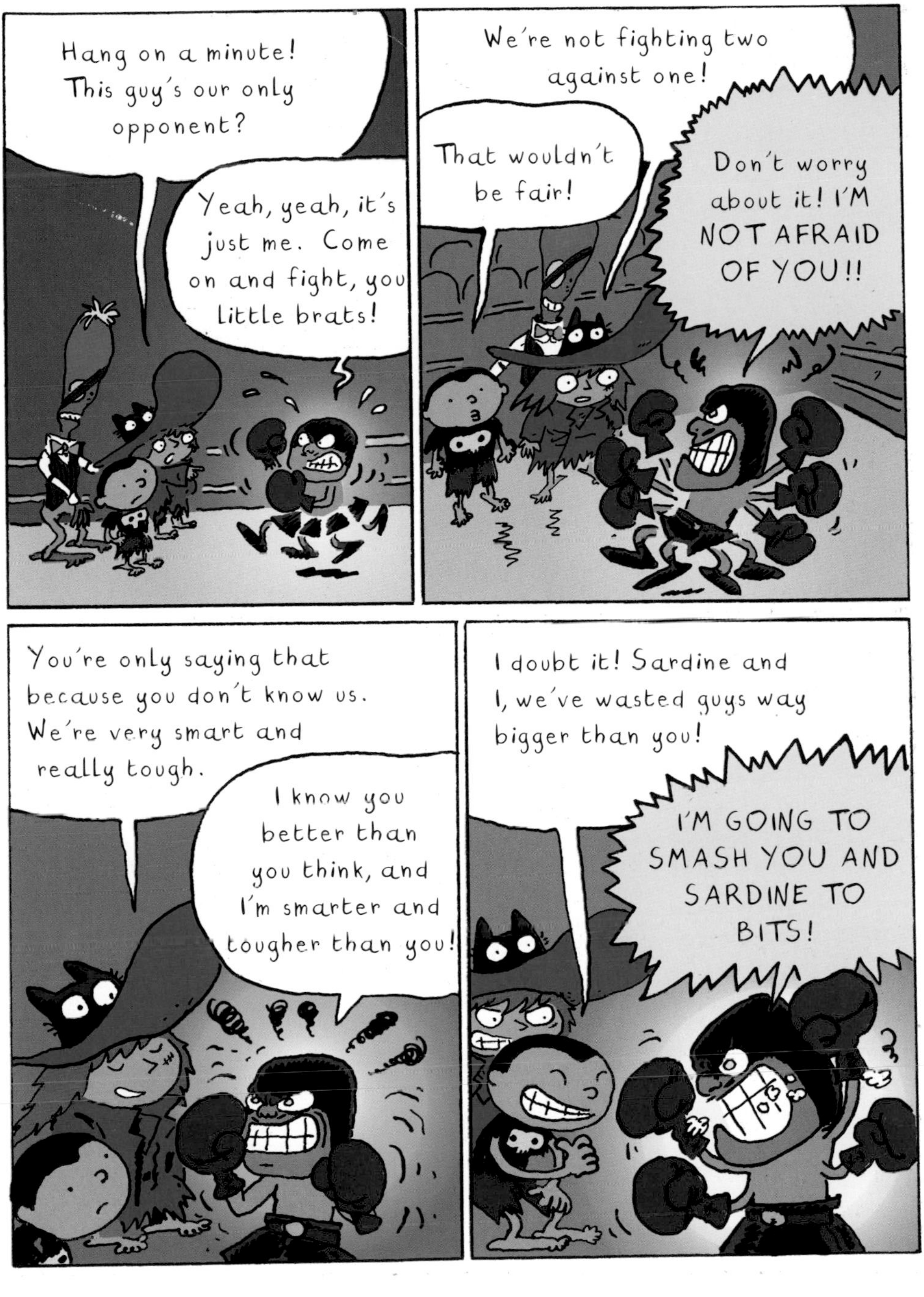
Hang on a minute! This guy's our only opponent?
Yeah, yeah, it's just me. Come on and fight, you little brats!
We're not fighting two against one!
That wouldn't be fair!
Don't worry about it! I'M NOT AFRAID OF YOU!!
You're only saying that because you don't know us. We're very smart and really tough.
I know you better than you think, and I'm smarter and tougher than you!
I doubt it! Sardine and I, we've wasted guys way bigger than you!
I'M GOING TO SMASH YOU AND SARDINE TO BITS!

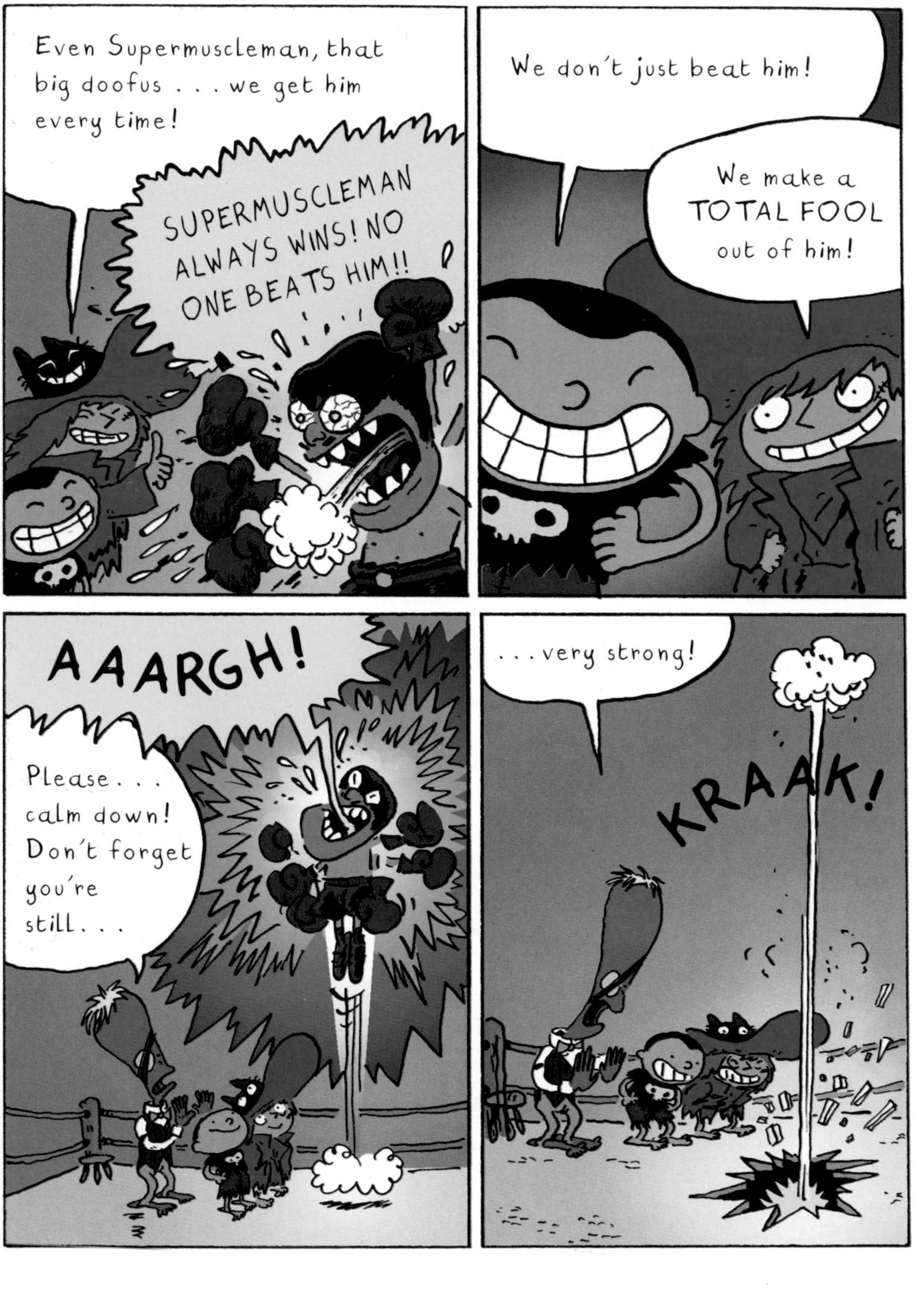
Even Supermuscleman, that big doofus . . . we get him every time!
SUPERMUSCLEMAN ALWAYS WINS! NO ONE BEATS HIM!!
We don't just beat him!
We make a TOTAL FOOL out of him!
AAARGH!
Please . . . calm down! Don't forget you're still . . .
. . . very strong!
KRAAK!

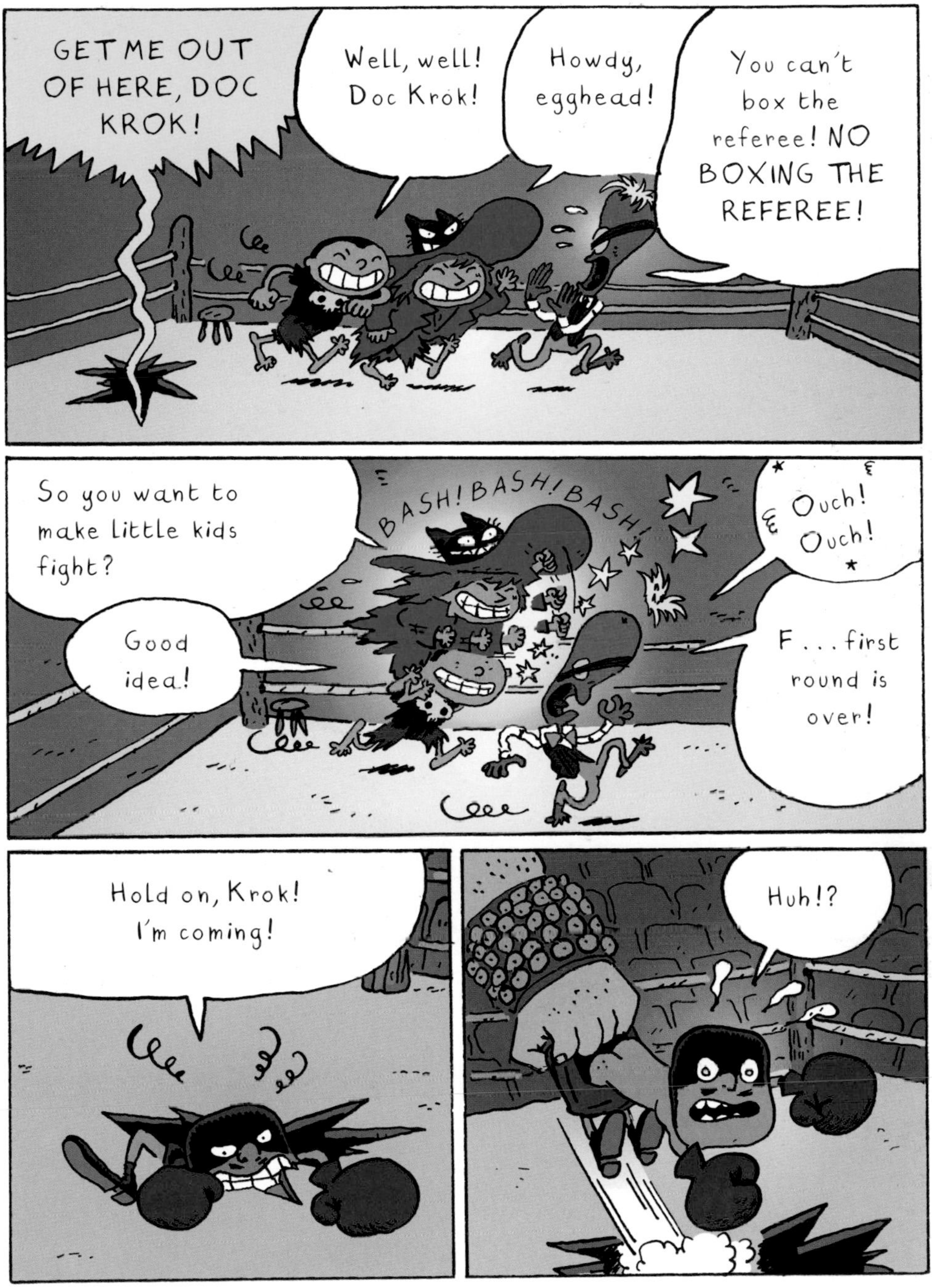
GET ME OUT OF HERE, DOC KROK!
Well, well! Doc Krok!
Howdy, egghead!
You can't box the referee! NO BOXING THE REFEREE!
So you want to make little kids fight?
BASH! BASH! BASH!
Ouch! Ouch!
Good idea!
F . . . first round is over!
Hold on, Krok! I'm coming!
Huh!?

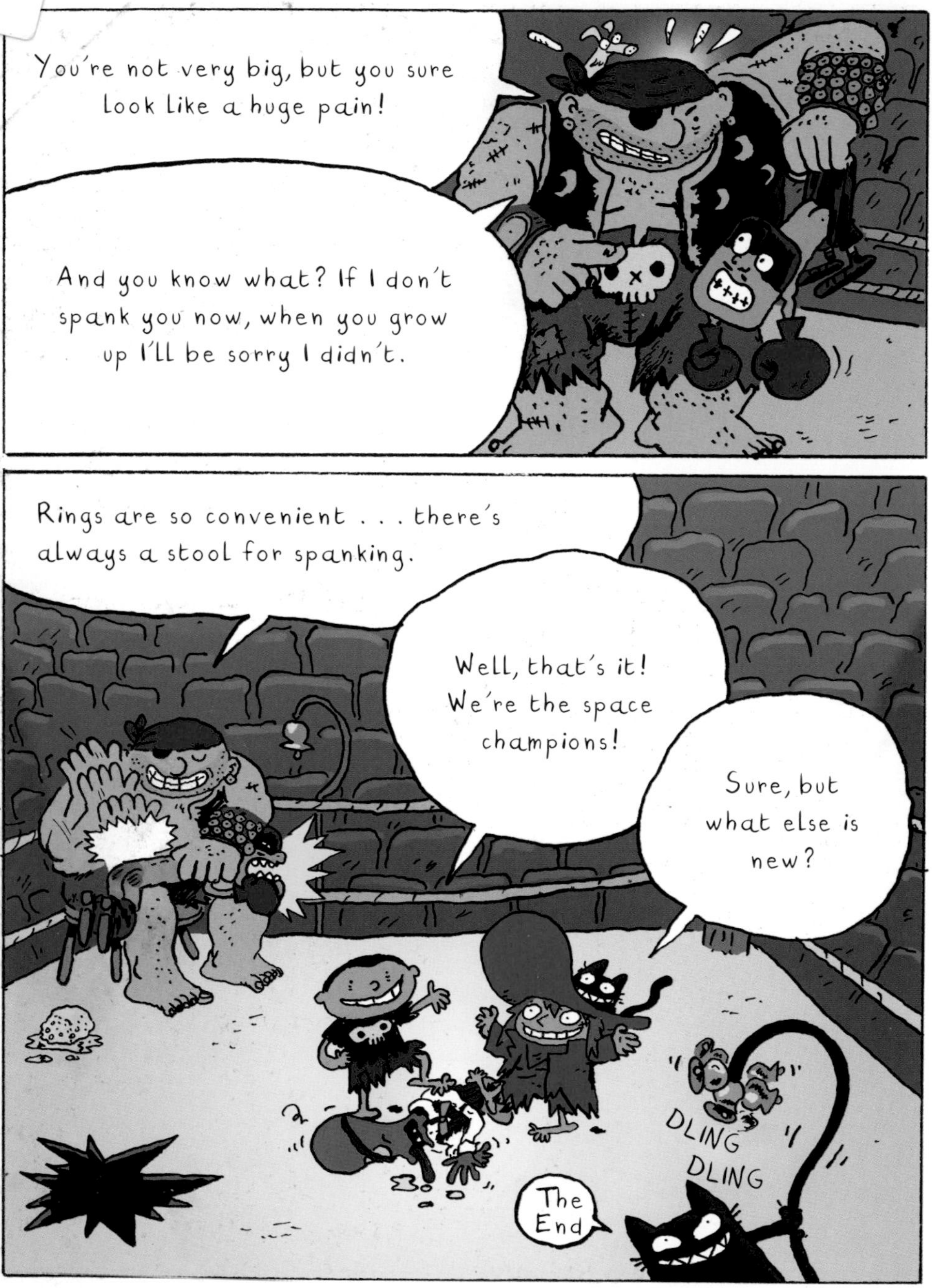
You're not very big, but you sure look like a huge pain!
And you know what? If I don't spank you now, when you grow up I'll be sorry I didn't.
Rings are so convenient . . . there's always a stool for spanking.
Well, that's it! We're the space champions!
Sure, but what else is new?
DLING DLING
The End

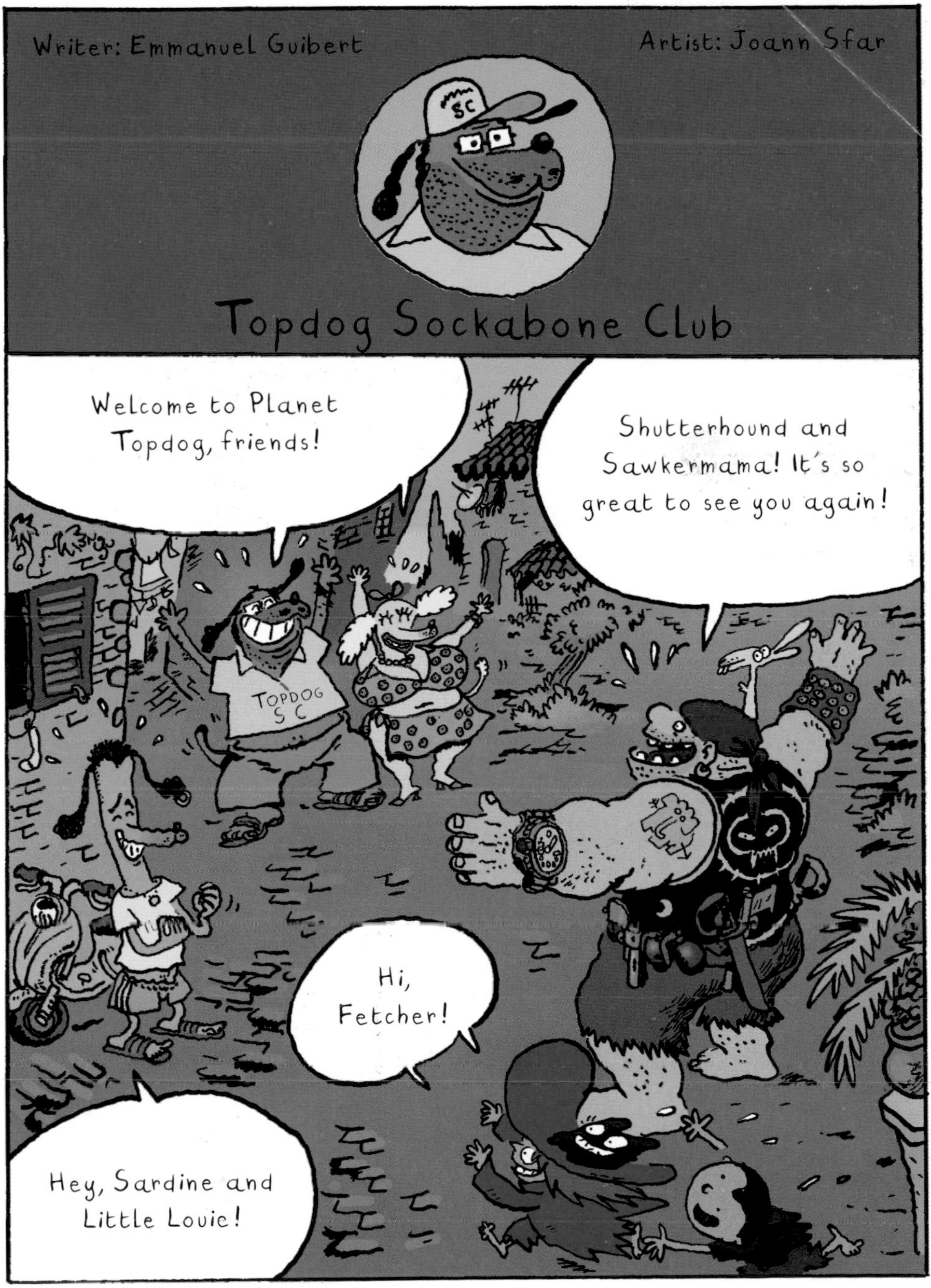
Writer: Emmanuel Guibert
Artist: Joann Sfar
SC
Topdog Sockabone Club
Welcome to Planet Topdog, friends!
Shutterhound and Sawkermama! It's so great to see you again!
TOPDOG SC
Hi, Fetcher!
Hey, Sardine and Little Louie!

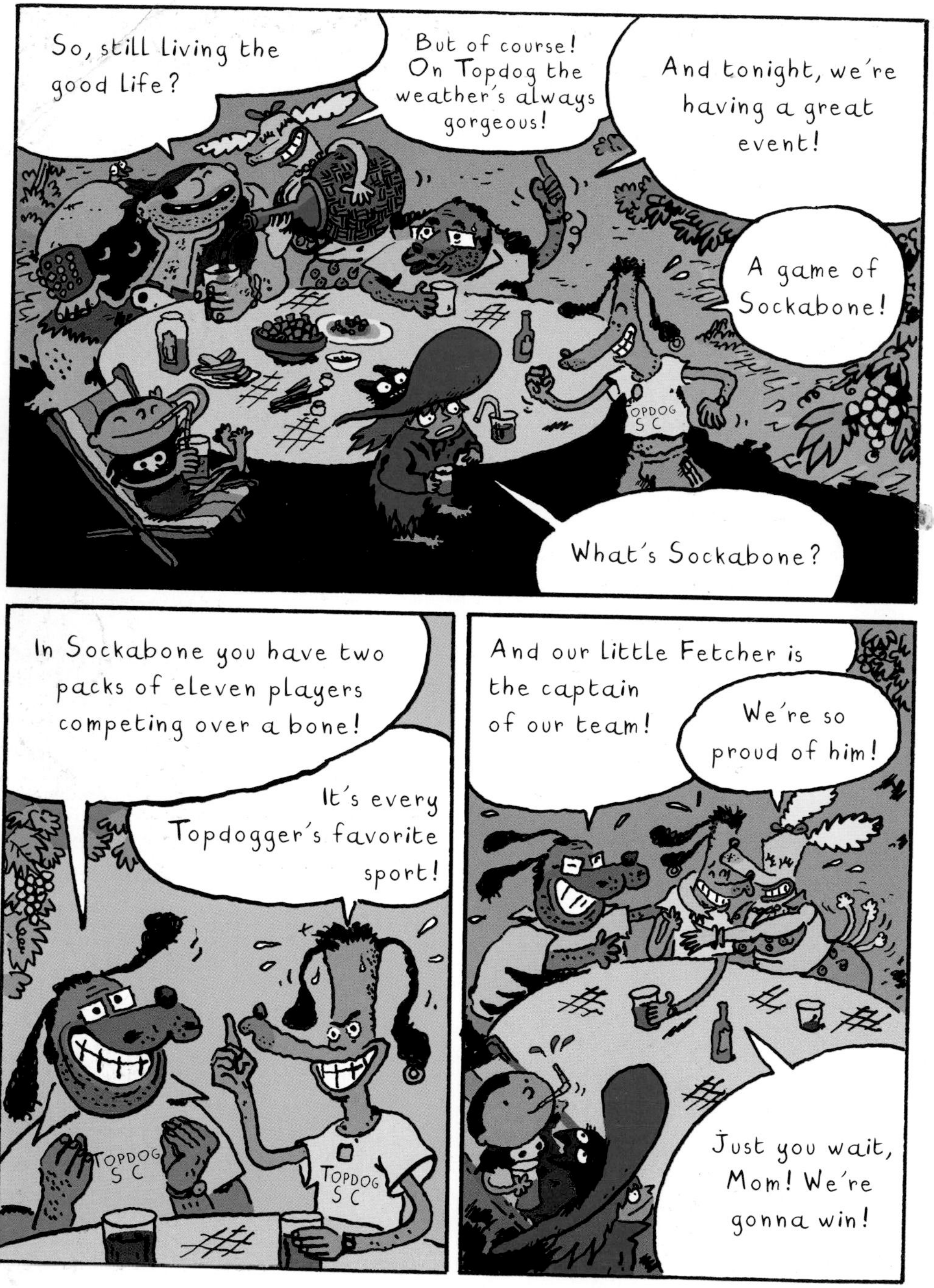
So, still living the good life?
But of course! On Topdog the weather's always gorgeous!
And tonight, we're having a great event!
A game of Sockabone!
TOPDOG S C
What's Sockabone?
In Sockabone you have two packs of eleven players competing over a bone!
It's every Topdogger's favorite sport!
TOPDOG S C
TOPDOG S C
And our little Fetcher is the captain of our team!
We're so proud of him!
Just you wait, Mom! We're gonna win!

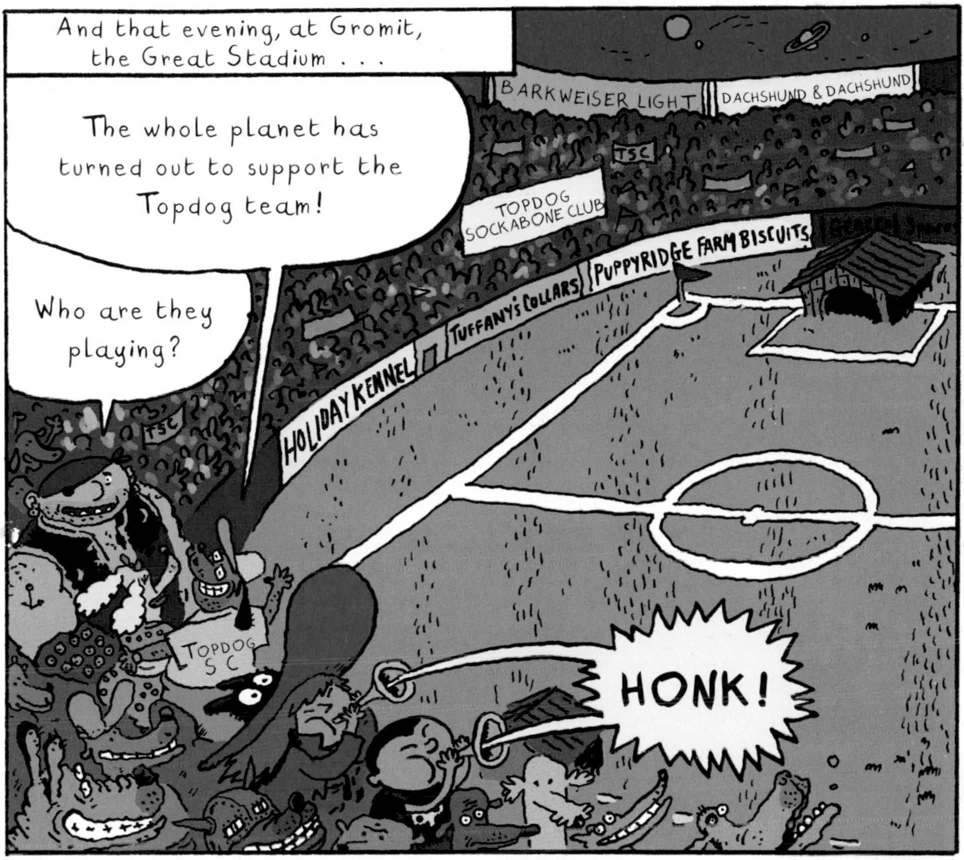
And that evening, at Gromit, the Great Stadium . . .
BARKWEISER LIGHT
DACHSHUND & DACHSHUND
TSC
TOPDOG SOCKABONE CLUB
PUPPYRIDGE FARM BISCUITS
TUFFANY'S COLLARS
HOLIDAY KENNEL
The whole planet has turned out to support the Topdog team!
Who are they playing?
TSC
TOPDOG S C
HONK!

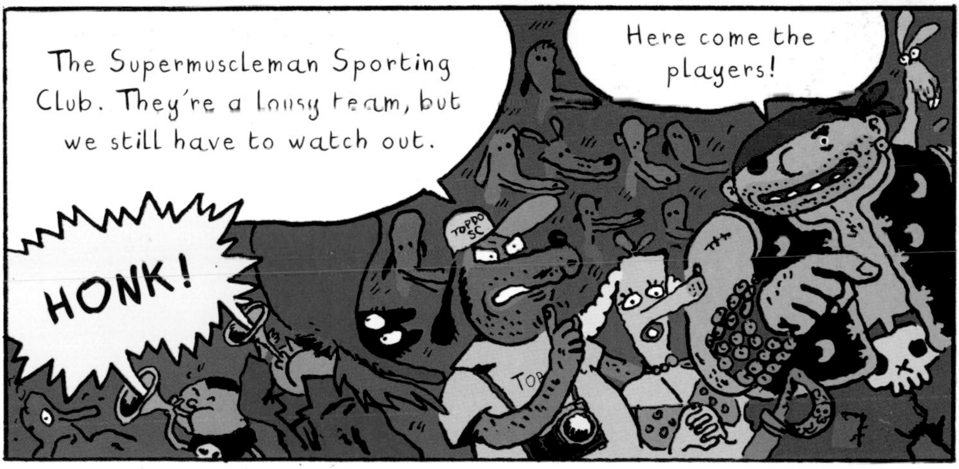
The Supermuscleman Sporting Club. They're a lousy team, but we still have to watch out.
Here come the players!
HONK!
TOPDOG SC

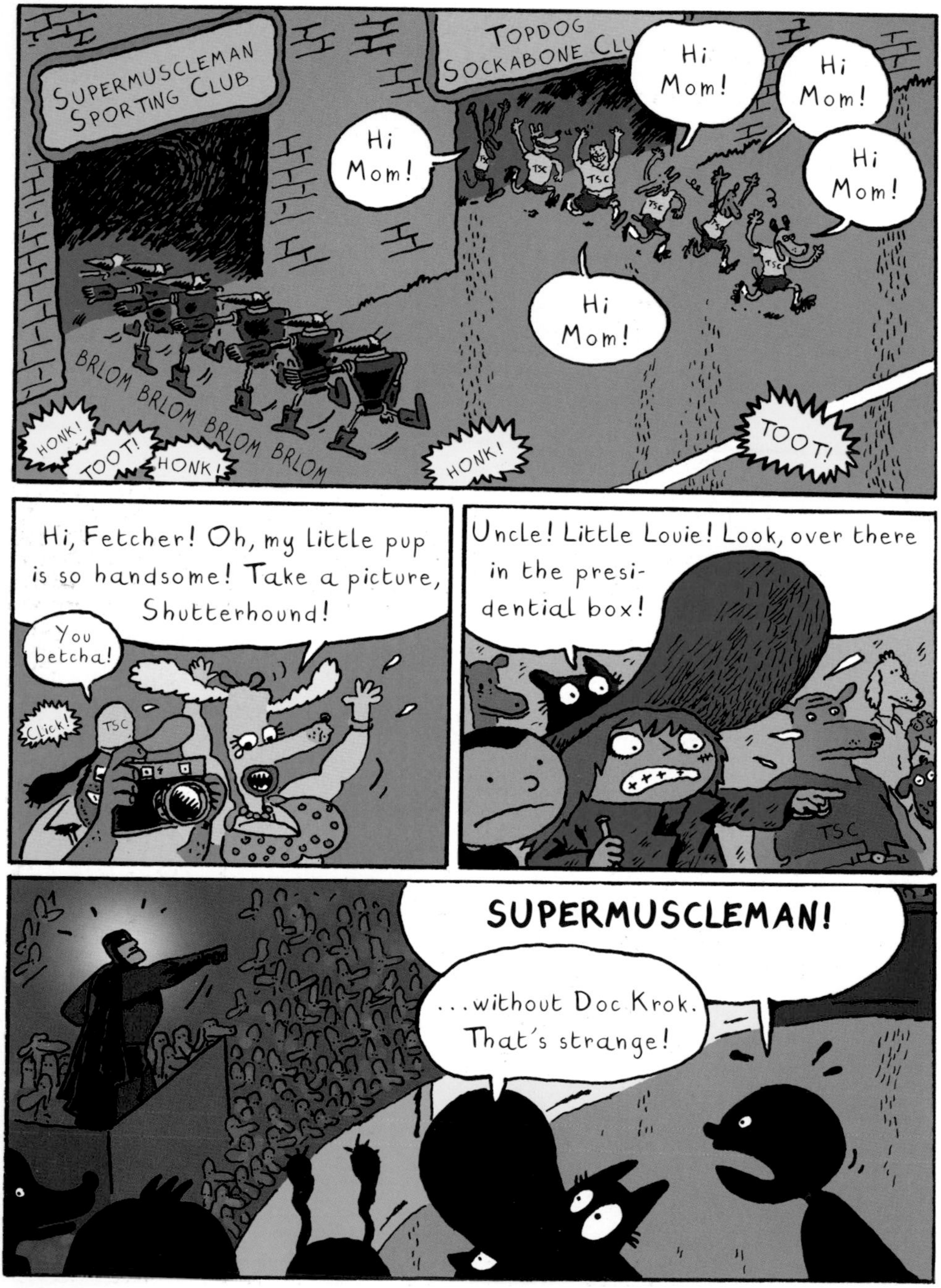
SUPERMUSCLEMAN SPORTING CLUB
TOPDOG SOCKABONE CLU
Hi Mom!
Hi Mom!
Hi Mom!
Hi Mom!
Hi Mom!
BRLOM BRLOM BRLOM BRLOM
HONK!
TOOT!
HONK!
HONK!
TOOT!
Hi, Fetcher! Oh, my little pup is so handsome! Take a picture, Shutterhound!
You betcha!
Click!
Uncle! Little Louie! Look, over there in the presi-dential box!
SUPERMUSCLEMAN!
...without Doc Krok. That's strange!

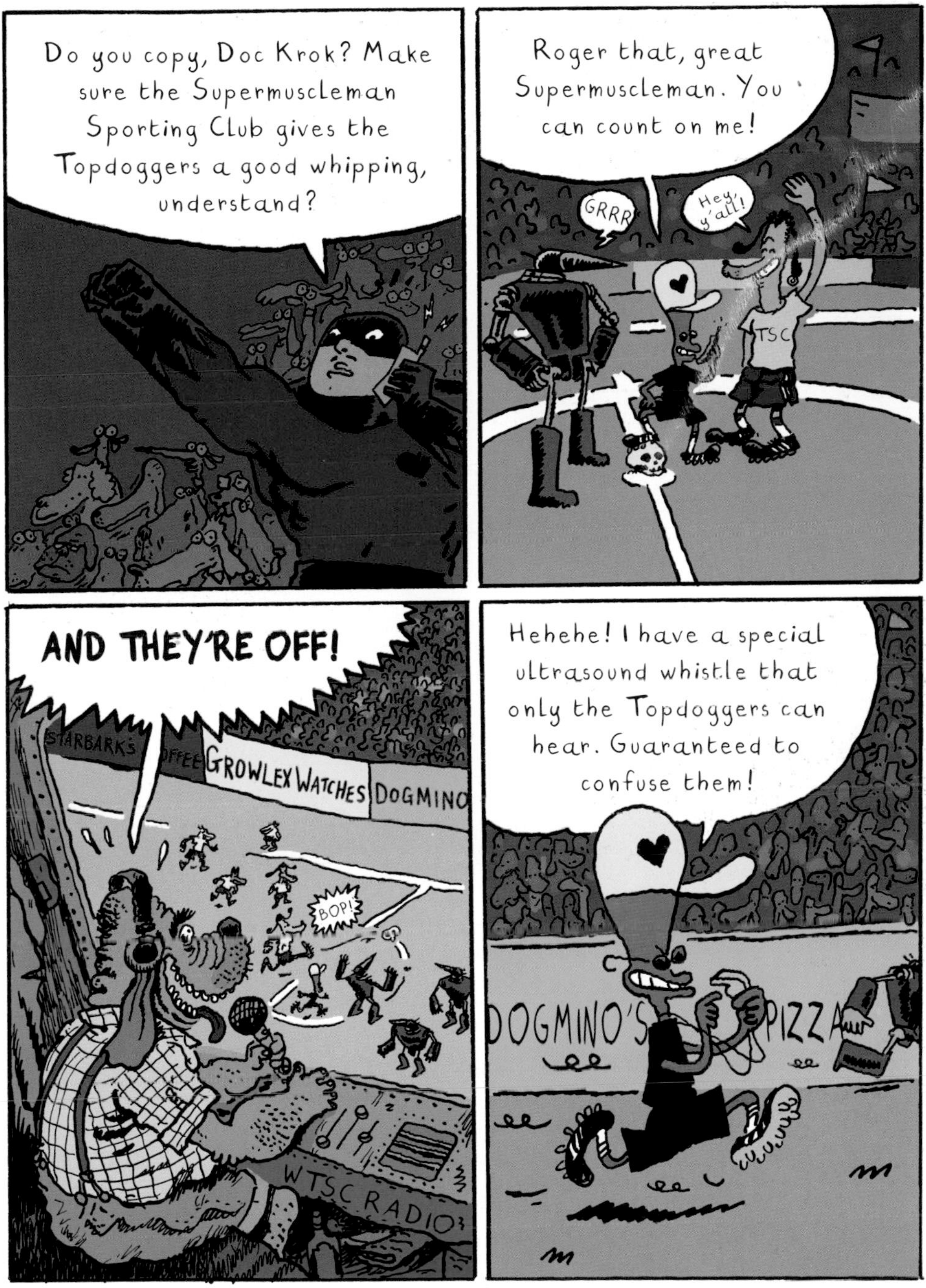
Do you copy, Doc Krok? Make sure the Supermuscleman Sporting Club gives the Topdoggers a good whipping, understand?
Roger that, great Supermuscleman. You can count on me!
GRRR
Hey, y'all!
TSC
AND THEY'RE OFF!
STARBARKS
OFFEE
GROWLEX WATCHES
DOGMINO
BOP!
WTSC RADIO
Hehehe! I have a special ultrasound whistle that only the Topdoggers can hear. Guaranteed to confuse them!
DOGMINO'S
PIZZA

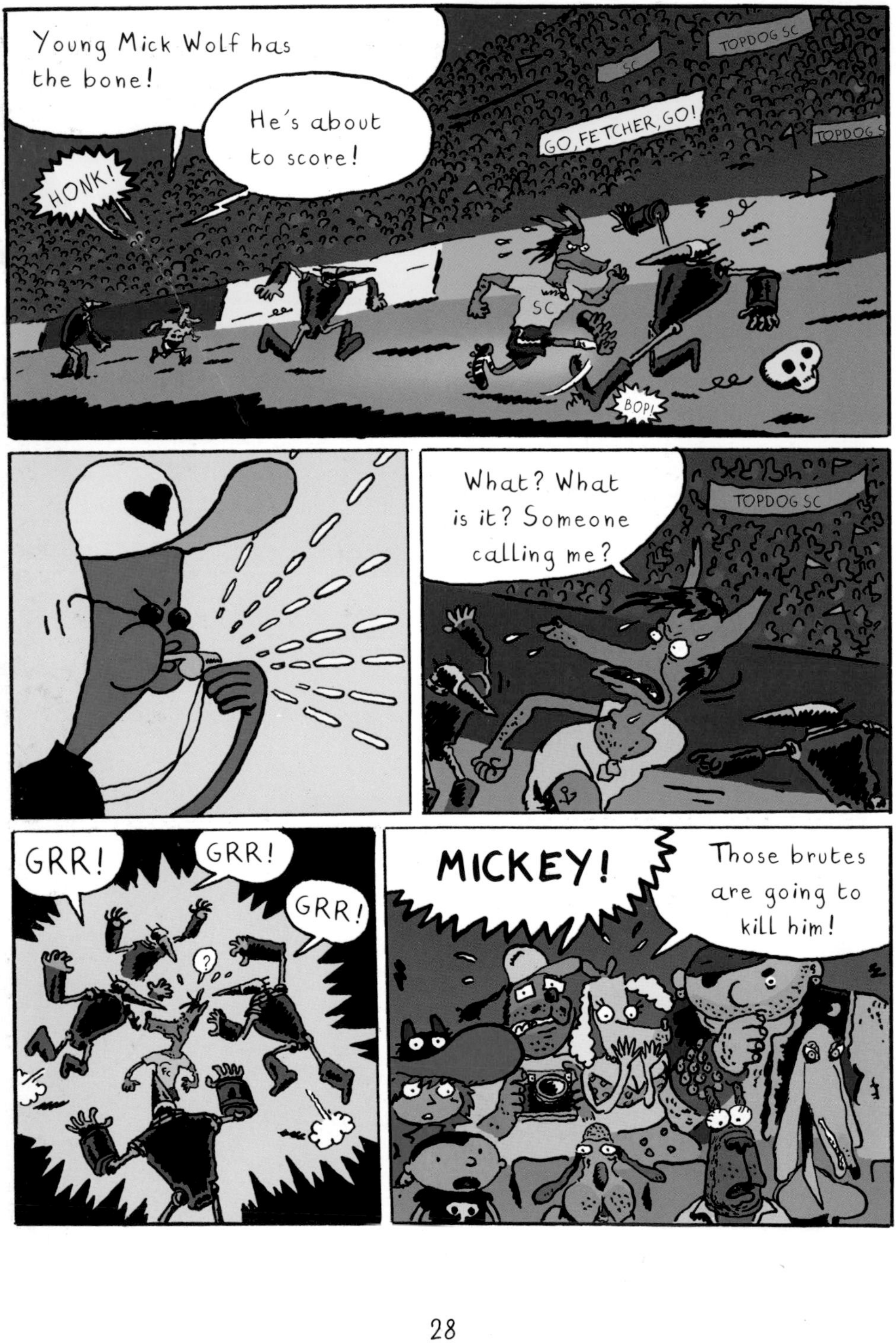
Young Mick Wolf has the bone!
He's about to score!
HONK!
TOPDOG SC
SC
GO, FETCHER, GO!
TOPDOG S
SC
BOP!
What? What is it? Someone calling me?
TOPDOG SC
GRR!
GRR!
GRR!
?
FC
MICKEY!
Those brutes are going to kill him!

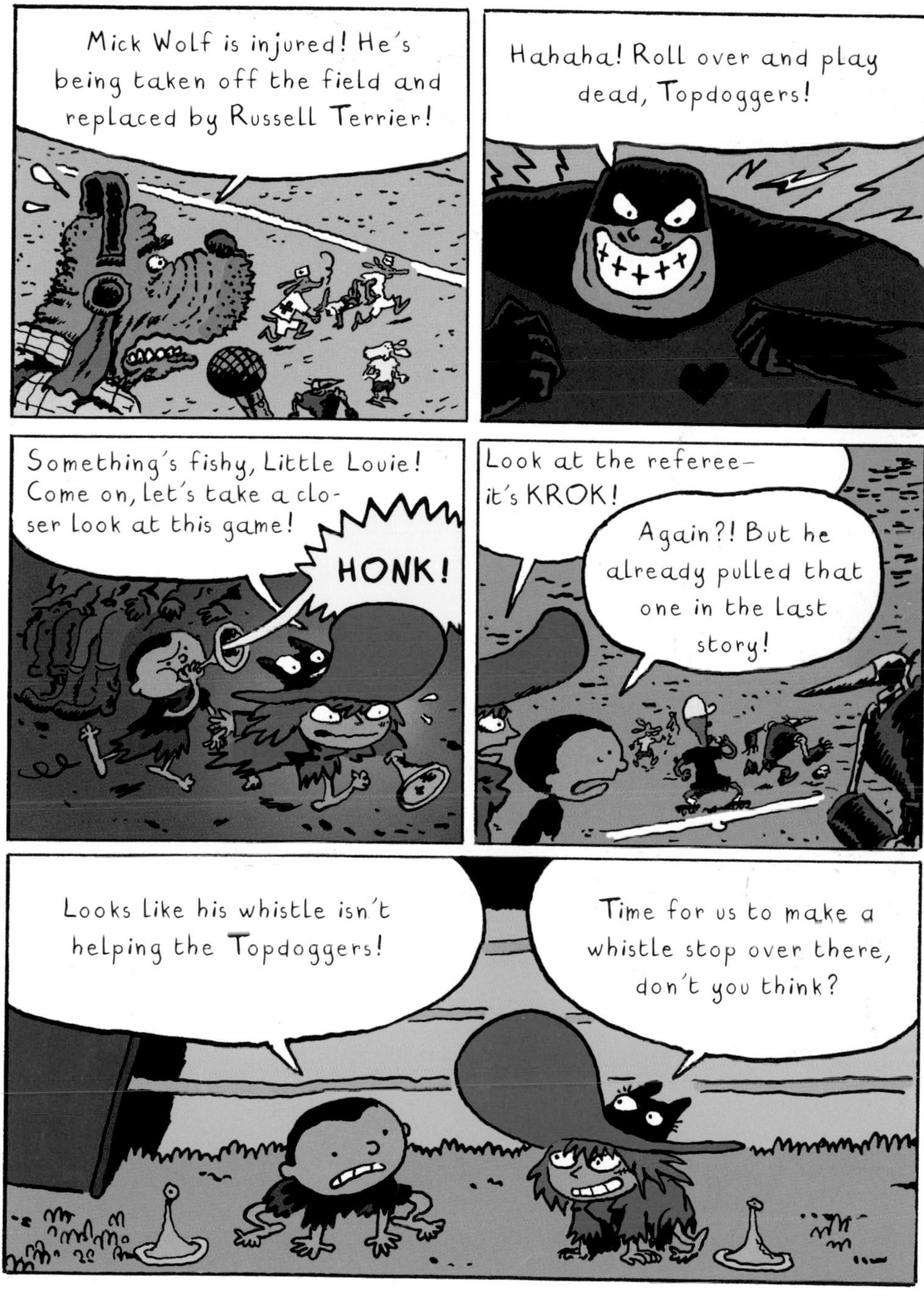
Mick Wolf is injured! He's being taken off the field and replaced by Russell Terrier!
Hahaha! Roll over and play dead, Topdoggers!
Something's fishy, Little Louie! Come on, let's take a clo-ser look at this game!
HONK!
Look at the referee— it's KROK!
Again?! But he already pulled that one in the last story!
Looks like his whistle isn't helping the Topdoggers!
Time for us to make a whistle stop over there, don't you think?

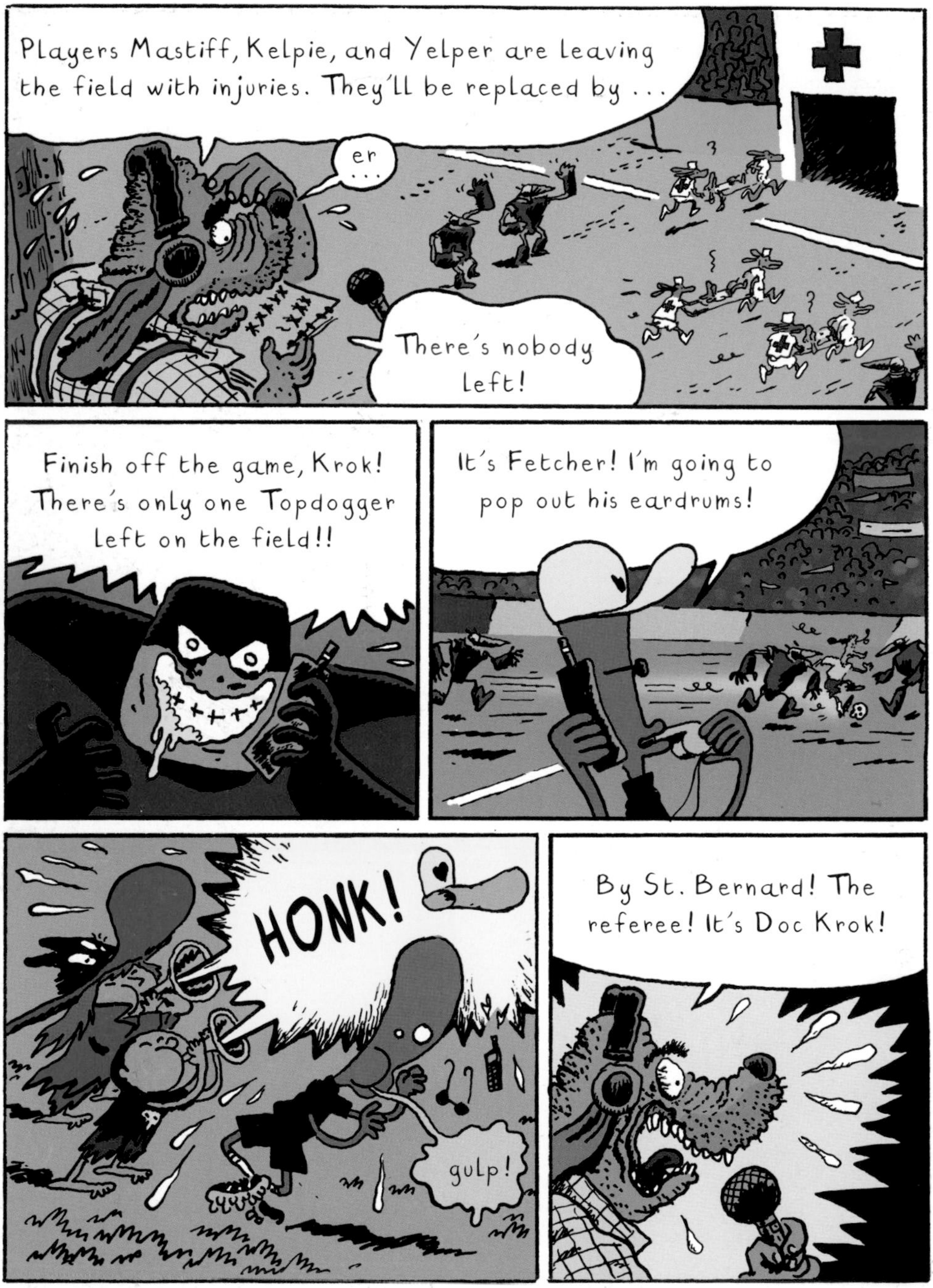

Players Mastiff, Kelpie, and Yelper are leaving the field with injuries. They'll be replaced by ...
er ...
There's nobody left!
Finish off the game, Krok! There's only one Topdogger left on the field!!
It's Fetcher! I'm going to pop out his eardrums!
HONK!
gulp!
By St. Bernard! The referee! It's Doc Krok!

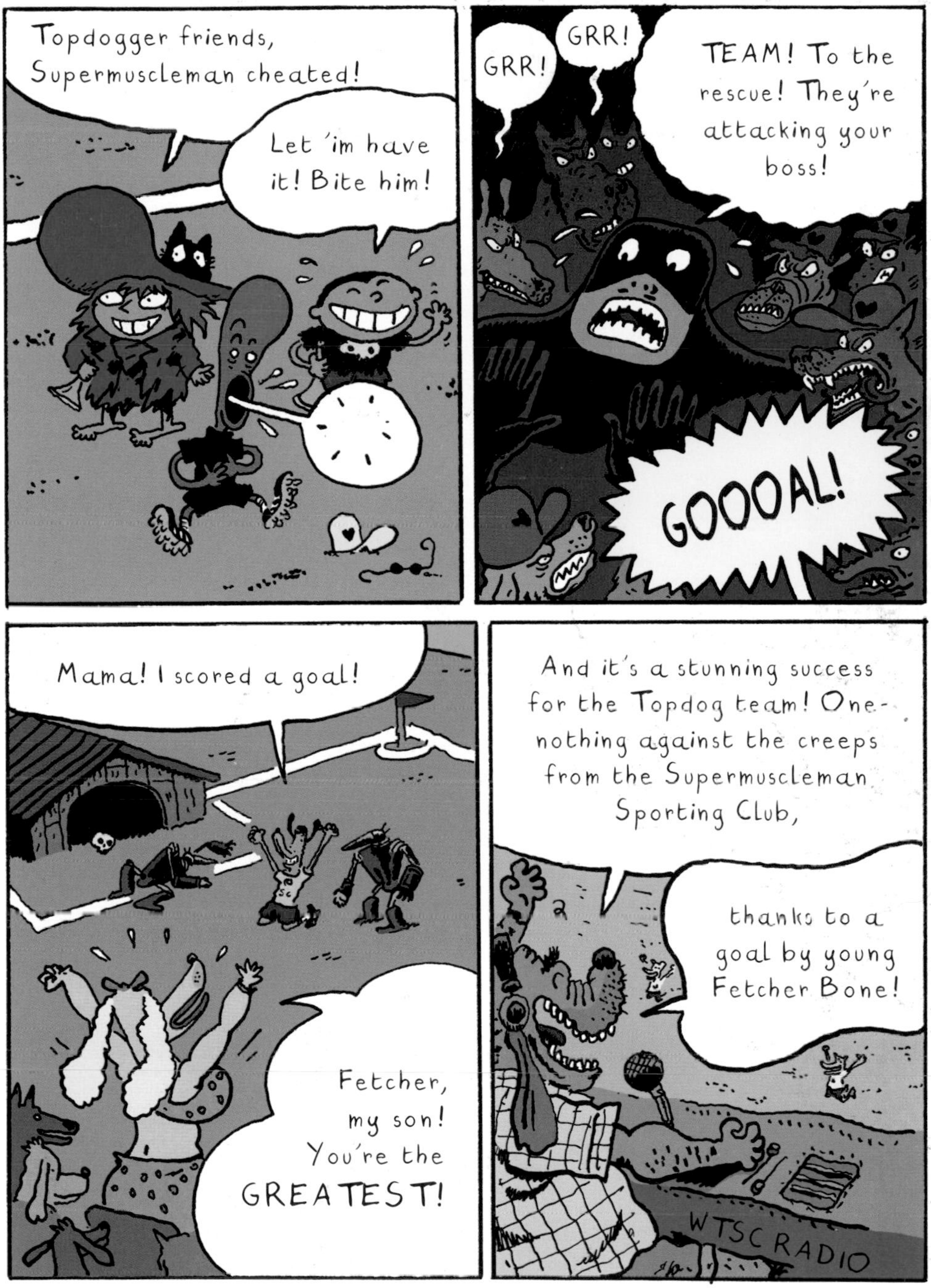
Topdogger friends, Supermuscleman cheated!
Let 'im have it! Bite him!
GRR!
GRR!
TEAM! To the rescue! They're attacking your boss!
GOOOAL!
Mama! I scored a goal!
Fetcher, my son! You're the GREATEST!
And it's a stunning success for the Topdog team! One-nothing against the creeps from the Supermuscleman Sporting Club,
thanks to a goal by young Fetcher Bone!
WTSC RADIO

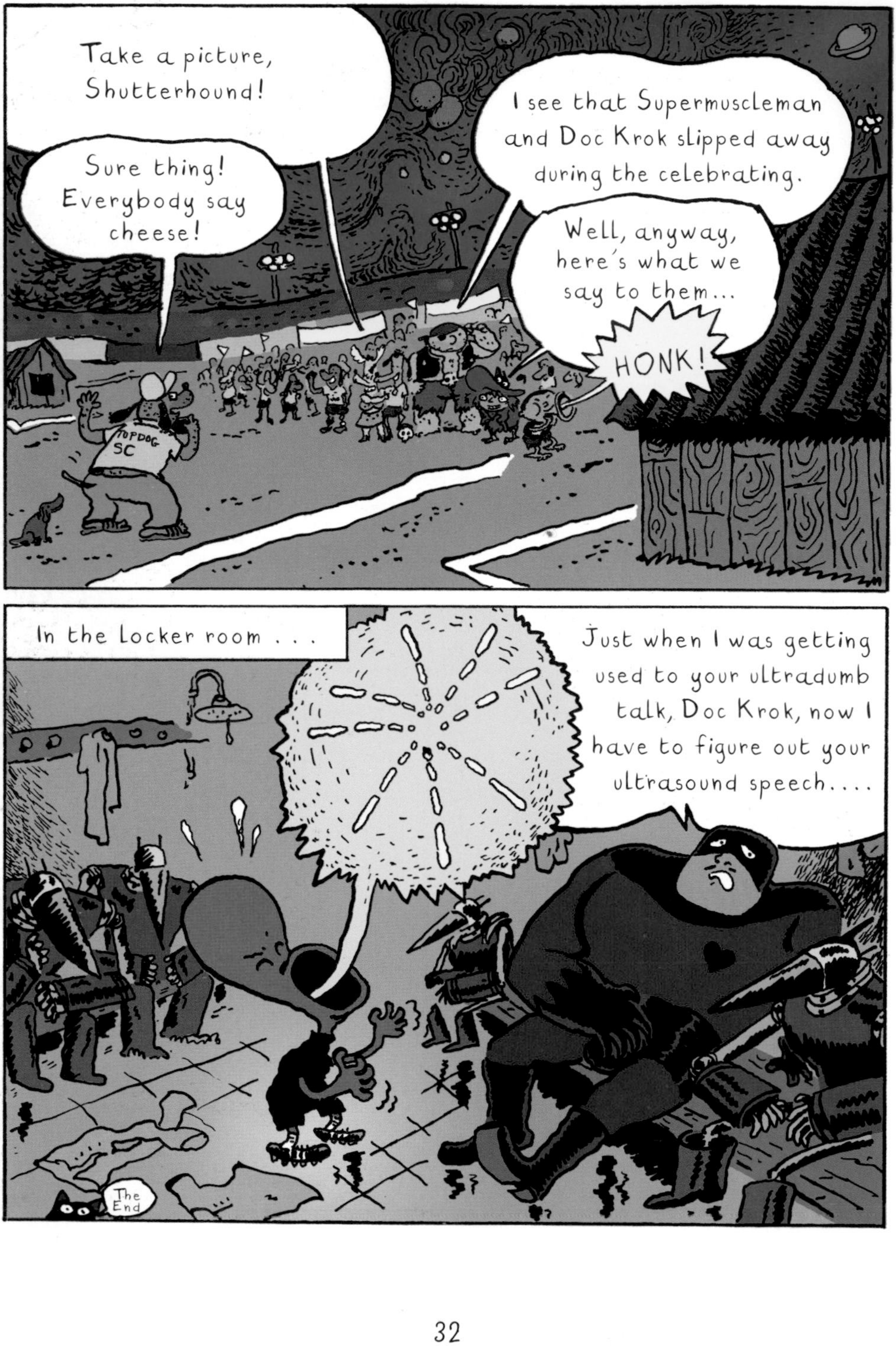
Take a picture, Shutterhound!
Sure thing! Everybody say cheese!
I see that Supermuscleman and Doc Krok slipped away during the celebrating.
Well, anyway, here's what we say to them...
HONK!
TOPDOG SC
In the locker room . . .
Just when I was getting used to your ultradumb talk, Doc Krok, now I have to figure out your ultrasound speech....
The End

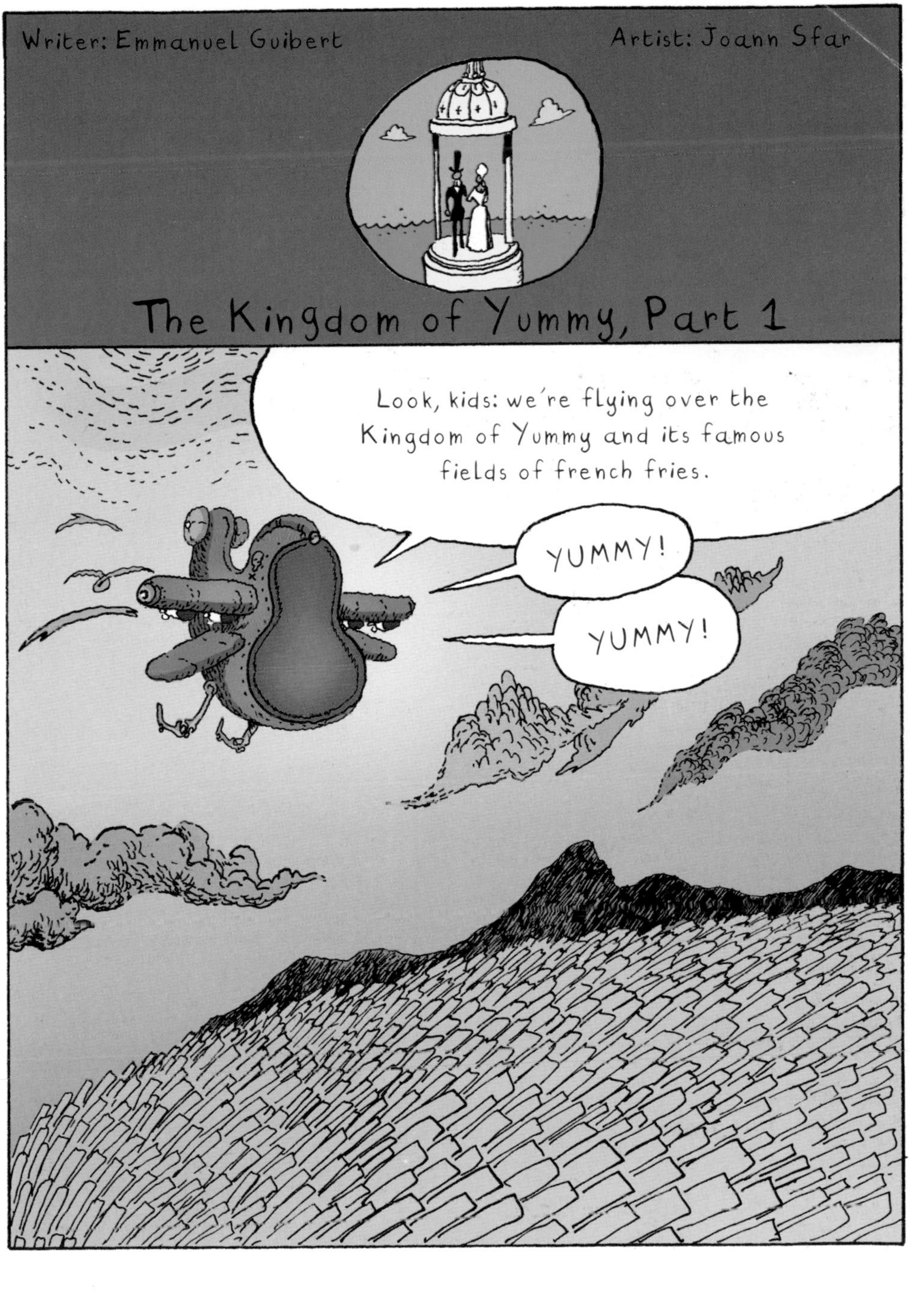
Writer: Emmanuel Guibert
Artist: Joann Sfar
The Kingdom of Yummy, Part 1
Look, kids: we're flying over the Kingdom of Yummy and its famous fields of french fries.
YUMMY!
YUMMY!

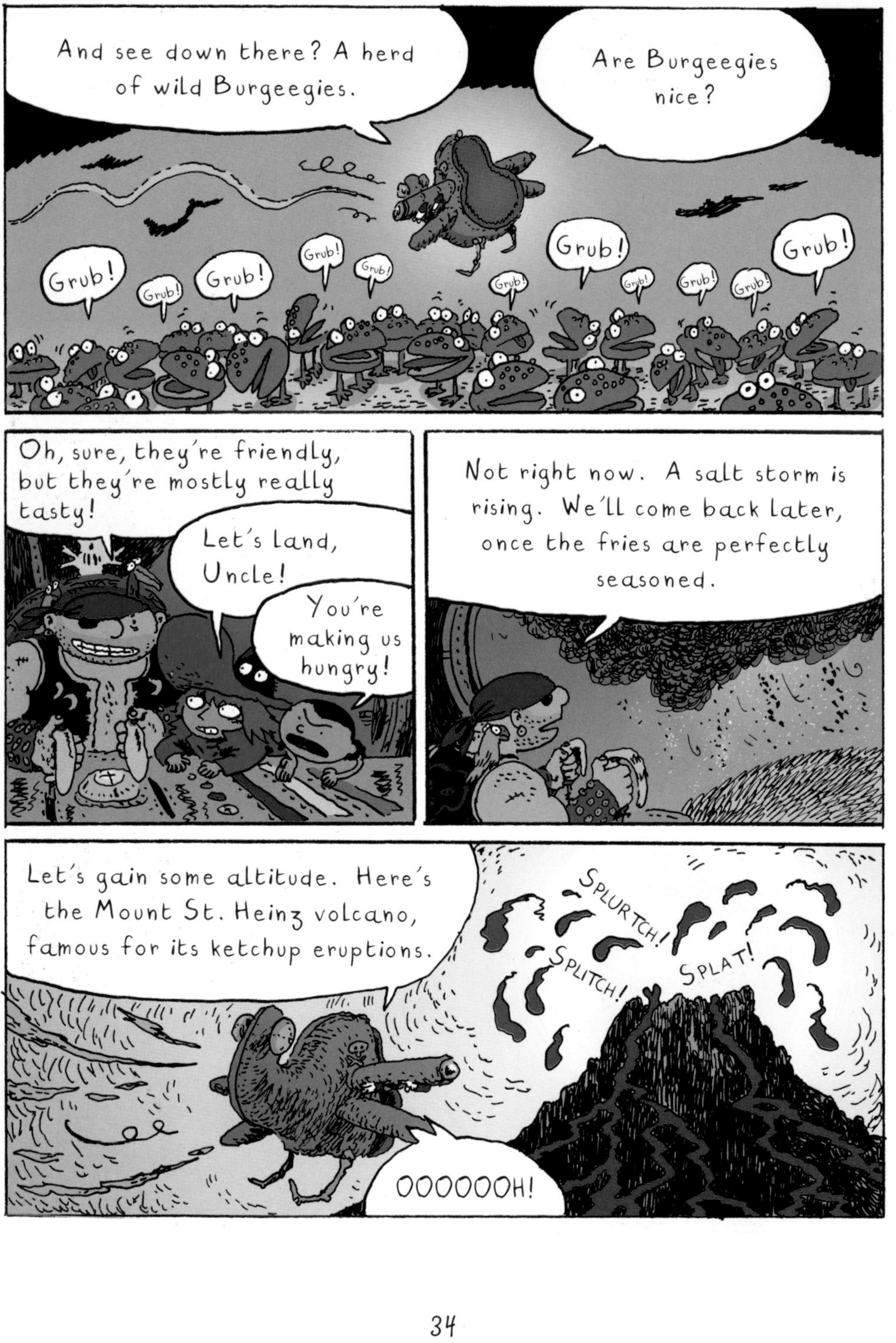
And see down there? A herd of wild Burgeegies.
Are Burgeegies nice?
Grub!
Grub!
Grub!
Grub!
Grub!
Grub!
Grub!
Grub!
Grub!
Grub!
Grub!
Oh, sure, they're friendly, but they're mostly really tasty!
Let's land, Uncle!
You're making us hungry!
Not right now. A salt storm is rising. We'll come back later, once the fries are perfectly seasoned.
Let's gain some altitude. Here's the Mount St. Heinz volcano, famous for its ketchup eruptions.
SPLURTCH!
SPLITCH!
SPLAT!
OOOOOOH!

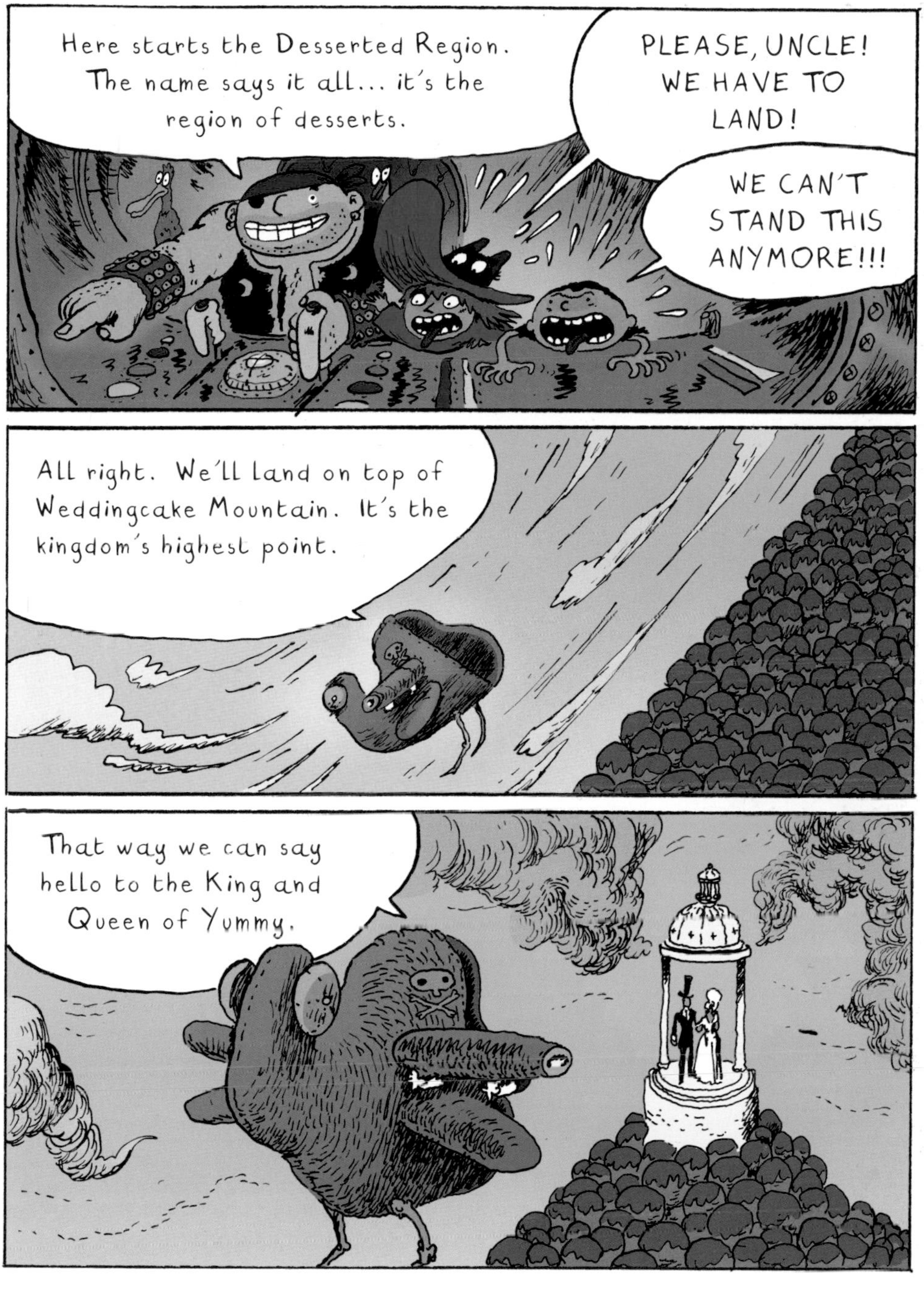
Here starts the Desserted Region. The name says it all... it's the region of desserts.
PLEASE, UNCLE! WE HAVE TO LAND!
WE CAN'T STAND THIS ANYMORE!!!
All right. We'll land on top of Weddingcake Mountain. It's the kingdom's highest point.
That way we can say hello to the King and Queen of Yummy.

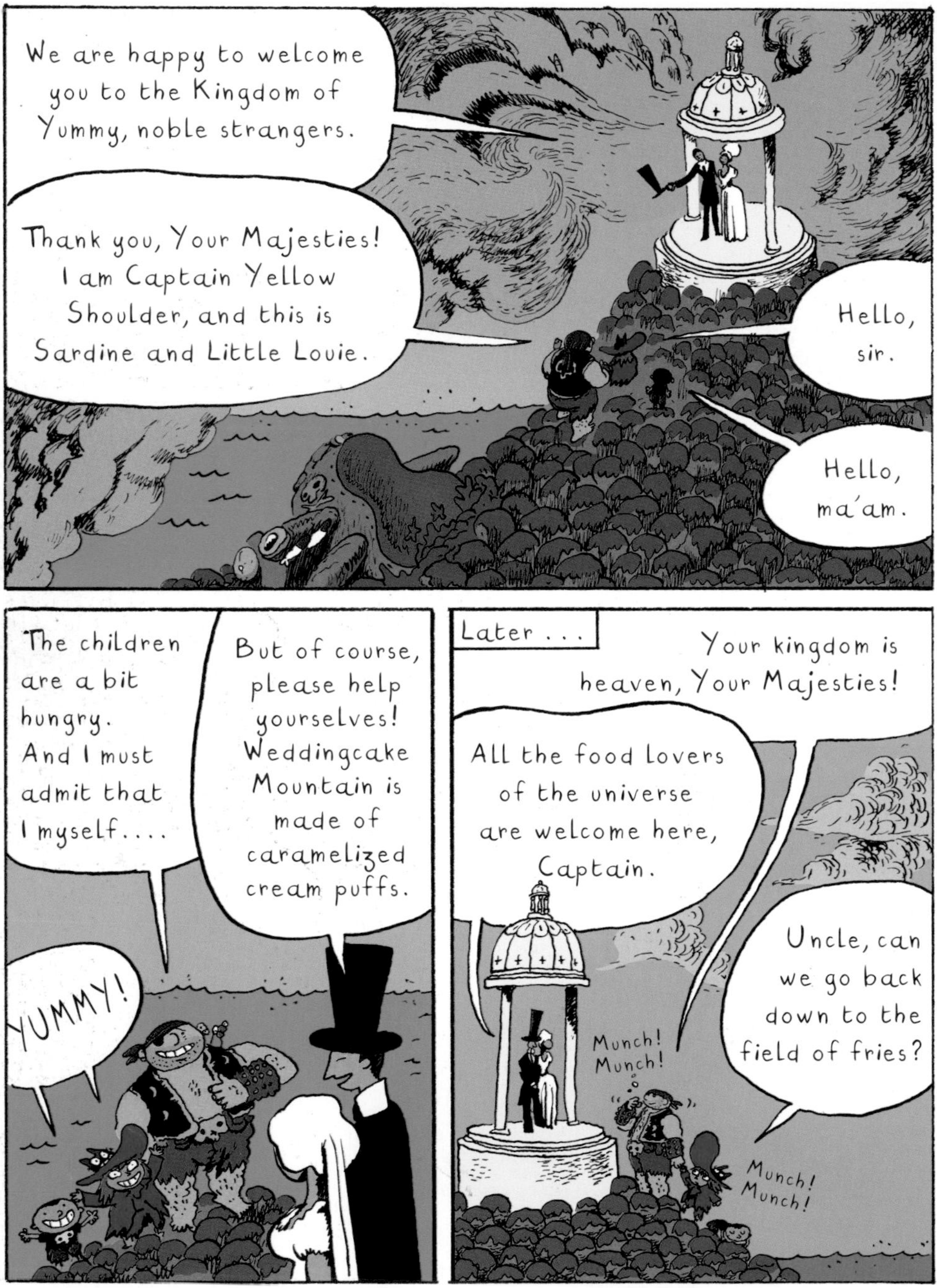
We are happy to welcome you to the Kingdom of Yummy, noble strangers.
Thank you, Your Majesties! I am Captain Yellow Shoulder, and this is Sardine and Little Louie.
Hello, sir.
Hello, ma'am.
The children are a bit hungry. And I must admit that I myself....
But of course, please help yourselves! Weddingcake Mountain is made of caramelized cream puffs.
YUMMY!
Later...
Your kingdom is heaven, Your Majesties!
All the food lovers of the universe are welcome here, Captain.
Munch! Munch!
Uncle, can we go back down to the field of fries?
Munch! Munch!

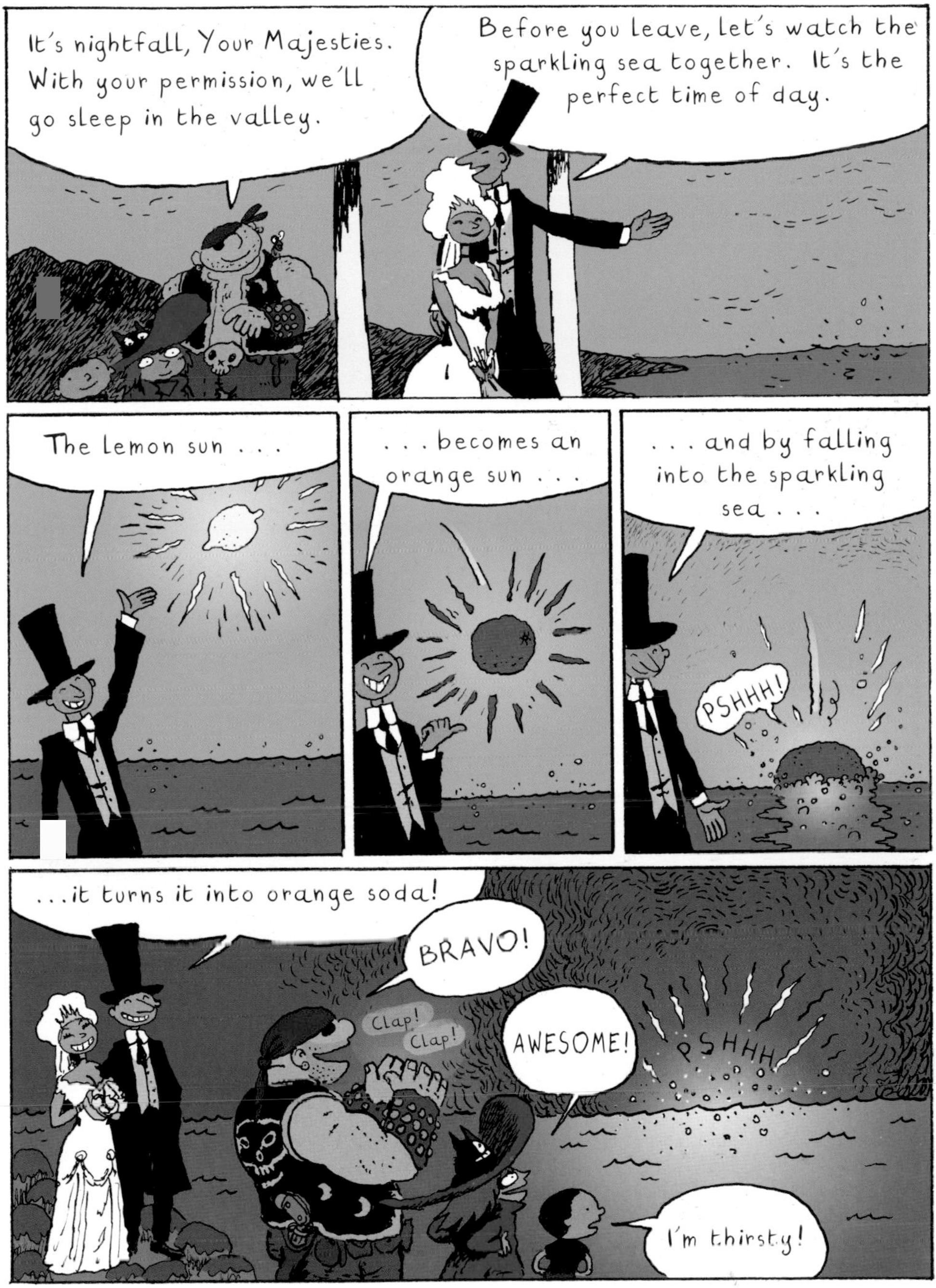
It's nightfall, Your Majesties. With your permission, we'll go sleep in the valley.
Before you leave, let's watch the sparkling sea together. It's the perfect time of day.
The lemon sun . . .
. . . becomes an orange sun . . .
. . . and by falling into the sparkling sea . . .
PSHHH!
. . .it turns it into orange soda!
BRAVO!
Clap!
Clap!
AWESOME!
PSHHH
I'm thirsty!

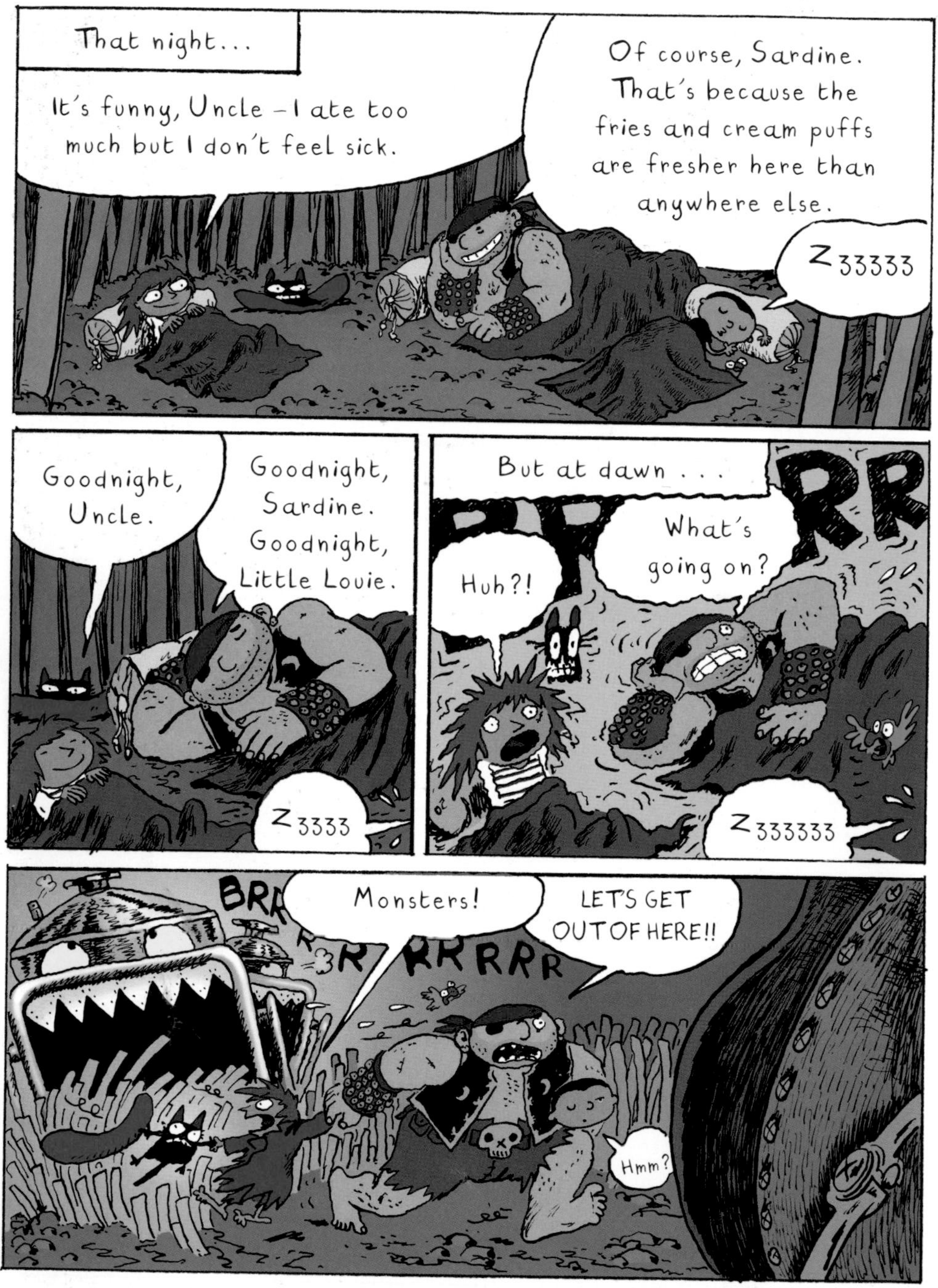
That night...
It's funny, Uncle – I ate too much but I don't feel sick.
Of course, Sardine. That's because the fries and cream puffs are fresher here than anywhere else.
Z33333
Goodnight, Uncle.
Goodnight, Sardine. Goodnight, Little Louie.
Z3333
But at dawn . . .
RR
Huh?!
What's going on?
Z333333
BRRRRRRRRR
Monsters!
LET'S GET OUT OF HERE!!
Hmm?

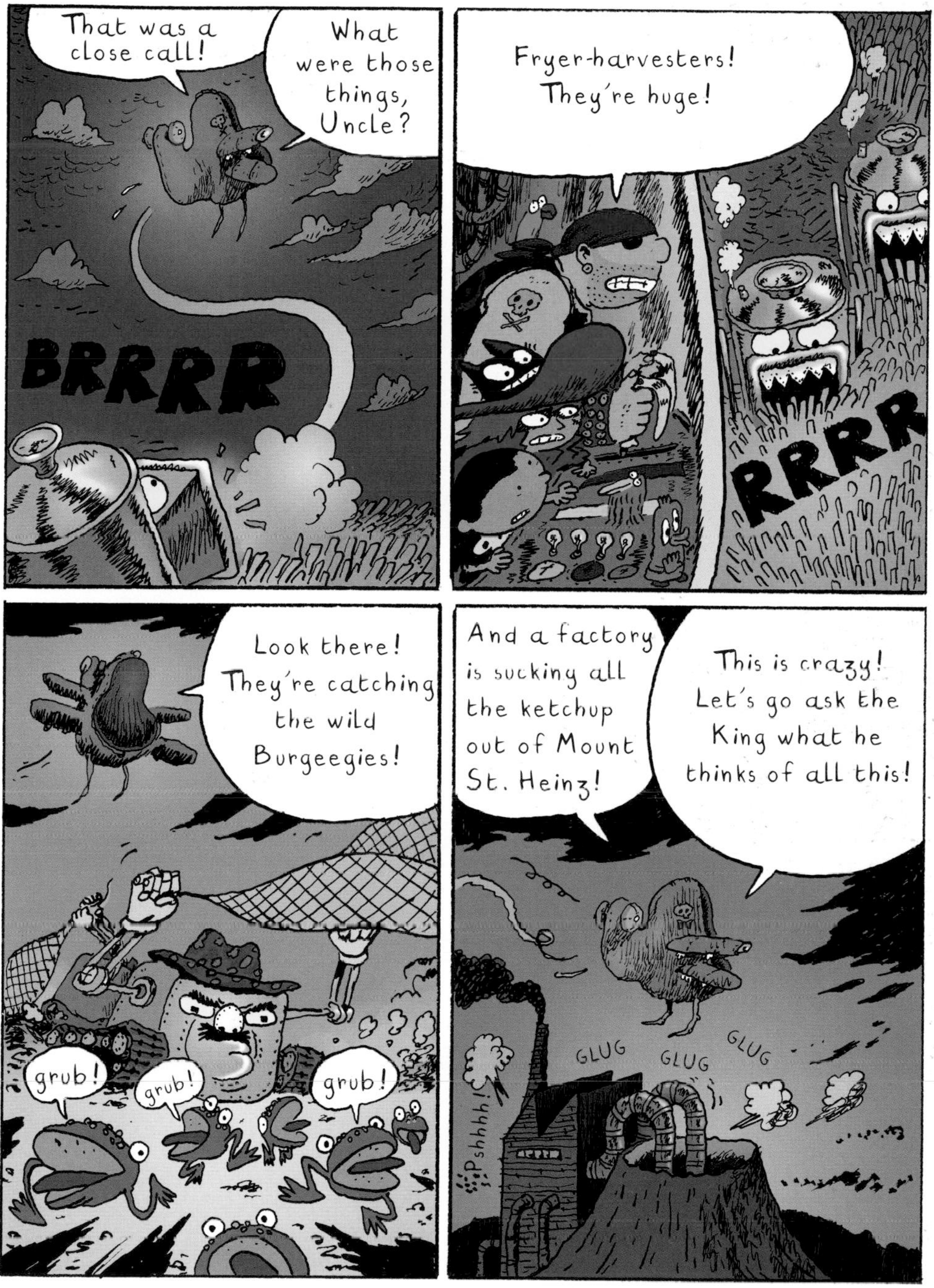

That was a close call!
What were those things, Uncle?
BRRRR
Fryer-harvesters! They're huge!
RRRR
Look there! They're catching the wild Burgeegies!
grub!
grub!
grub!
And a factory is sucking all the ketchup out of Mount St. Heinz!
This is crazy! Let's go ask the King what he thinks of all this!
GLUG
GLUG
GLUG
Pshhhh!

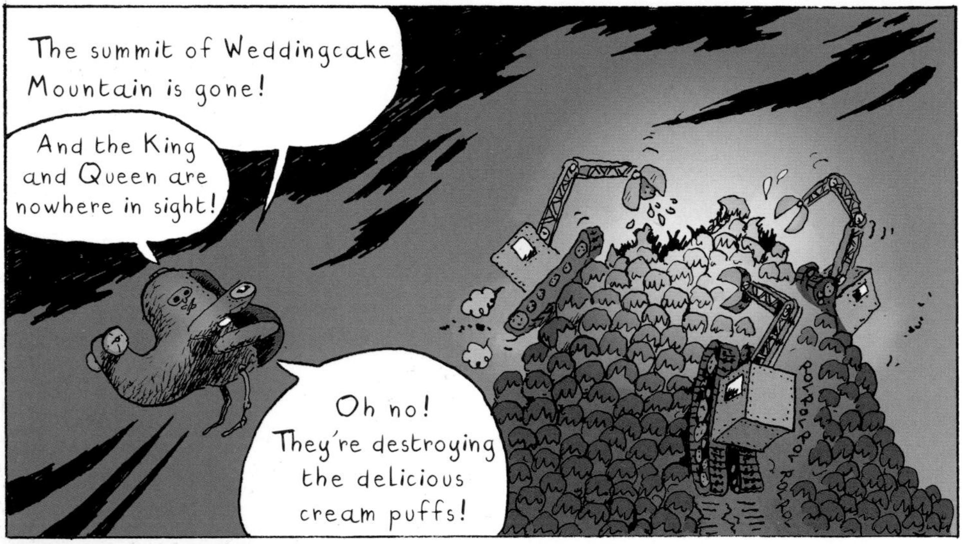
The summit of Weddingcake Mountain is gone!
And the King and Queen are nowhere in sight!
Oh no! They're destroying the delicious cream puffs!

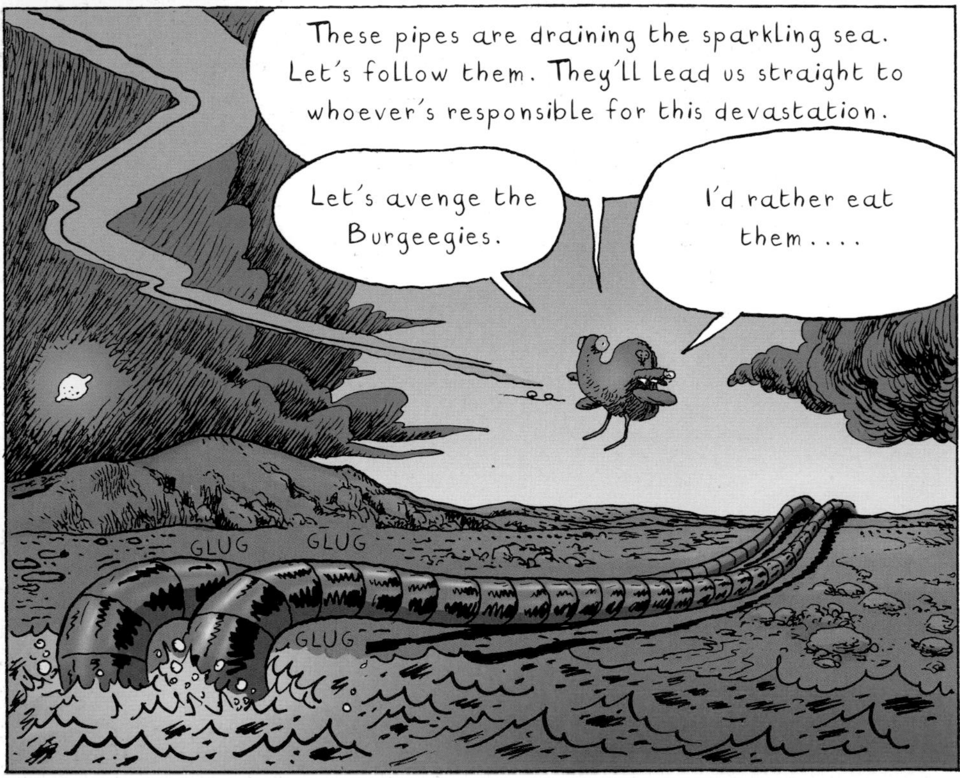
These pipes are draining the sparkling sea. Let's follow them. They'll lead us straight to whoever's responsible for this devastation.
Let's avenge the Burgeegies.
I'd rather eat them....
GLUG
GLUG
GLUG

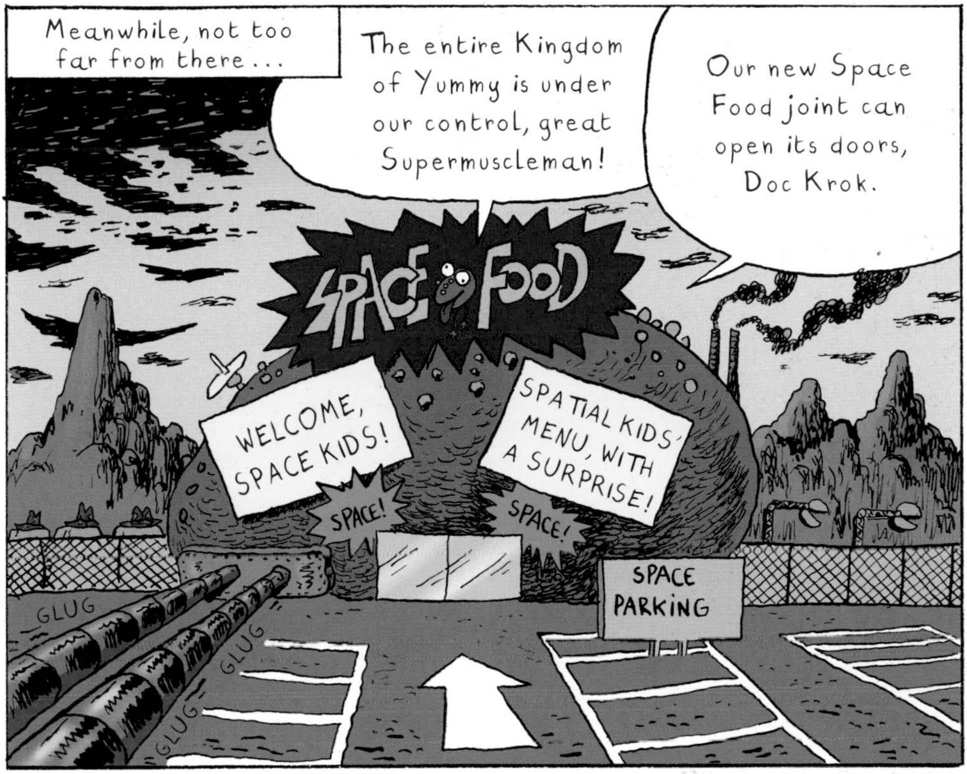
Meanwhile, not too far from there...
The entire Kingdom of Yummy is under our control, great Supermuscleman!
Our new Space Food joint can open its doors, Doc Krok.
SPACE FOOD
WELCOME, SPACE KIDS!
SPATIAL KIDS' MENU, WITH A SURPRISE!
SPACE!
SPACE!
SPACE PARKING
GLUG
GLUG
GLUG
GLUG

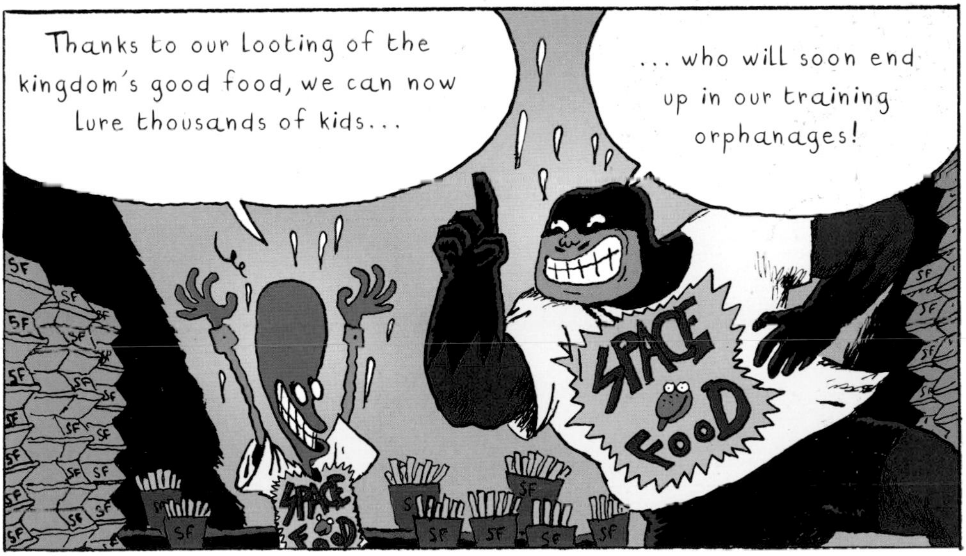
Thanks to our looting of the kingdom's good food, we can now lure thousands of kids...
... who will soon end up in our training orphanages!
SPACE FOOD
SPACE FOOD

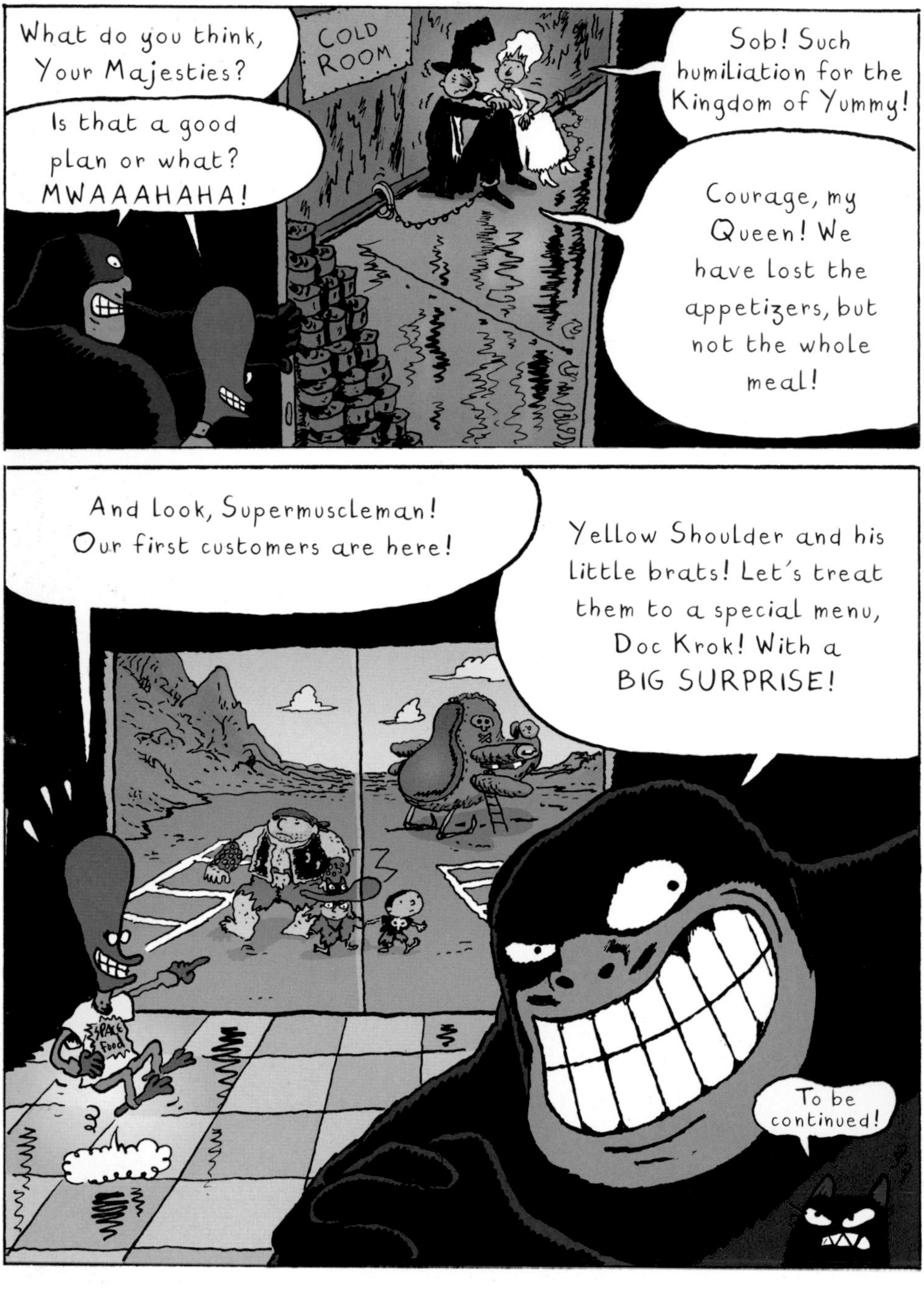
What do you think, Your Majesties?
Is that a good plan or what? MWAAAHAHA!
COLD ROOM
Sob! Such humiliation for the Kingdom of Yummy!
Courage, my Queen! We have lost the appetizers, but not the whole meal!
And look, Supermuscleman! Our first customers are here!
Yellow Shoulder and his little brats! Let's treat them to a special menu, Doc Krok! With a BIG SURPRISE!
SPACE Food
To be continued!

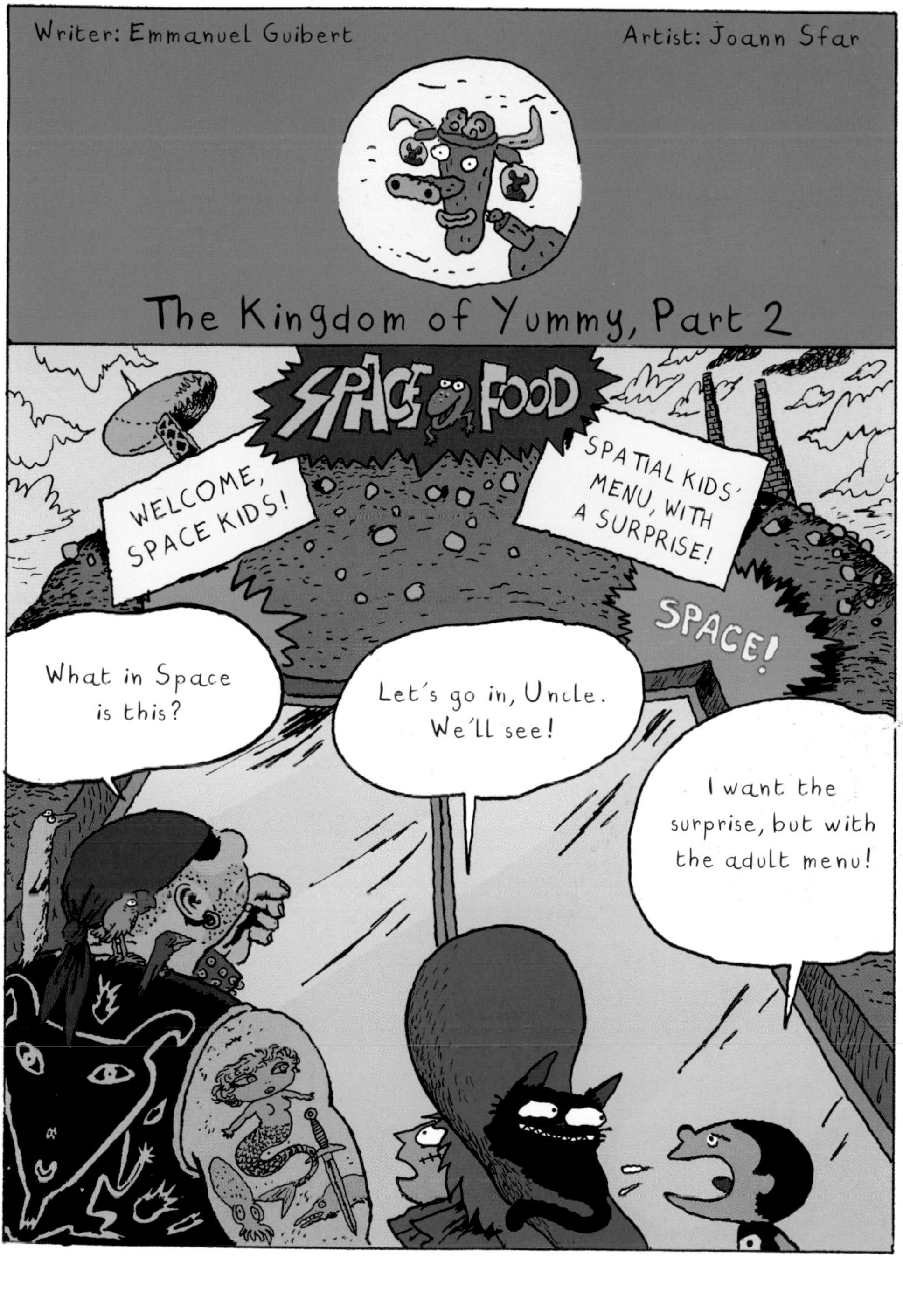
Writer: Emmanuel Guibert
Artist: Joann Sfar
The Kingdom of Yummy, Part 2
SPACE FOOD
WELCOME, SPACE KIDS!
SPATIAL KIDS' MENU, WITH A SURPRISE!
SPACE!
What in Space is this?
Let's go in, Uncle. We'll see!
I want the surprise, but with the adult menu!

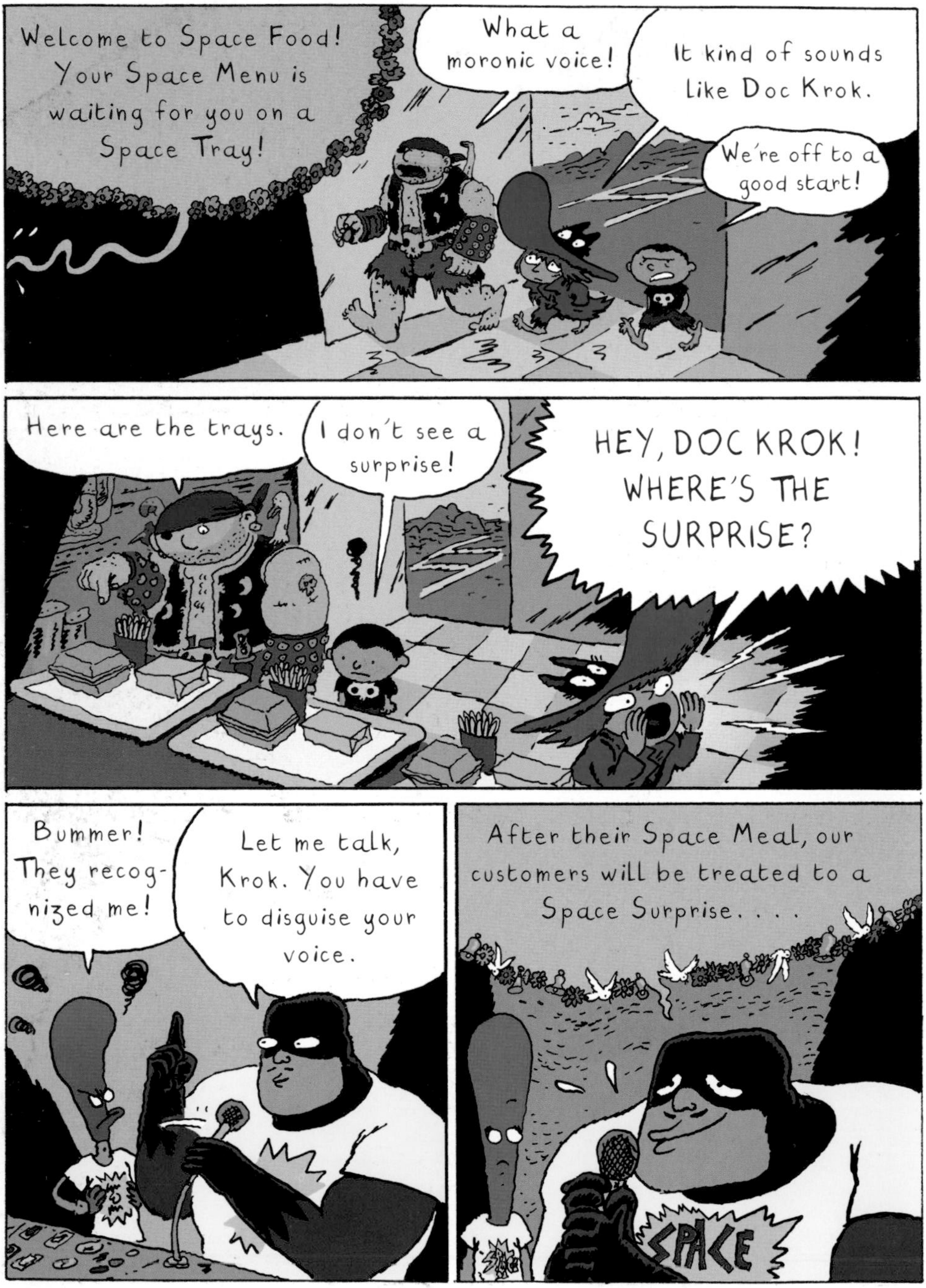

Welcome to Space Food! Your Space Menu is waiting for you on a Space Tray!
What a moronic voice!
It kind of sounds like Doc Krok.
We're off to a good start!
Here are the trays.
I don't see a surprise!
HEY, DOC KROK! WHERE'S THE SURPRISE?
Bummer! They recog-nized me!
Let me talk, Krok. You have to disguise your voice.
After their Space Meal, our customers will be treated to a Space Surprise. . . .
SPACE

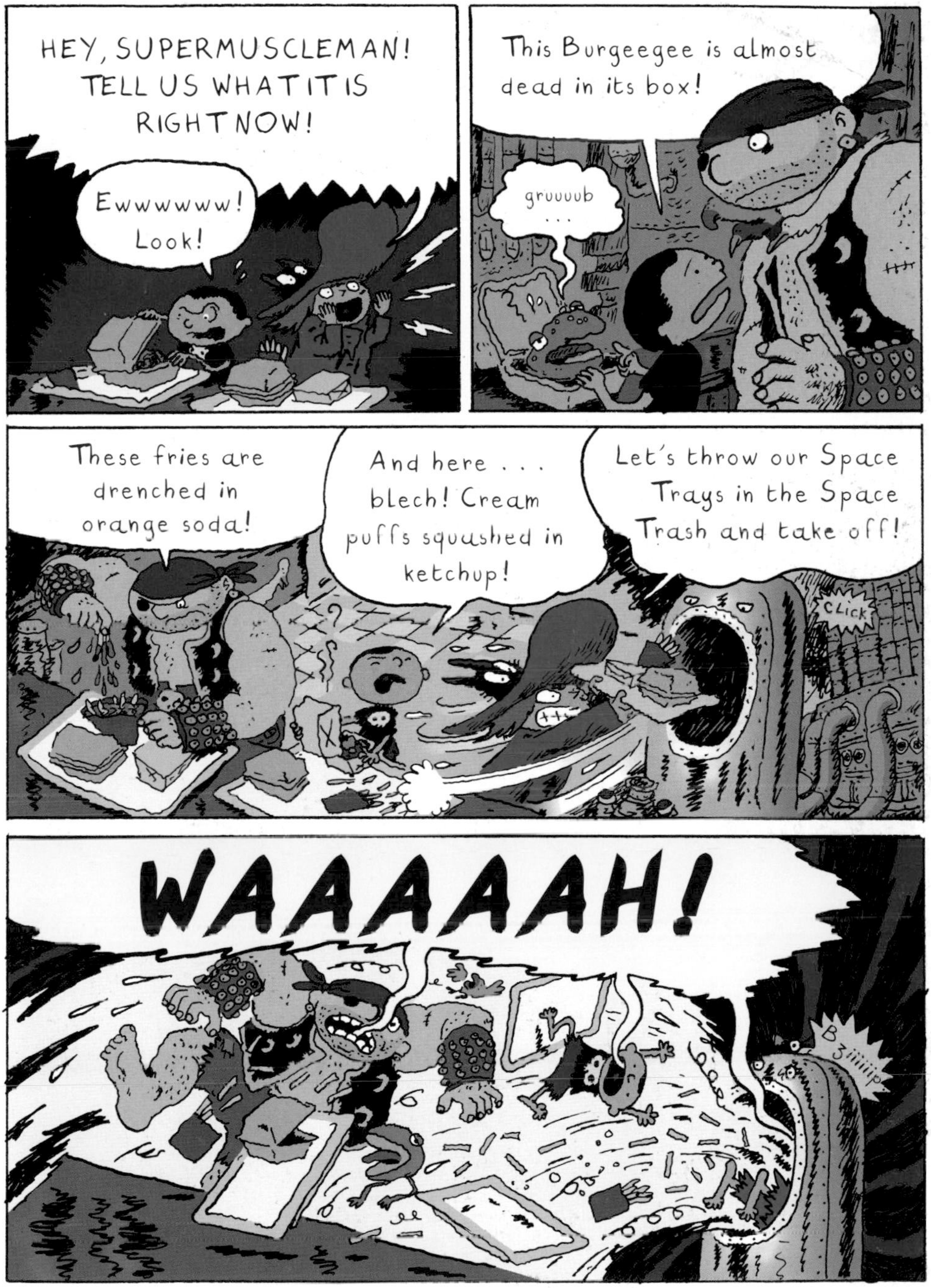
HEY, SUPERMUSCLEMAN! TELL US WHAT IT IS RIGHT NOW!
Ewwwwww! Look!
This Burgeegee is almost dead in its box!
grouuub . . .
These fries are drenched in orange soda!
And here . . . blech! Cream puffs squashed in ketchup!
Let's throw our Space Trays in the Space Trash and take off!
CLICK
WAAAAAH!
B3iiiiiip

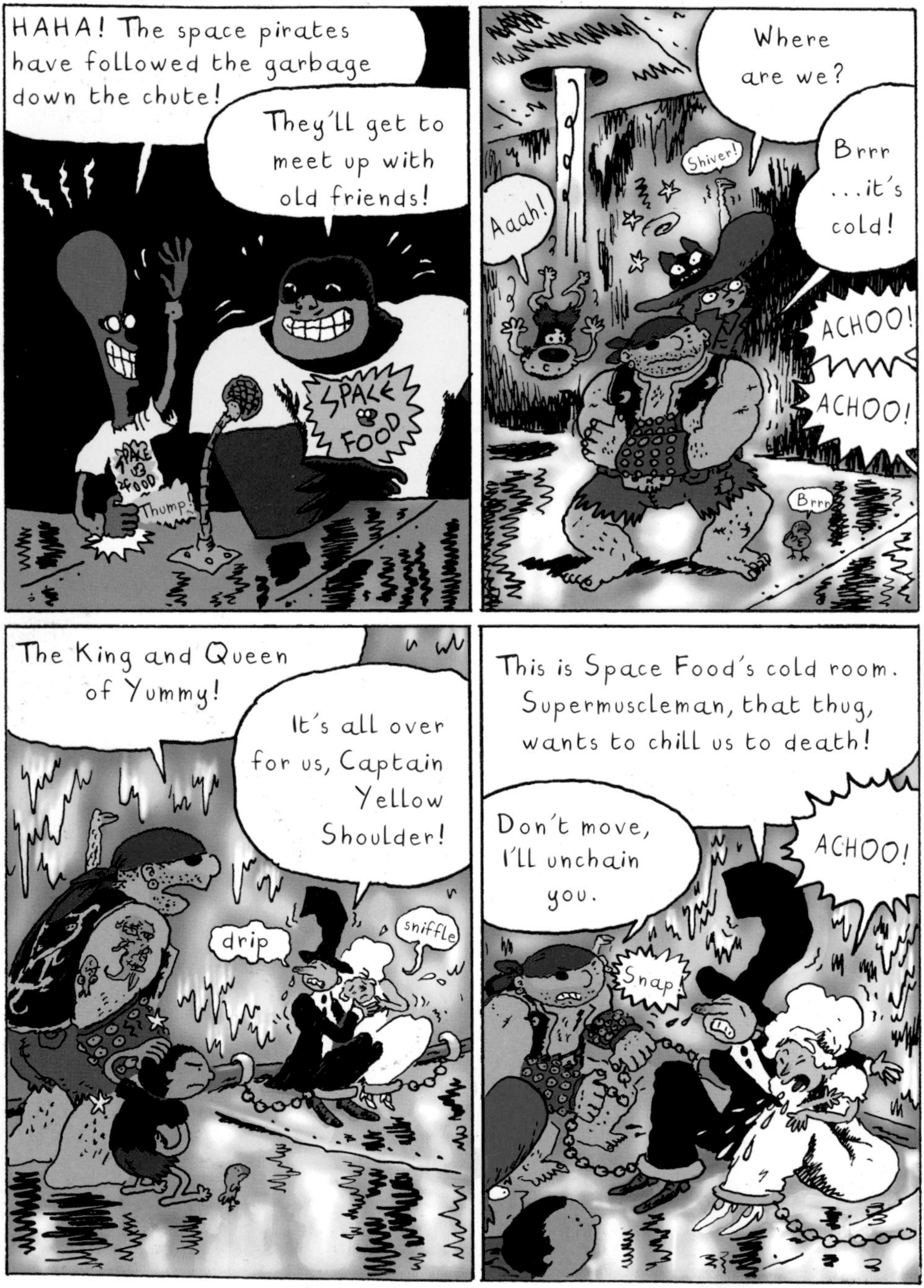
HAHA! The space pirates have followed the garbage down the chute!
They'll get to meet up with old friends!
SPACE FOOD
Thump!
Where are we?
Shiver!
Brrr ...it's cold!
Aaah!
ACHOO!
ACHOO!
Brrr
The King and Queen of Yummy!
It's all over for us, Captain Yellow Shoulder!
drip
sniffle
This is Space Food's cold room. Supermuscleman, that thug, wants to chill us to death!
Don't move, I'll unchain you.
ACHOO!
Snap!

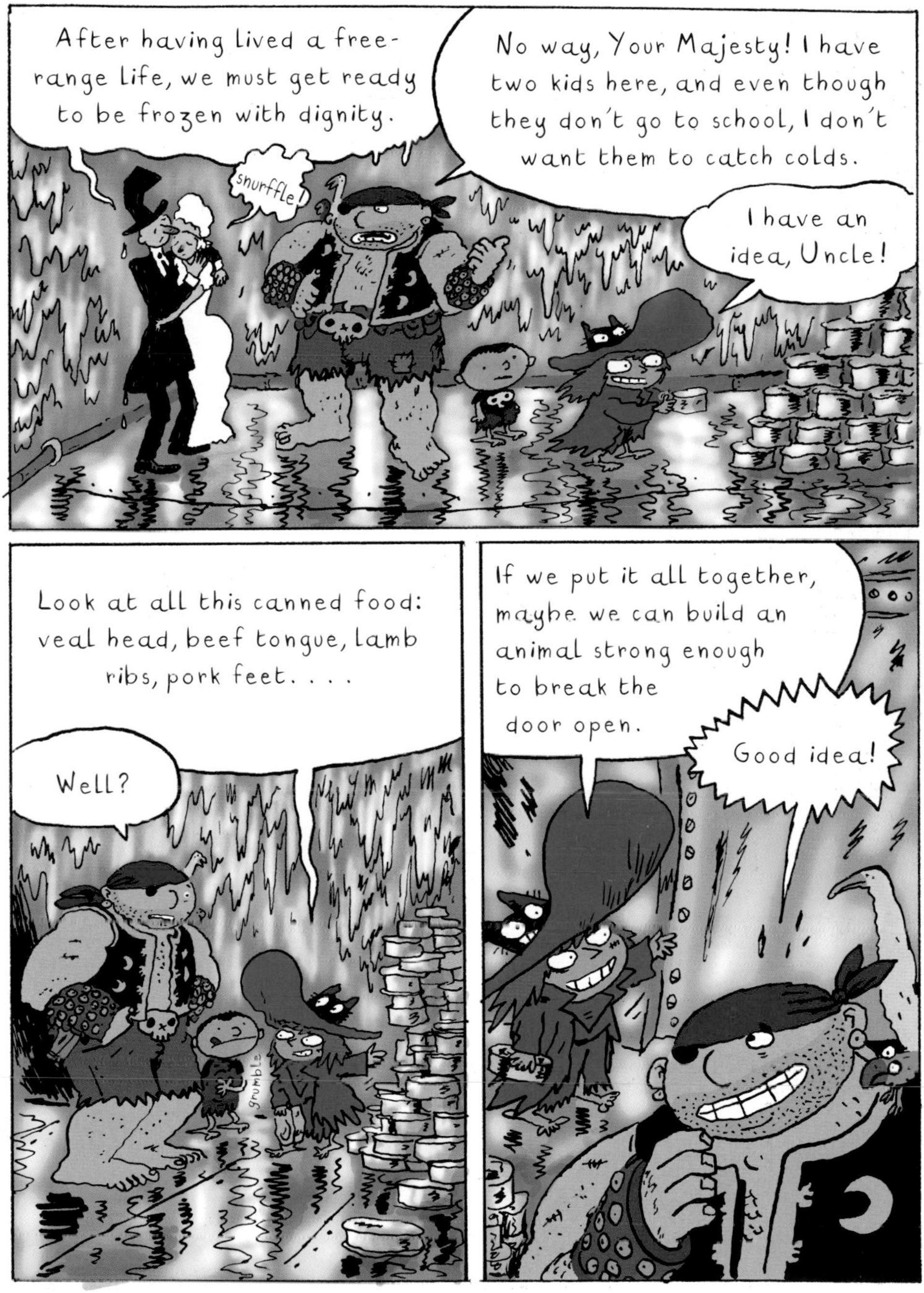
After having lived a free-range life, we must get ready to be frozen with dignity.
snuffle!
No way, Your Majesty! I have two kids here, and even though they don't go to school, I don't want them to catch colds.
I have an idea, Uncle!
Look at all this canned food: veal head, beef tongue, lamb ribs, pork feet. . . .
Well?
grumble
If we put it all together, maybe we can build an animal strong enough to break the door open.
Good idea!

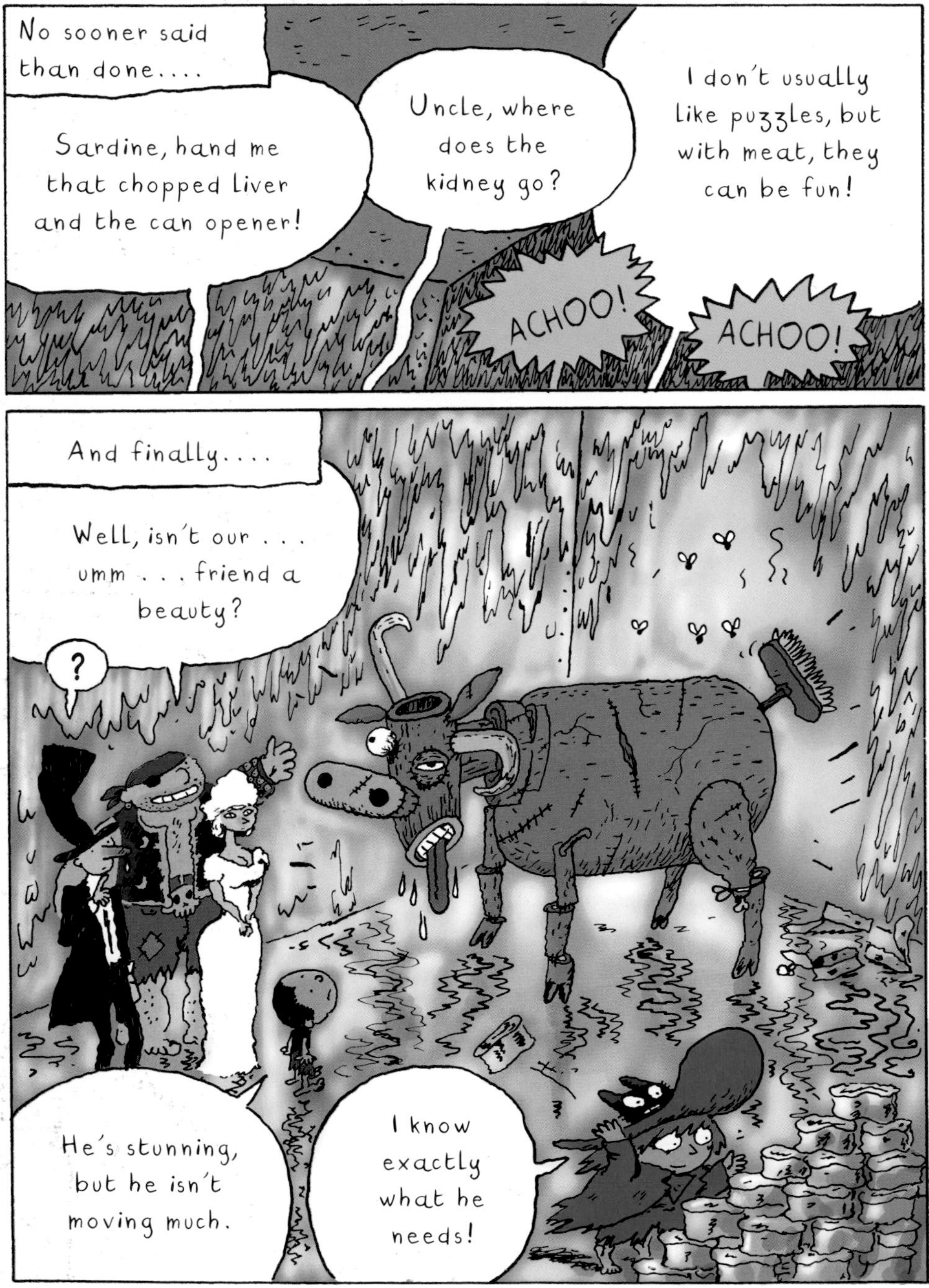
No sooner said than done....
Sardine, hand me that chopped liver and the can opener!
Uncle, where does the kidney go?
I don't usually like puzzles, but with meat, they can be fun!
ACHOO!
ACHOO!
And finally....
Well, isn't our . . . umm . . . friend a beauty?
?
He's stunning, but he isn't moving much.
I know exactly what he needs!

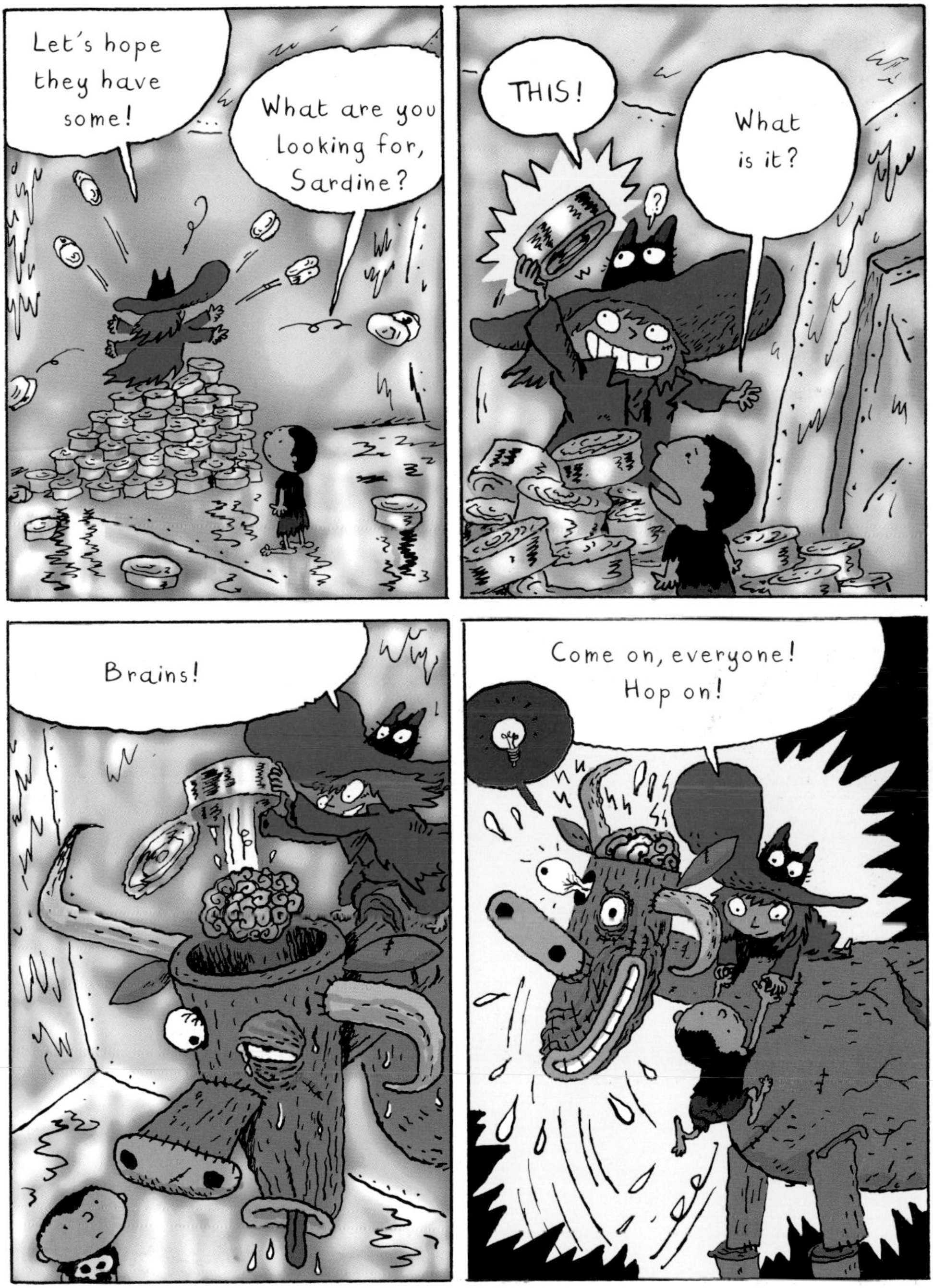
Let's hope they have some!
What are you looking for, Sardine?
THIS!
?
What is it?
Brains!
Come on, everyone! Hop on!

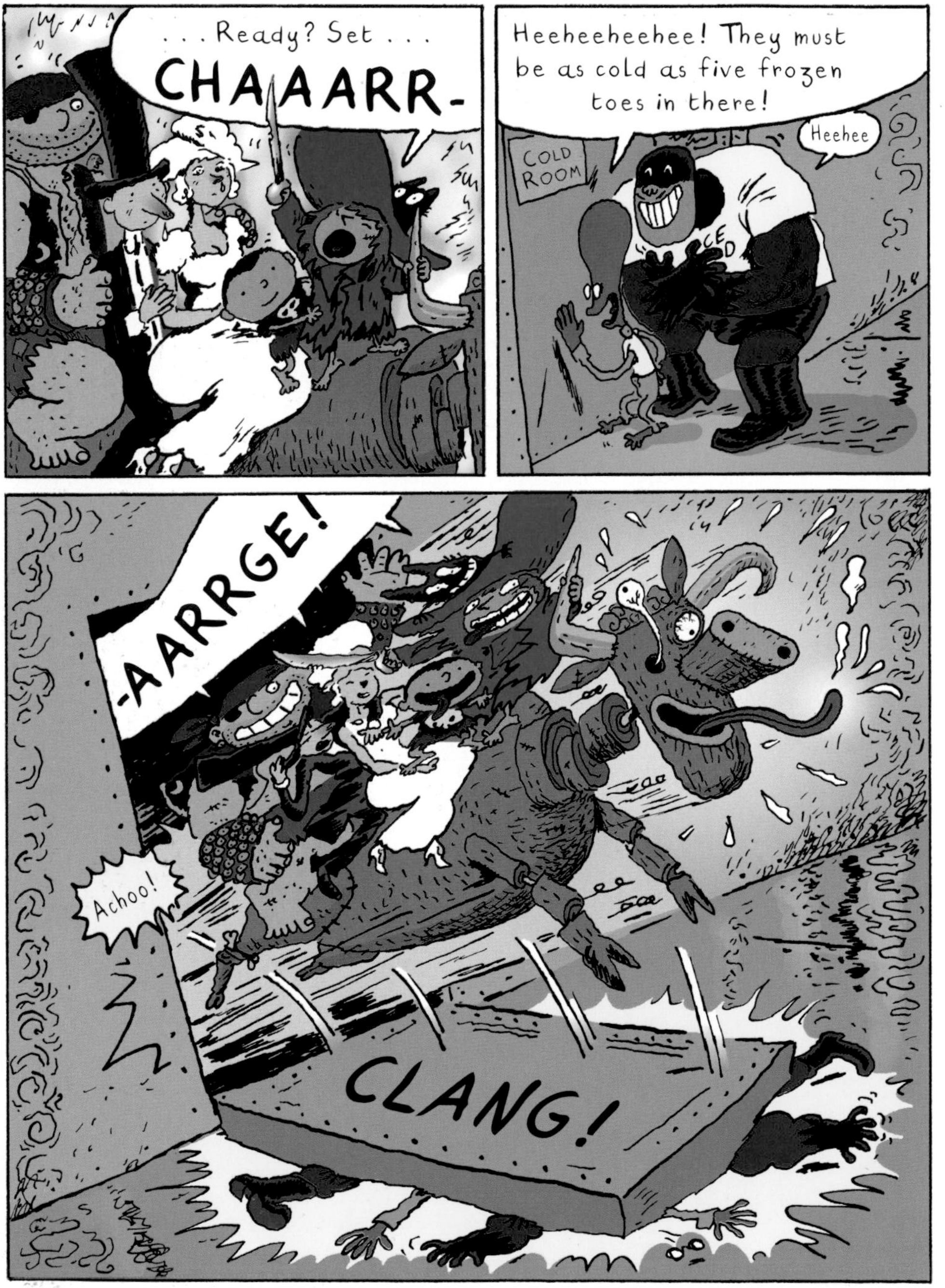
. . . Ready? Set . . .
CHAAARR-
Heeheeheehee! They must be as cold as five frozen toes in there!
COLD ROOM
Heehee
-AARRGE!
Achoo!
CLANG!

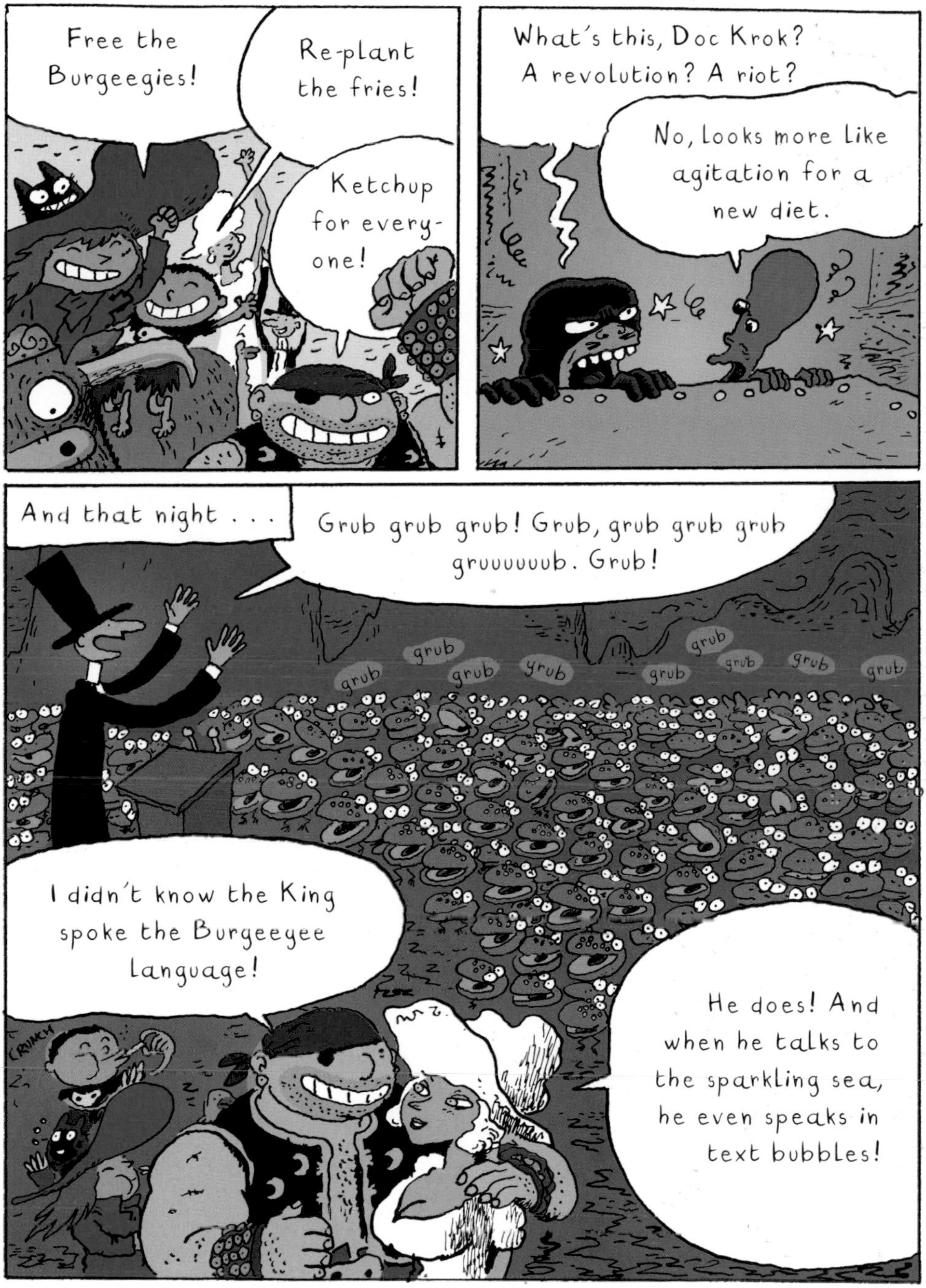
Free the Burgeegies!
Re-plant the fries!
Ketchup for every-one!
What's this, Doc Krok? A revolution? A riot?
No, looks more like agitation for a new diet.
And that night . . .
Grub grub grub! Grub, grub grub grub gruuuuuub. Grub!
grub
grub
grub
grub
grub
grub
grub
grub
grub
I didn't know the King spoke the Burgeeyee language!
He does! And when he talks to the sparkling sea, he even speaks in text bubbles!

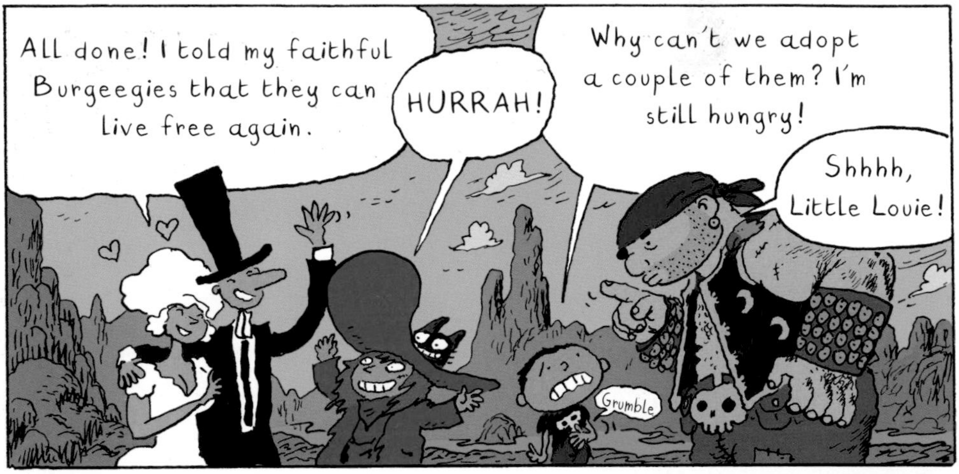
All done! I told my faithful Burgeegies that they can live free again.
HURRAH!
Why can't we adopt a couple of them? I'm still hungry!
Shhhh, Little Louie!
Grumble

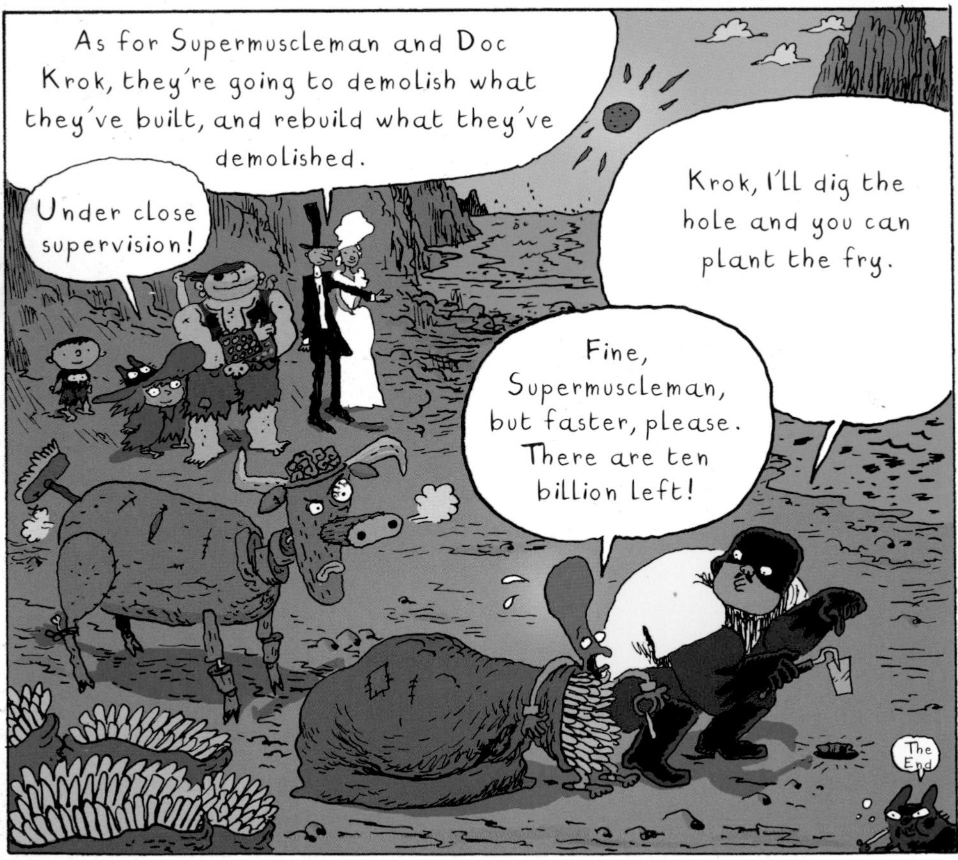
As for Supermuscleman and Doc Krok, they're going to demolish what they've built, and rebuild what they've demolished.
Under close supervision!
Krok, I'll dig the hole and you can plant the fry.
Fine, Supermuscleman, but faster, please. There are ten billion left!
The End

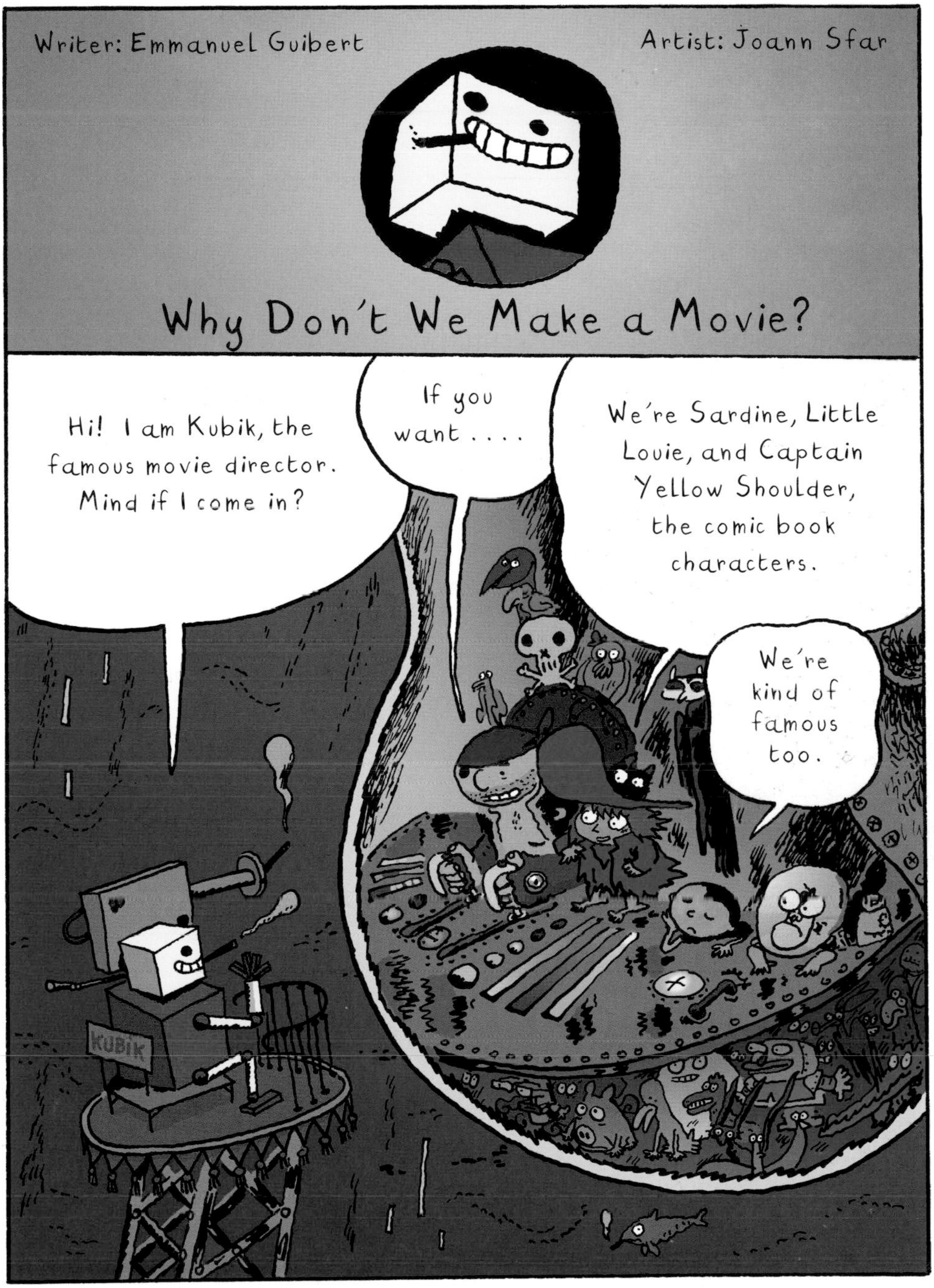
Writer: Emmanuel Guibert
Artist: Joann Sfar
Why Don't We Make a Movie?
Hi! I am Kubik, the famous movie director. Mind if I come in?
If you want....
We're Sardine, Little Louie, and Captain Yellow Shoulder, the comic book characters.
We're kind of famous too.
KUBIK

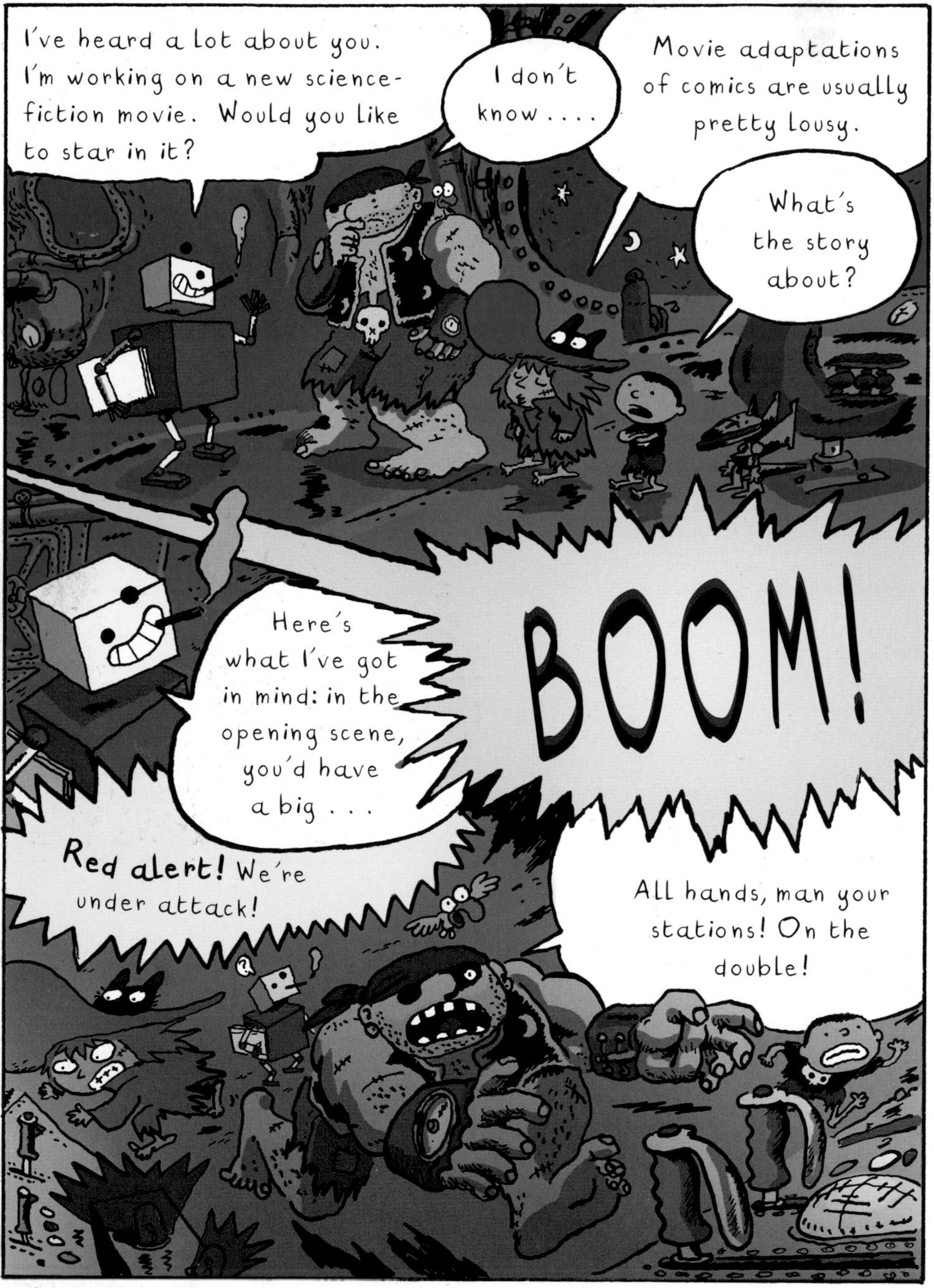
I've heard a lot about you. I'm working on a new science-fiction movie. Would you like to star in it?
I don't know....
Movie adaptations of comics are usually pretty lousy.
What's the story about?
Here's what I've got in mind: in the opening scene, you'd have a big . . .
BOOM!
Red alert! We're under attack!
All hands, man your stations! On the double!

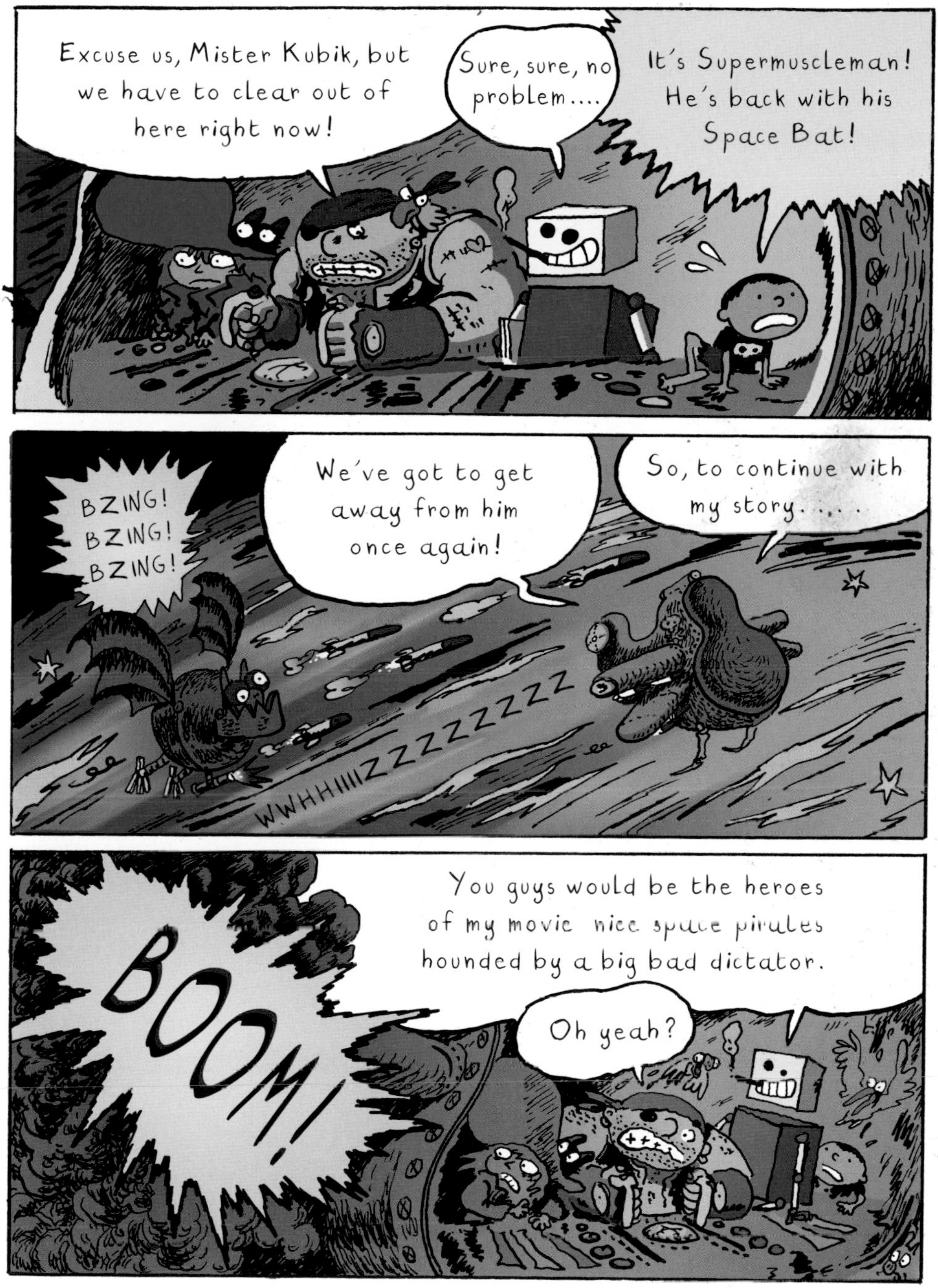
Excuse us, Mister Kubik, but we have to clear out of here right now!
Sure, sure, no problem....
It's Supermuscleman! He's back with his Space Bat!
BZING! BZING! BZING!
We've got to get away from him once again!
So, to continue with my story.....
WWHHIIIZZZZZZZZZ
BOOM!
You guys would be the heroes of my movie nice space pirates hounded by a big bad dictator.
Oh yeah?

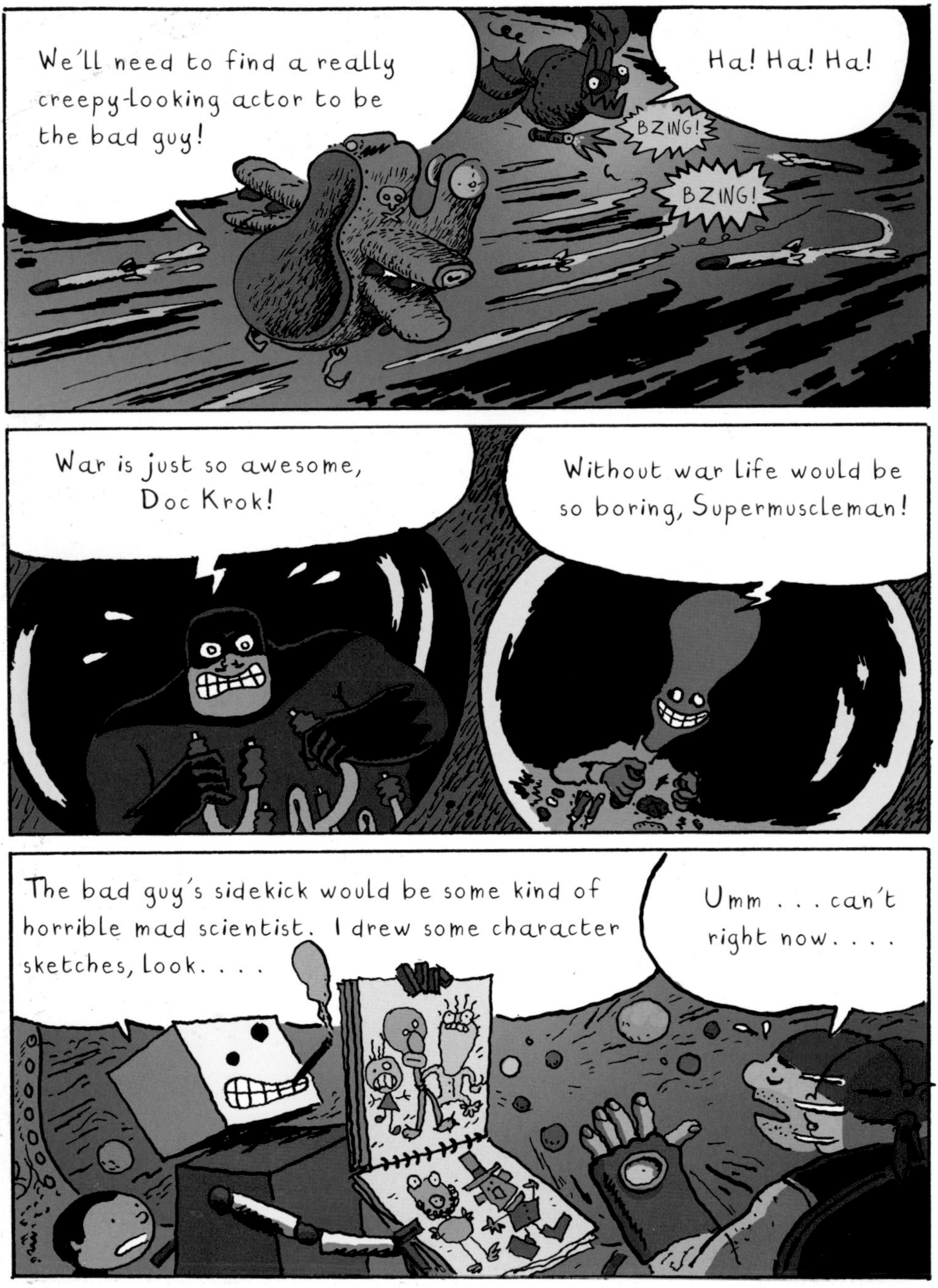
We'll need to find a really creepy-looking actor to be the bad guy!
Ha! Ha! Ha!
BZING!
BZING!
War is just so awesome, Doc Krok!
Without war life would be so boring, Supermuscleman!
The bad guy's sidekick would be some kind of horrible mad scientist. I drew some character sketches, look. . . .
Umm . . . can't right now. . . .

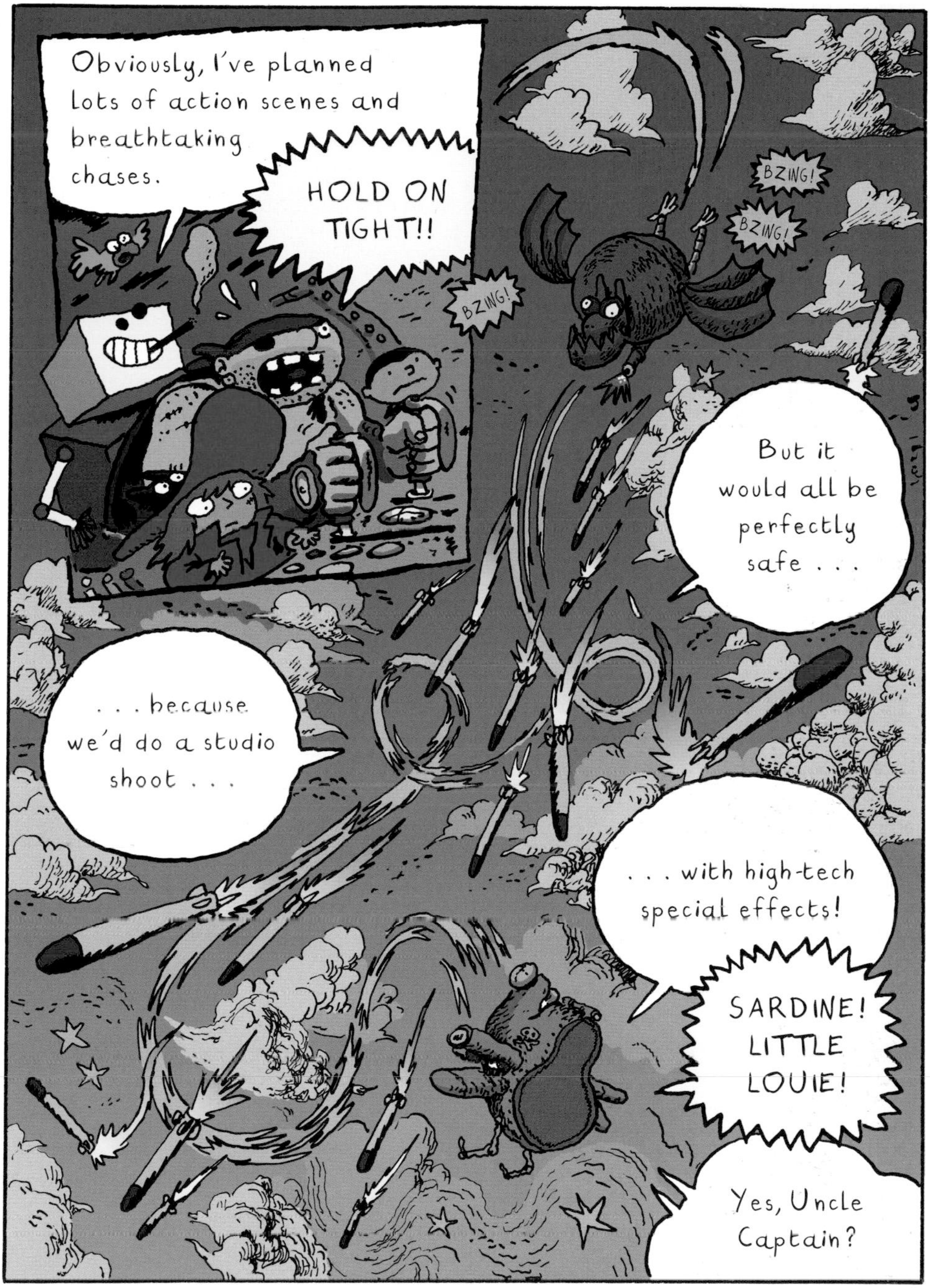
Obviously, I've planned lots of action scenes and breathtaking chases.
HOLD ON TIGHT!!
BZING!
BZING!
BZING!
But it would all be perfectly safe . . .
. . . because we'd do a studio shoot . . .
. . . with high-tech special effects!
SARDINE! LITTLE LOUIE!
Yes, Uncle Captain?

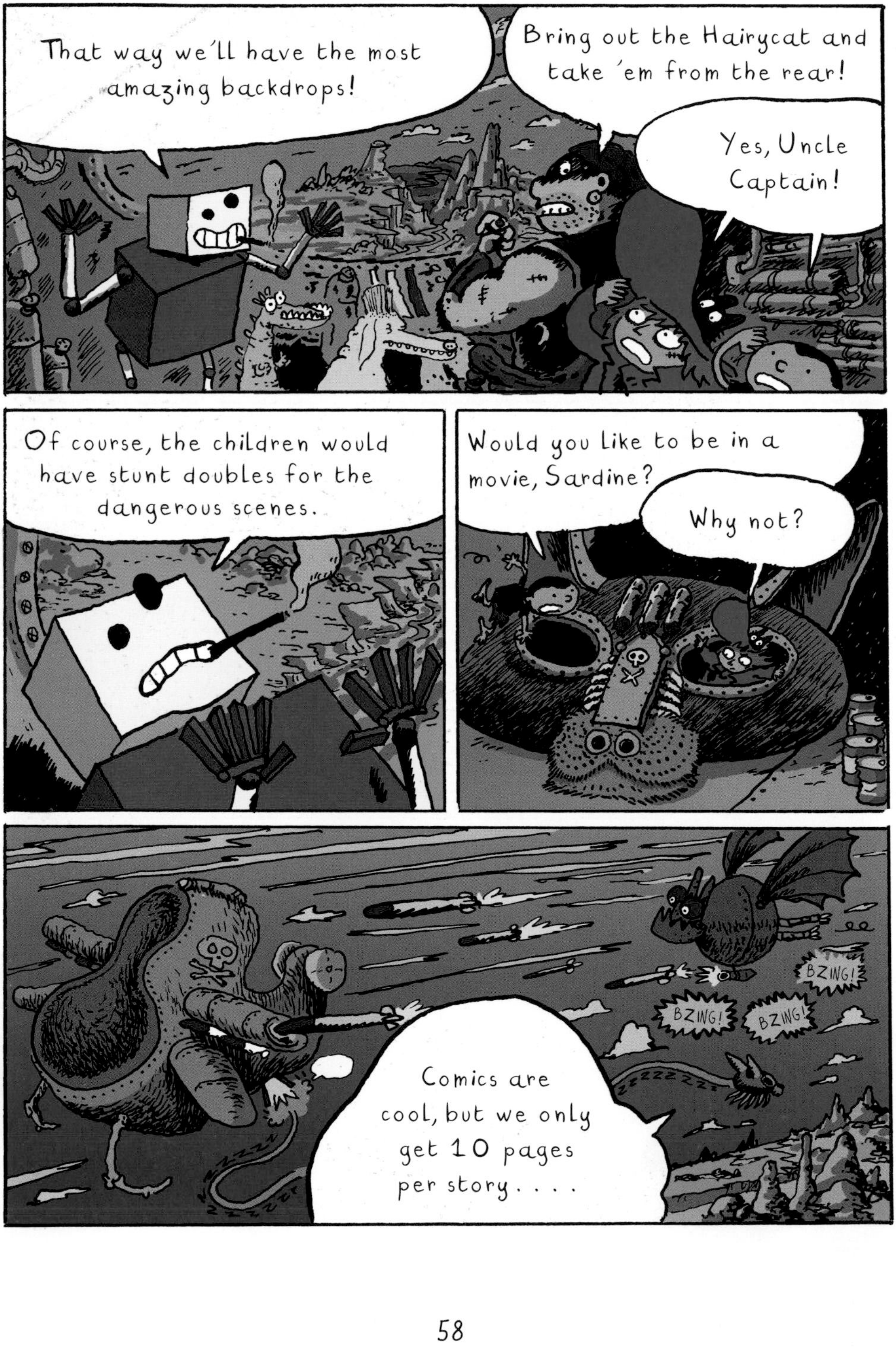
That way we'll have the most amazing backdrops!
Bring out the Hairycat and take 'em from the rear!
Yes, Uncle Captain!
Of course, the children would have stunt doubles for the dangerous scenes.
Would you like to be in a movie, Sardine?
Why not?
BZING!
BZING!
BZING!
Comics are cool, but we only get 10 pages per story . . . .

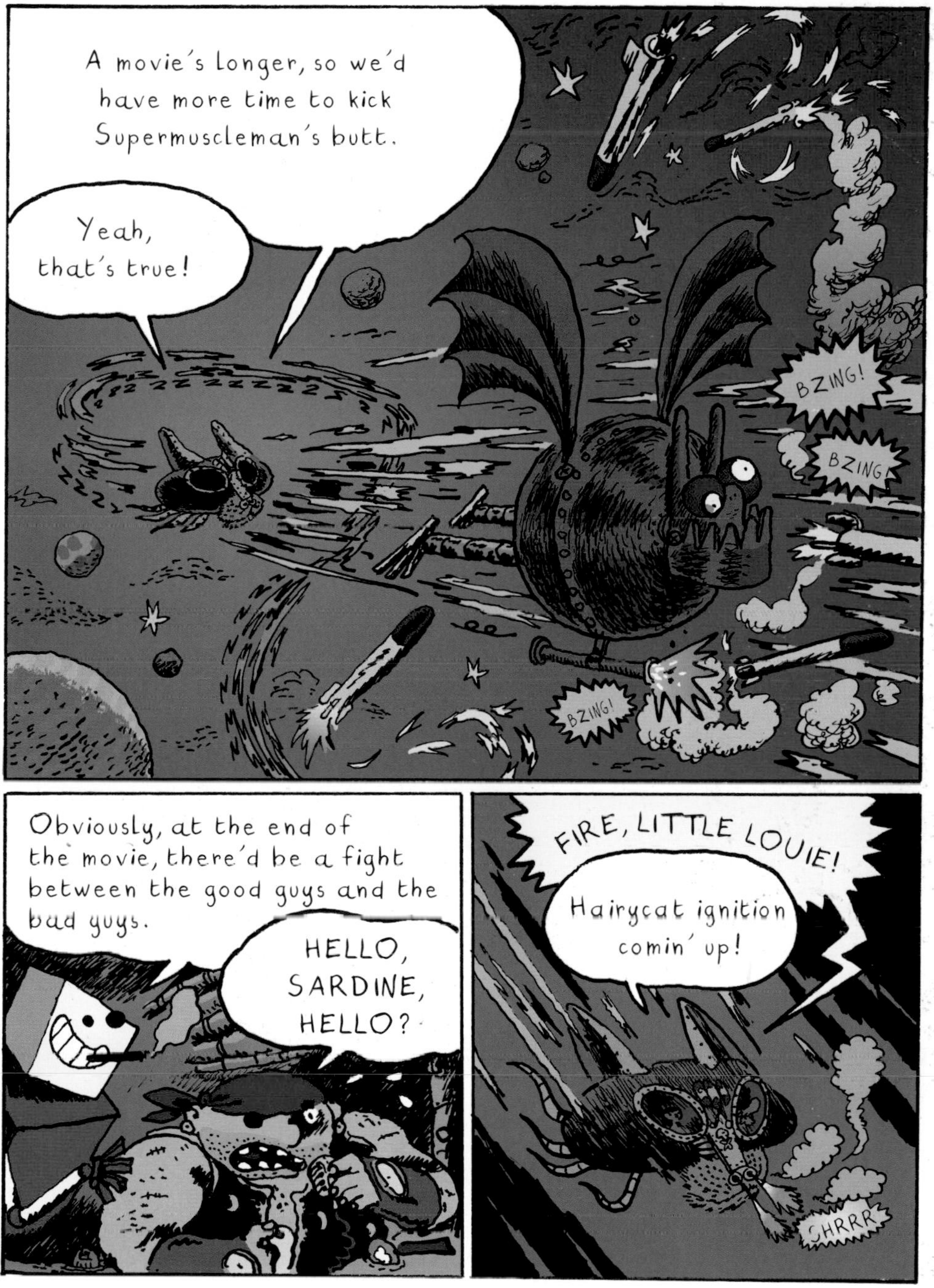
A movie's longer, so we'd have more time to kick Supermuscleman's butt.
Yeah, that's true!
BZING!
BZING!
BZING!
Obviously, at the end of the movie, there'd be a fight between the good guys and the bad guys.
HELLO, SARDINE, HELLO?
FIRE, LITTLE LOUIE!
Hairycat ignition comin' up!
CHRRR

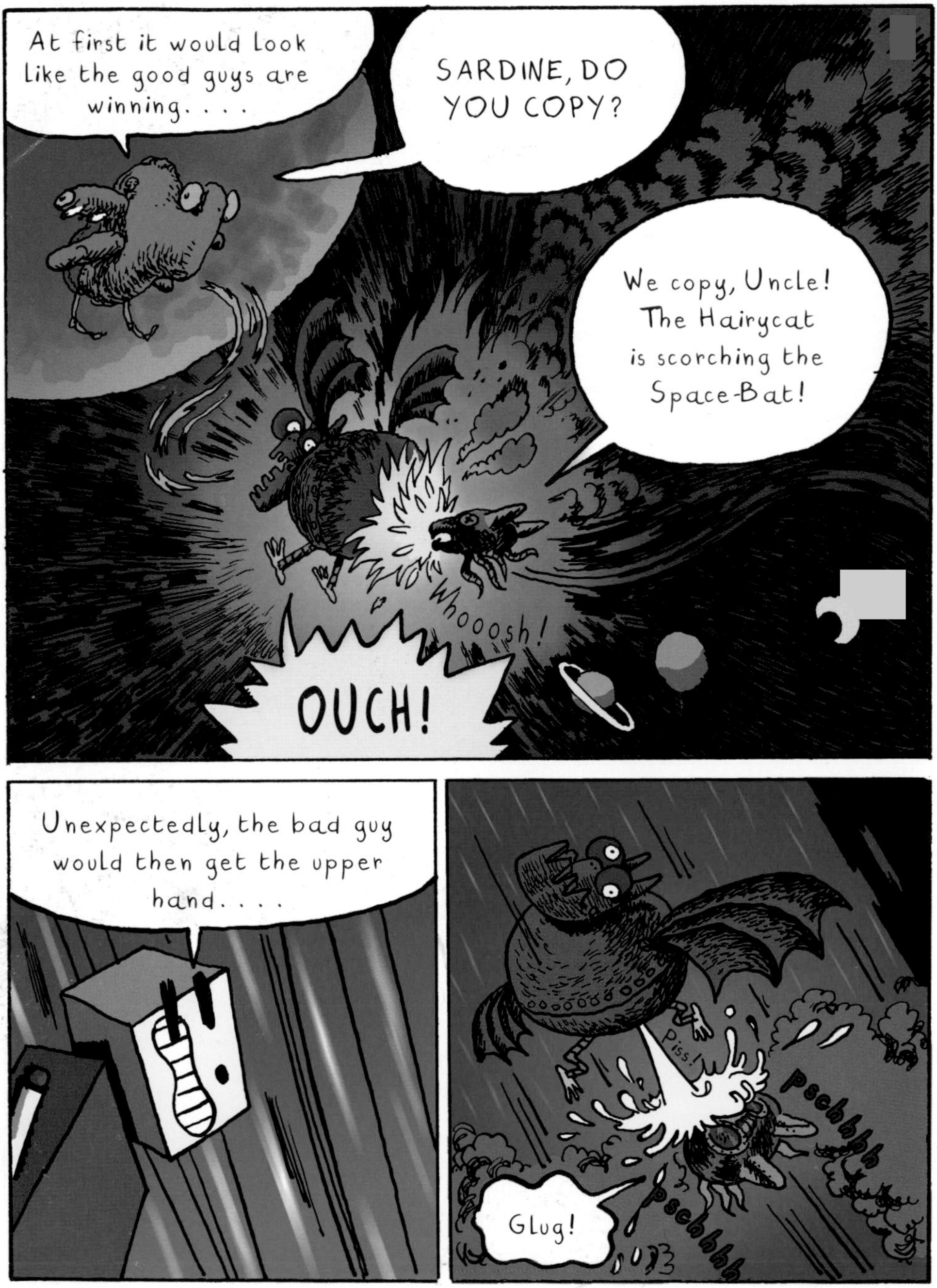
At first it would look like the good guys are winning. . . .
SARDINE, DO YOU COPY?
We copy, Uncle! The Hairycat is scorching the Space-Bat!
Whoooosh!
OUCH!
Unexpectedly, the bad guy would then get the upper hand. . . .
Piss!
Pschhhh
Pschhhh
Glug!

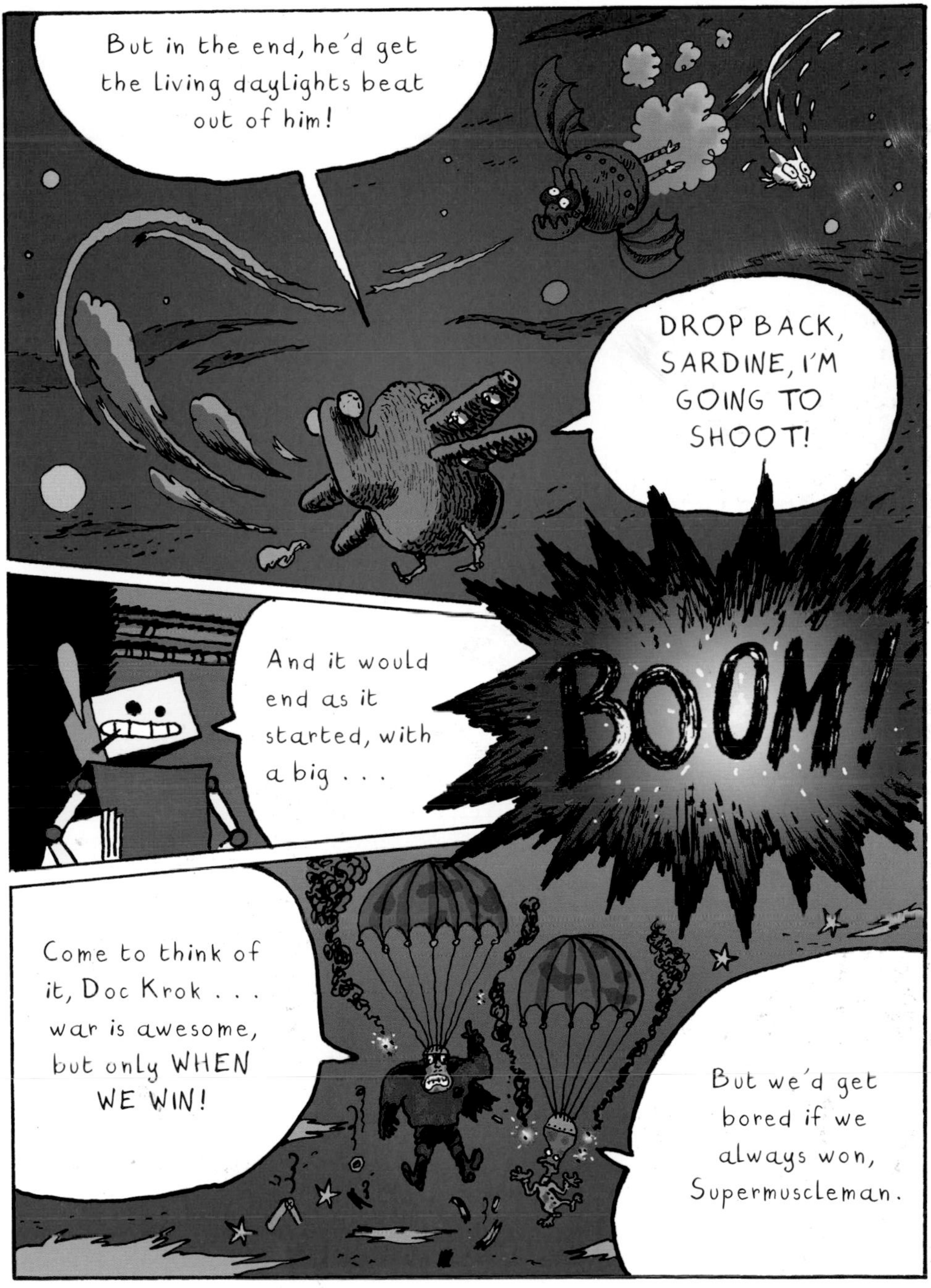
But in the end, he'd get the living daylights beat out of him!
DROP BACK, SARDINE, I'M GOING TO SHOOT!
And it would end as it started, with a big . . .
BOOM!
Come to think of it, Doc Krok . . . war is awesome, but only WHEN WE WIN!
But we'd get bored if we always won, Supermuscleman.

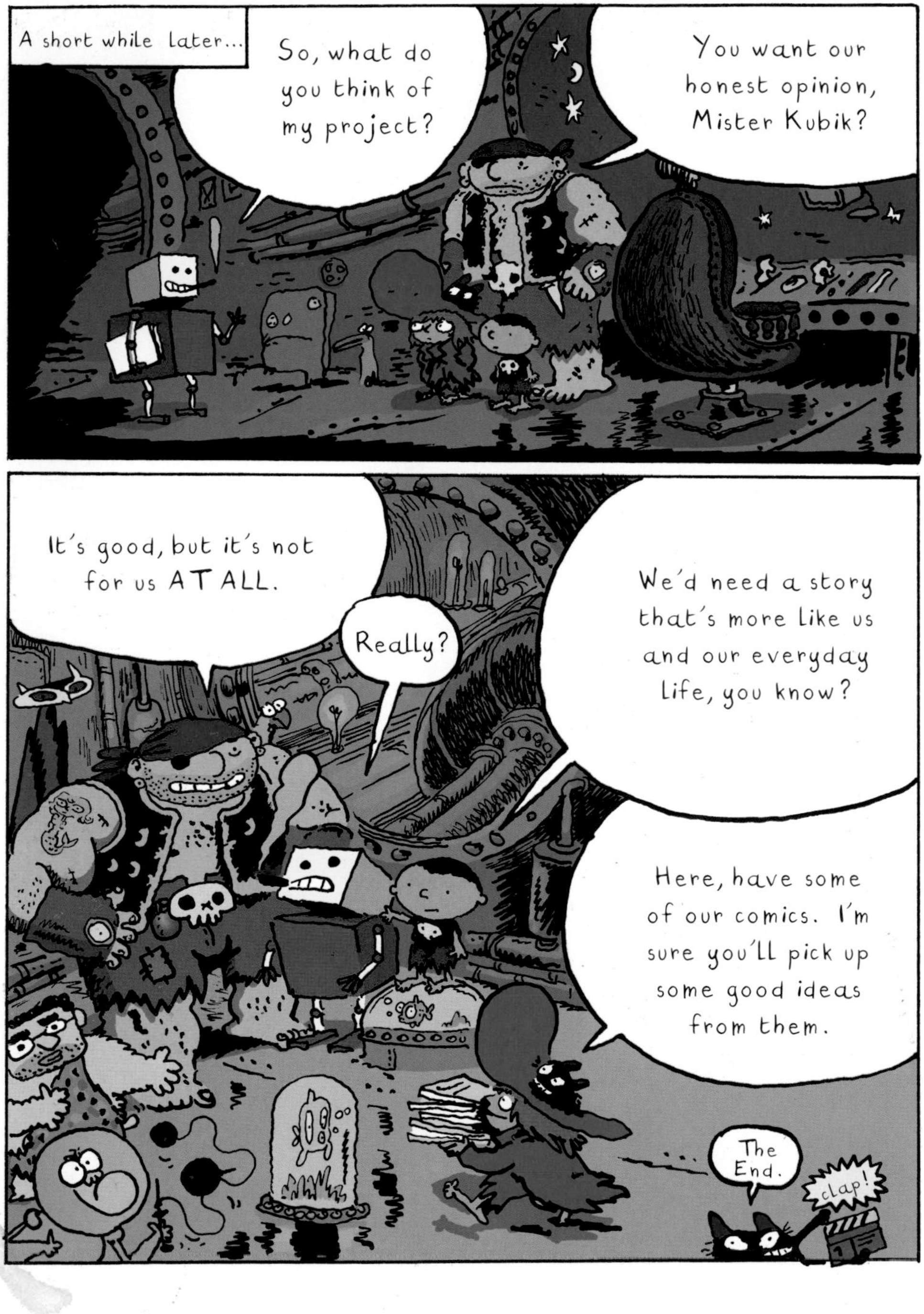
A short while later...
So, what do you think of my project?
You want our honest opinion, Mister Kubik?
It's good, but it's not for us AT ALL.
Really?
We'd need a story that's more like us and our everyday life, you know?
Here, have some of our comics. I'm sure you'll pick up some good ideas from them.
The End.
clap!

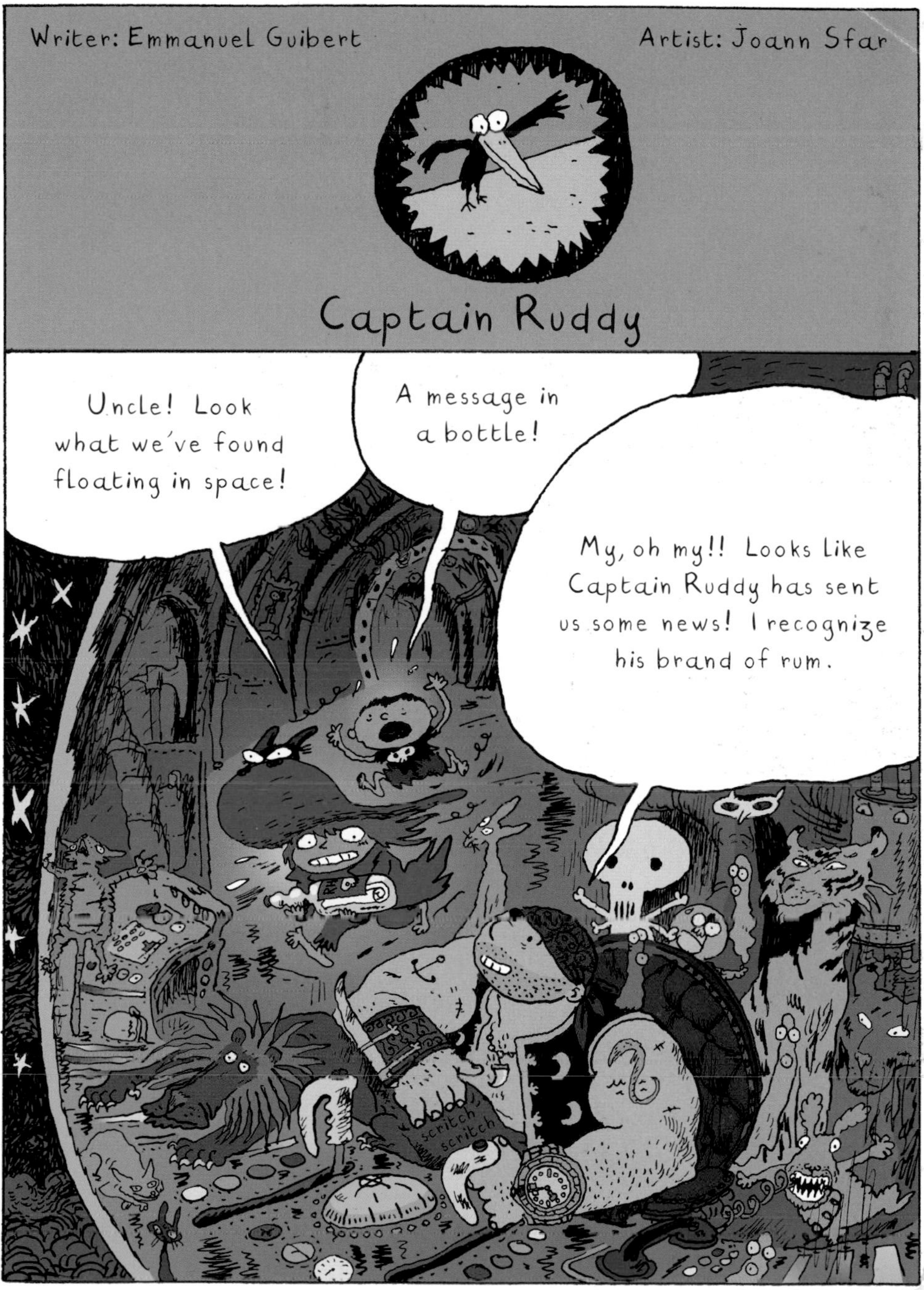
Writer: Emmanuel Guibert
Artist: Joann Sfar
Captain Ruddy
Uncle! Look what we've found floating in space!
A message in a bottle!
My, oh my!! Looks like Captain Ruddy has sent us some news! I recognize his brand of rum.
scritch scritch

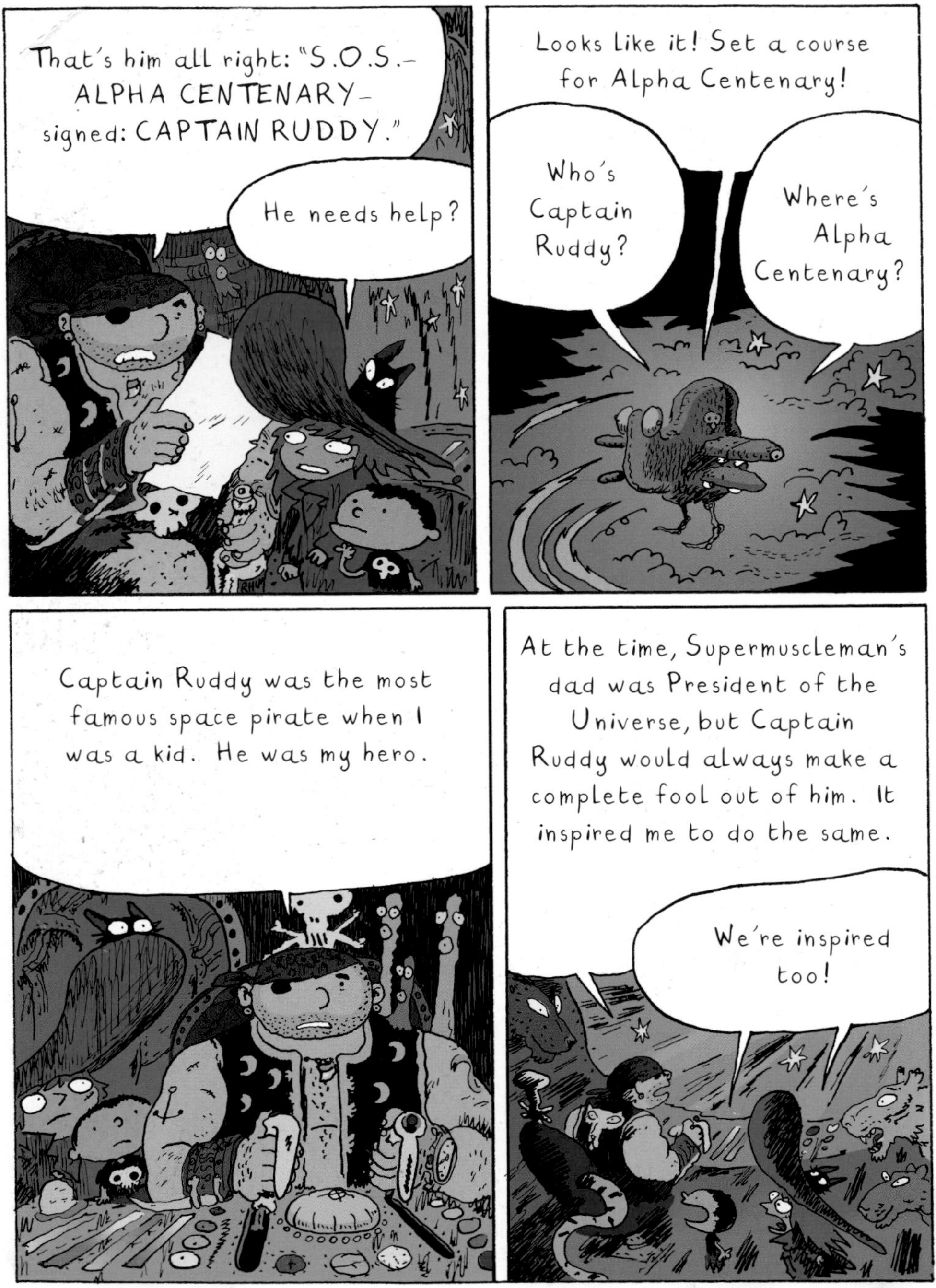

That's him all right: "S.O.S.– ALPHA CENTENARY– signed: CAPTAIN RUDDY."
He needs help?
Looks like it! Set a course for Alpha Centenary!
Who's Captain Ruddy?
Where's Alpha Centenary?
Captain Ruddy was the most famous space pirate when I was a kid. He was my hero.
At the time, Supermuscleman's dad was President of the Universe, but Captain Ruddy would always make a complete fool out of him. It inspired me to do the same.
We're inspired too!

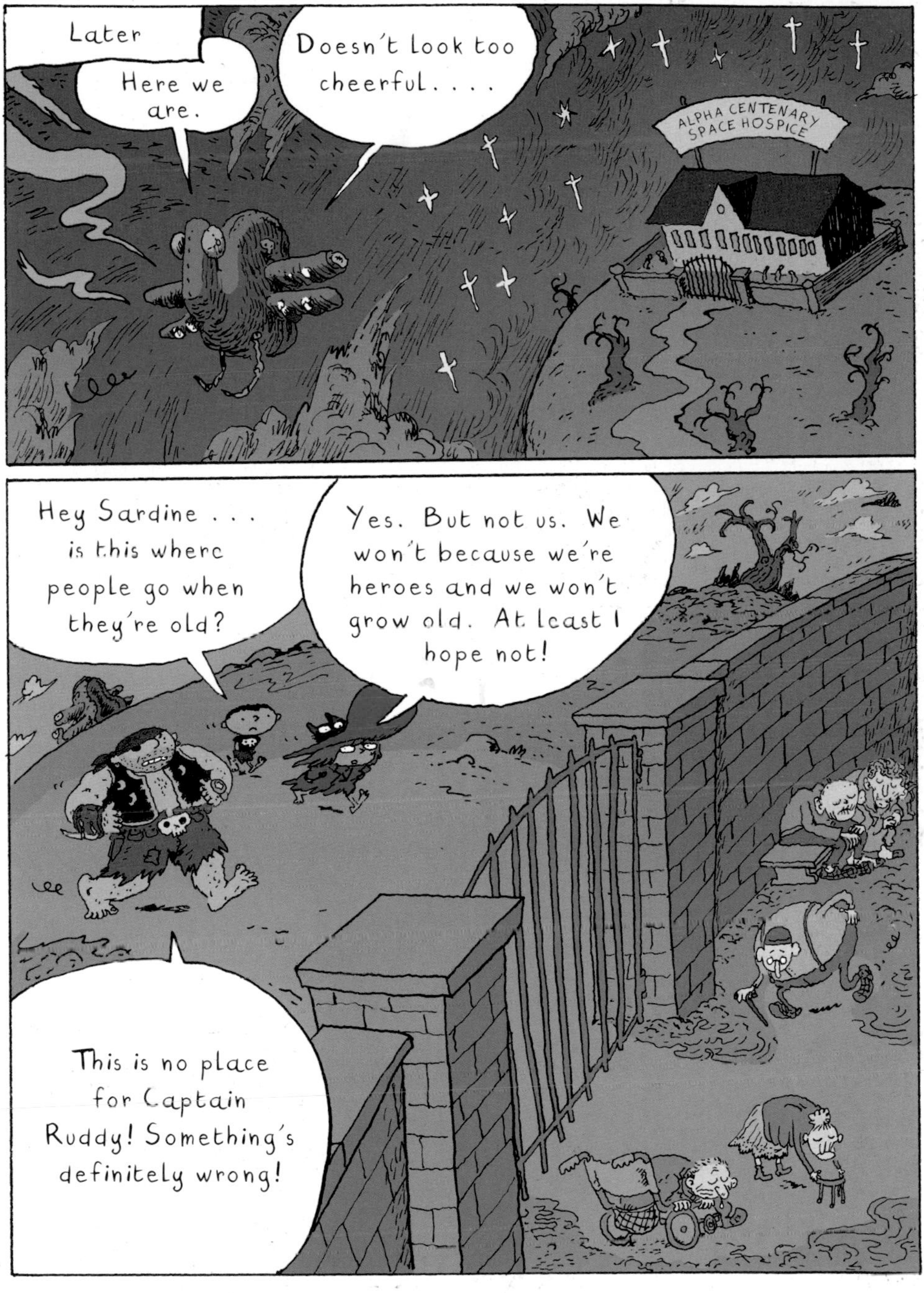
Later
Here we are.
Doesn't look too cheerful....
ALPHA CENTENARY SPACE HOSPICE
Hey Sardine ... is this where people go when they're old?
Yes. But not us. We won't because we're heroes and we won't grow old. At least I hope not!
This is no place for Captain Ruddy! Something's definitely wrong!

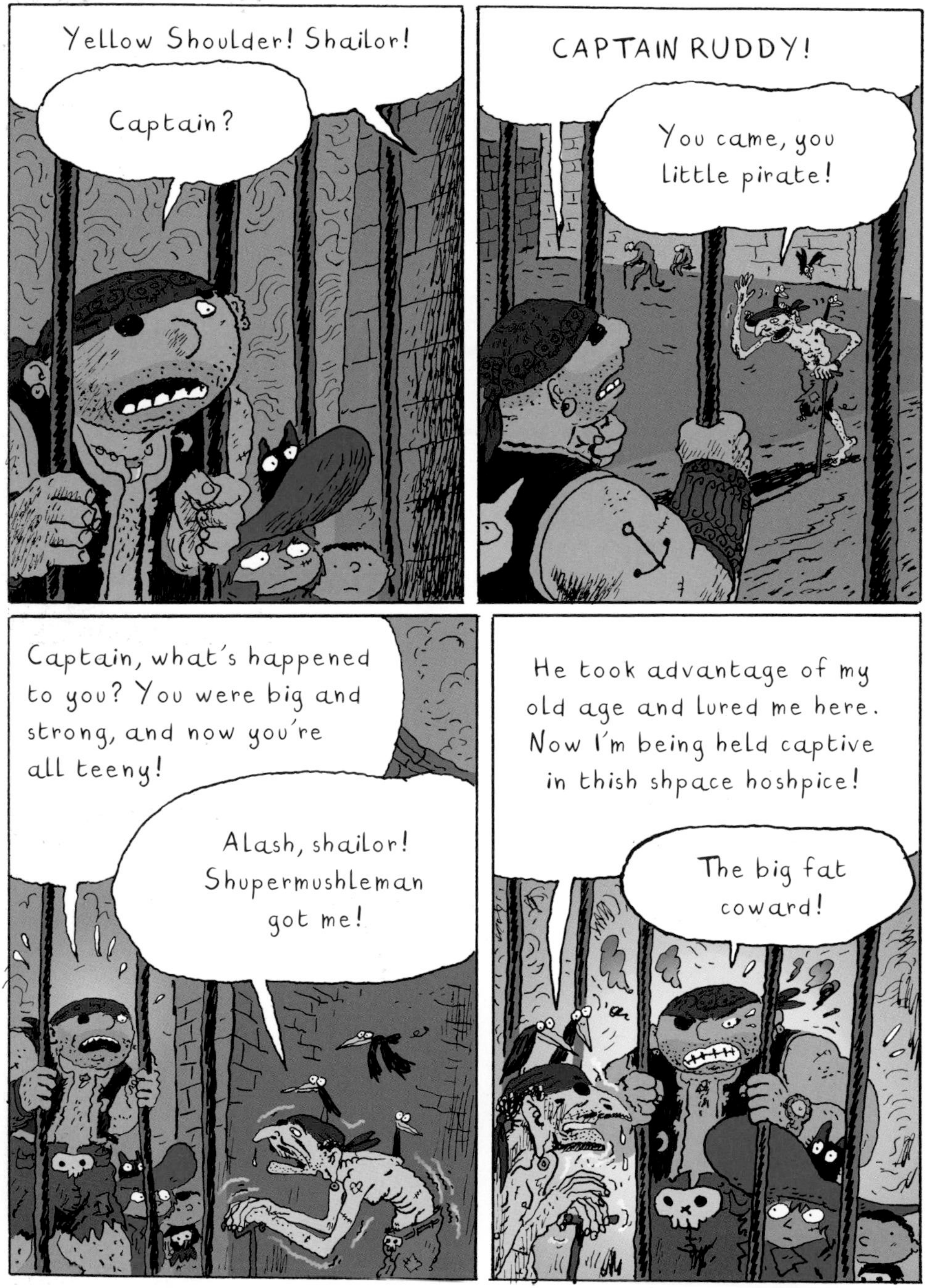
Yellow Shoulder! Shailor!
Captain?
CAPTAIN RUDDY!
You came, you little pirate!
Captain, what's happened to you? You were big and strong, and now you're all teeny!
Alash, shailor! Shupermushleman got me!
He took advantage of my old age and lured me here. Now I'm being held captive in thish shpace hoshpice!
The big fat coward!

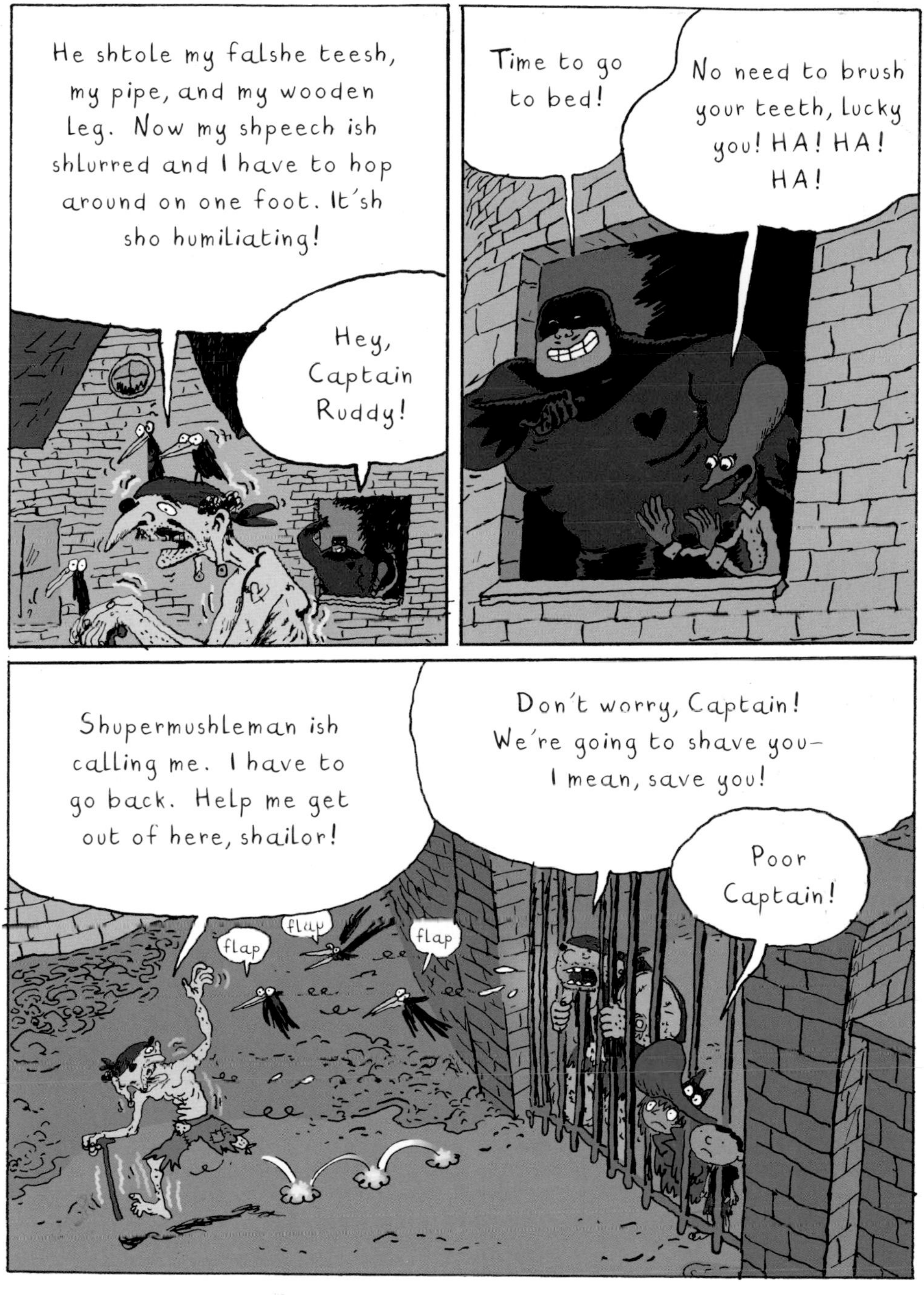
He shtole my falshe teesh, my pipe, and my wooden leg. Now my shpeech ish shlurred and I have to hop around on one foot. It'sh sho humiliating!
Hey, Captain Ruddy!
Time to go to bed!
No need to brush your teeth, lucky you! HA! HA! HA!
Shupermushleman ish calling me. I have to go back. Help me get out of here, shailor!
Don't worry, Captain! We're going to shave you— I mean, save you!
Poor Captain!
flap
flap
flap

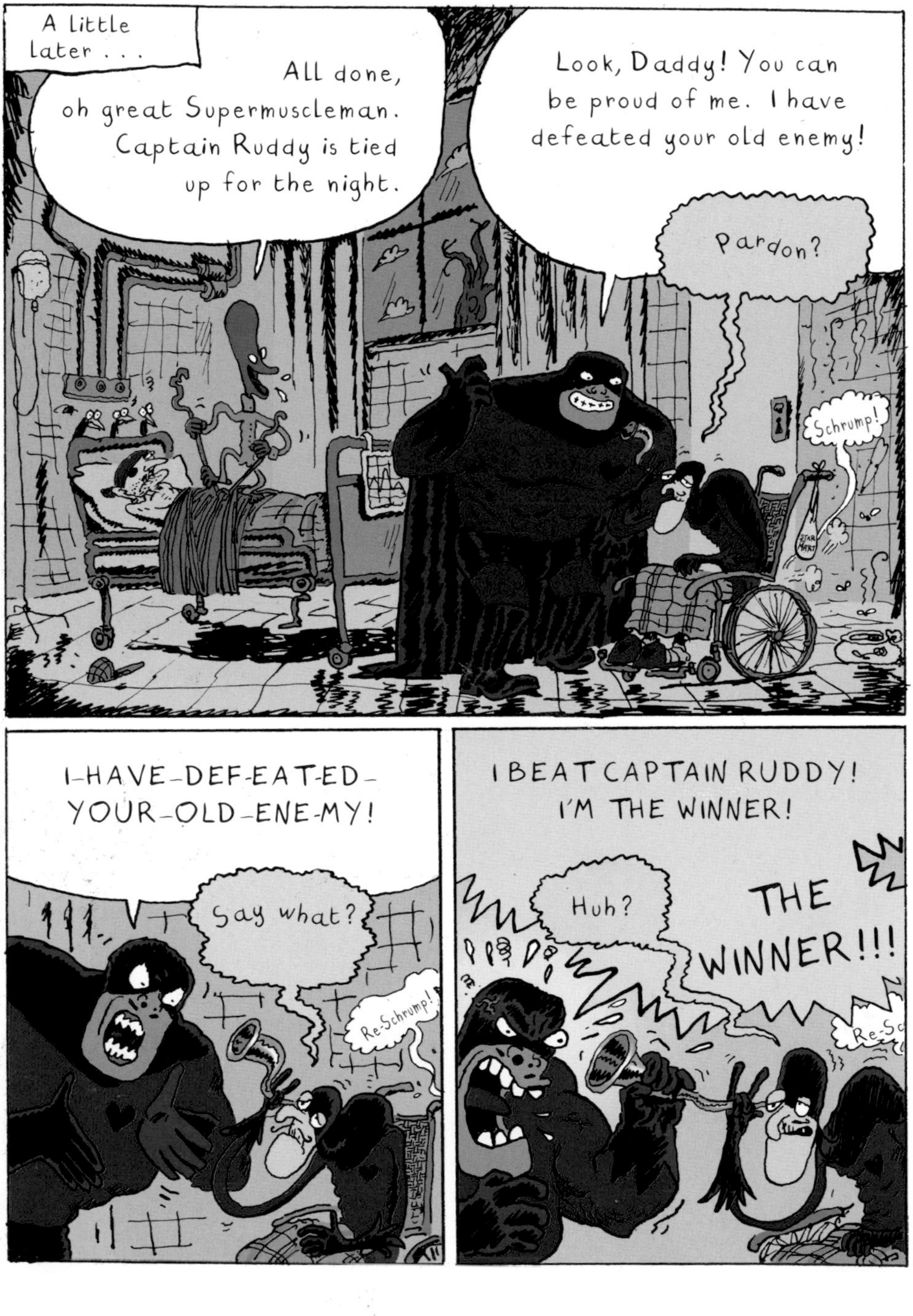

A little later . . .
All done, oh great Supermuscleman. Captain Ruddy is tied up for the night.
Look, Daddy! You can be proud of me. I have defeated your old enemy!
Pardon?
Schrump!
I-HAVE-DEF-EAT-ED-YOUR-OLD-ENE-MY!
Say what?
Re-Schrump!
I BEAT CAPTAIN RUDDY! I'M THE WINNER!
Huh?
THE WINNER!!!

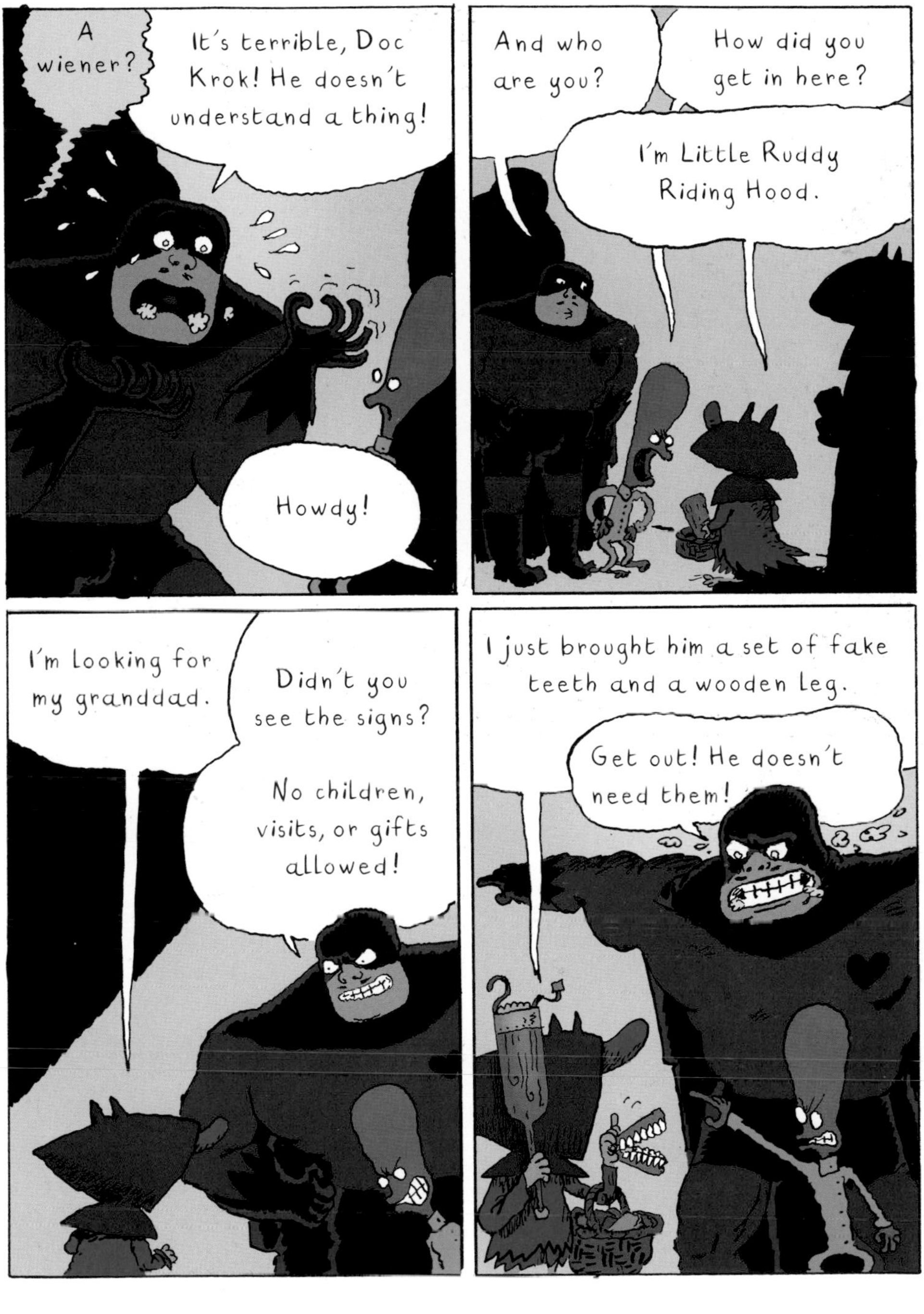
A wiener?
It's terrible, Doc Krok! He doesn't understand a thing!
Howdy!
And who are you?
How did you get in here?
I'm Little Ruddy Riding Hood.
I'm looking for my granddad.
Didn't you see the signs?
No children, visits, or gifts allowed!
I just brought him a set of fake teeth and a wooden leg.
Get out! He doesn't need them!

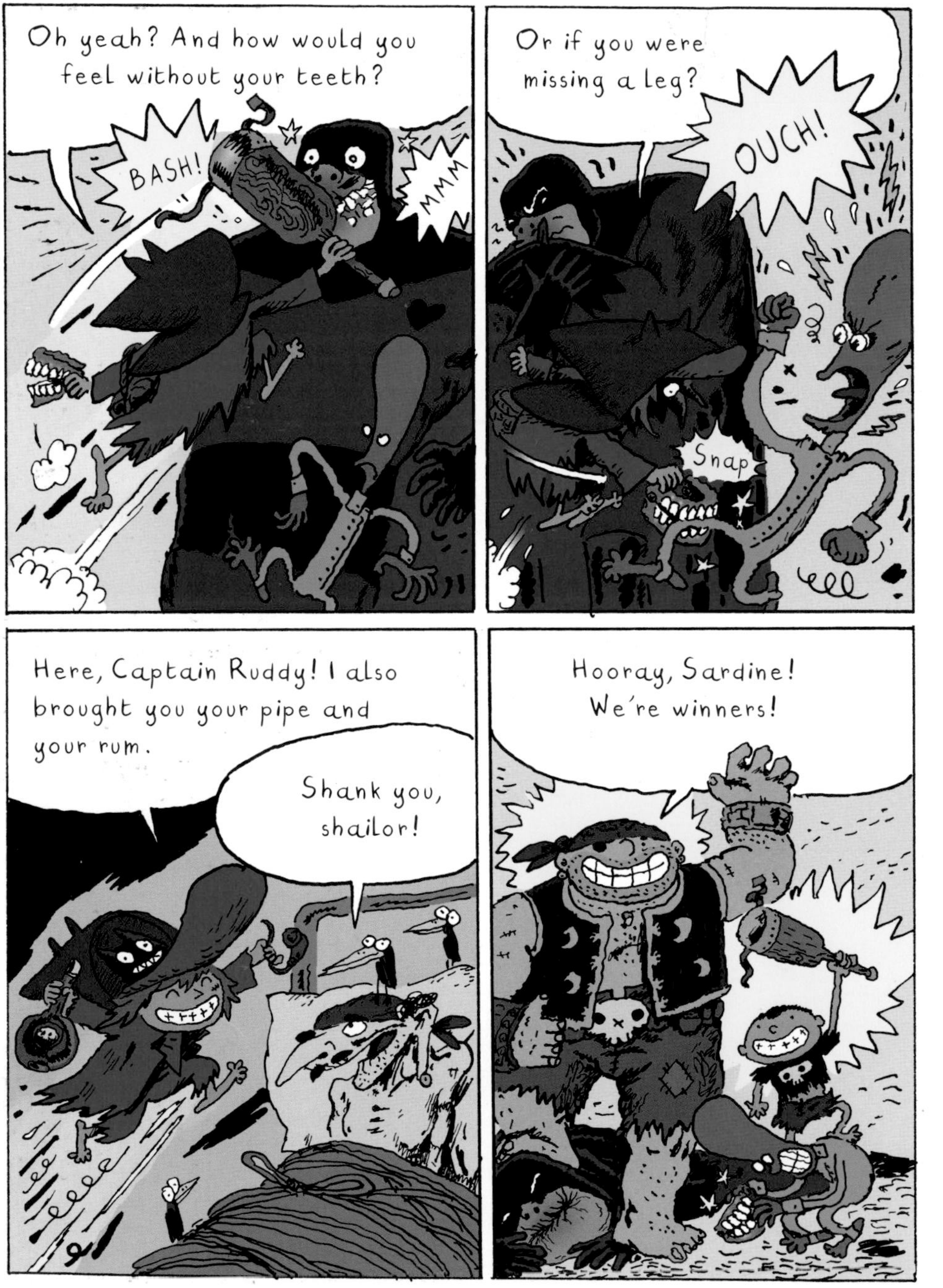
Oh yeah? And how would you feel without your teeth?
BASH!
MMM
Or if you were missing a leg?
OUCH!
Snap
Here, Captain Ruddy! I also brought you your pipe and your rum.
Shank you, shailor!
Hooray, Sardine! We're winners!

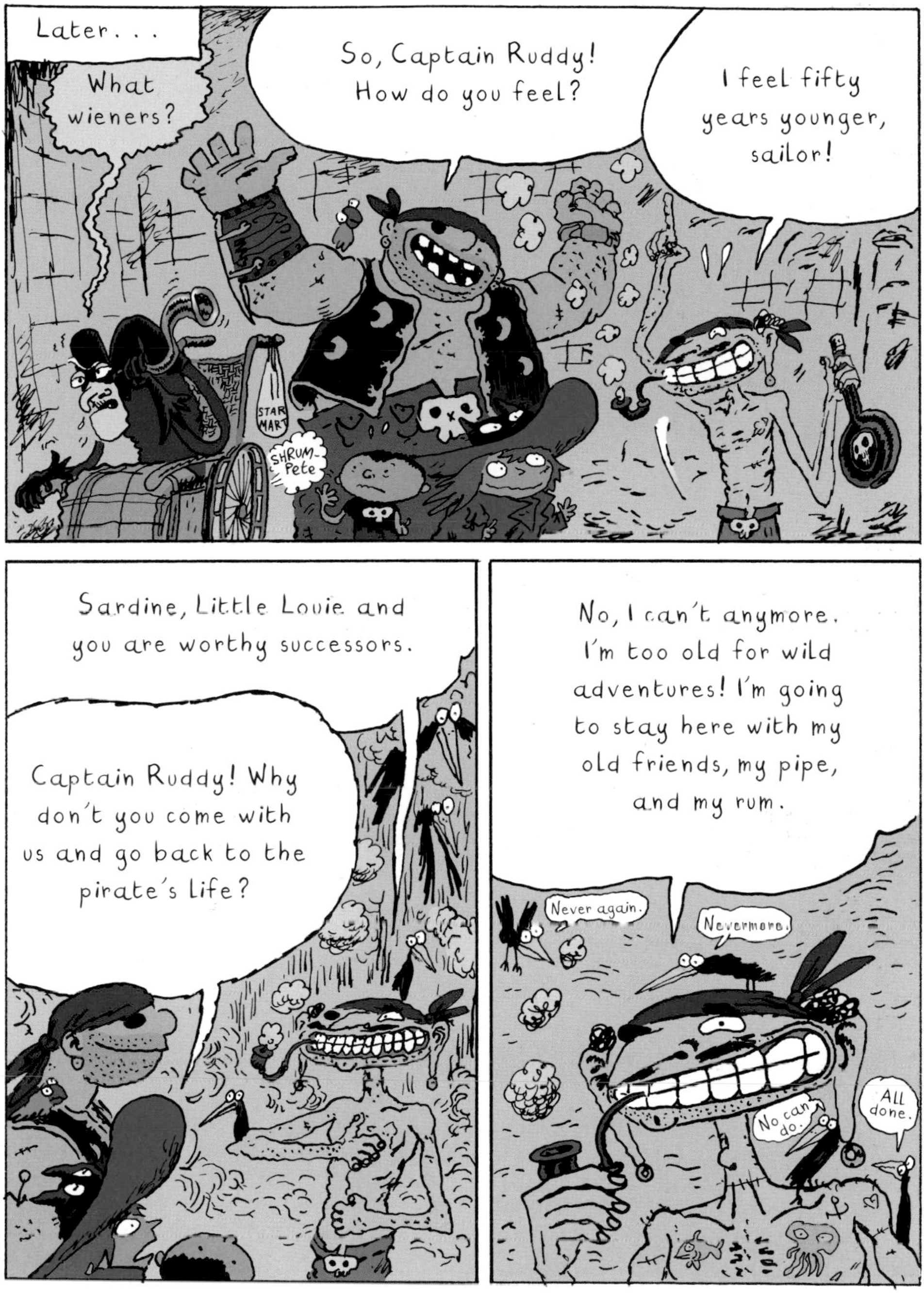
Later...
What wieners?
So, Captain Ruddy! How do you feel?
I feel fifty years younger, sailor!
STAR MART
SHRUM-Pete
Sardine, Little Louie and you are worthy successors.
Captain Ruddy! Why don't you come with us and go back to the pirate's life?
No, I can't anymore. I'm too old for wild adventures! I'm going to stay here with my old friends, my pipe, and my rum.
Never again.
Nevermore.
No can do.
All done.

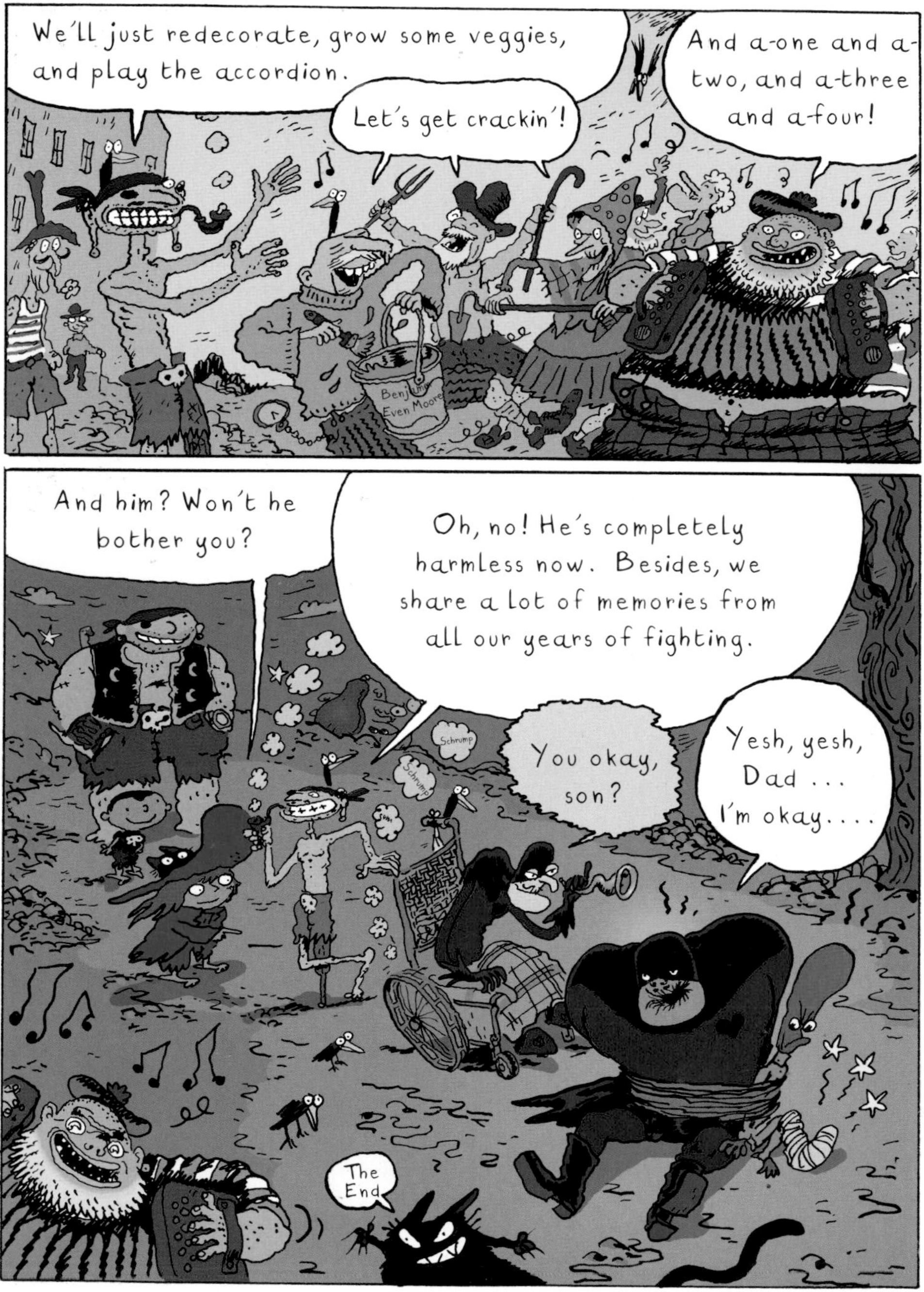
We'll just redecorate, grow some veggies, and play the accordion.
Let's get crackin'!
And a-one and a-two, and a-three and a-four!
And him? Won't he bother you?
Oh, no! He's completely harmless now. Besides, we share a lot of memories from all our years of fighting.
Schrump
Schrump
You okay, son?
Yesh, yesh, Dad . . . I'm okay. . . .
The End

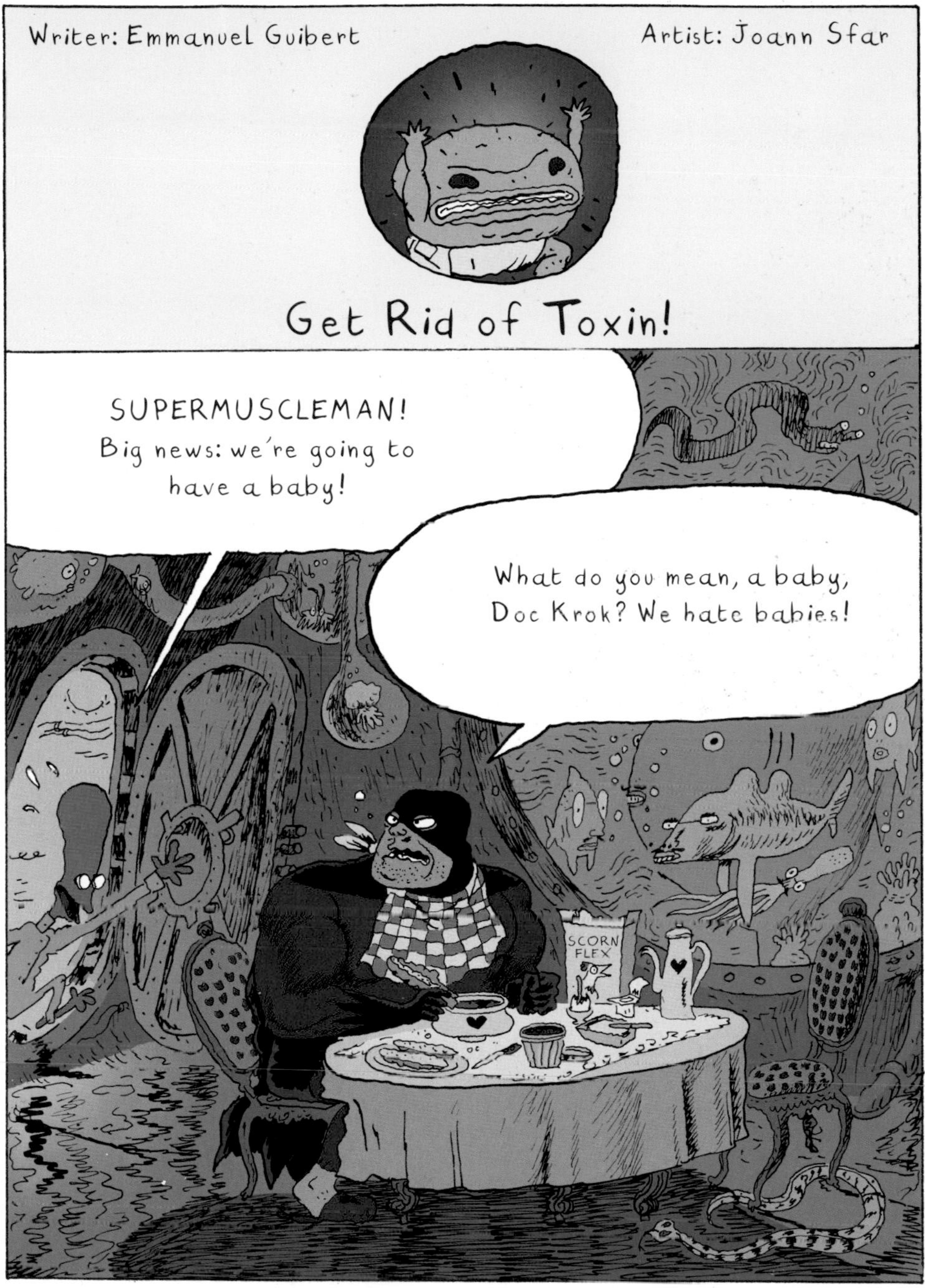
Writer: Emmanuel Guibert
Artist: Joann Sfar
Get Rid of Toxin!
SUPERMUSCLEMAN! Big news: we're going to have a baby!
What do you mean, a baby, Doc Krok? We hate babies!
SCORN FLEX

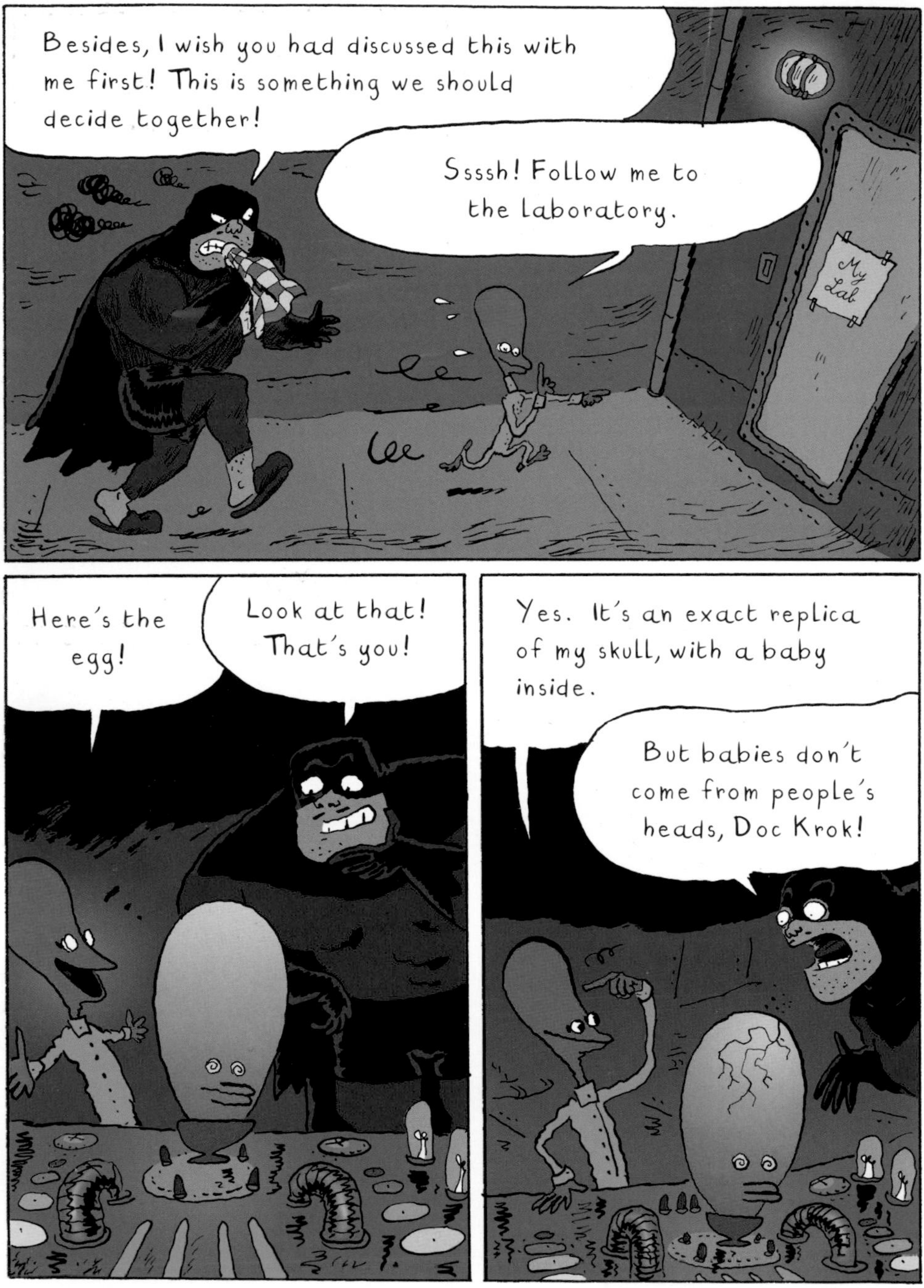
Besides, I wish you had discussed this with me first! This is something we should decide together!
Ssssh! Follow me to the laboratory.
My Lab
Here's the egg!
Look at that! That's you!
Yes. It's an exact replica of my skull, with a baby inside.
But babies don't come from people's heads, Doc Krok!

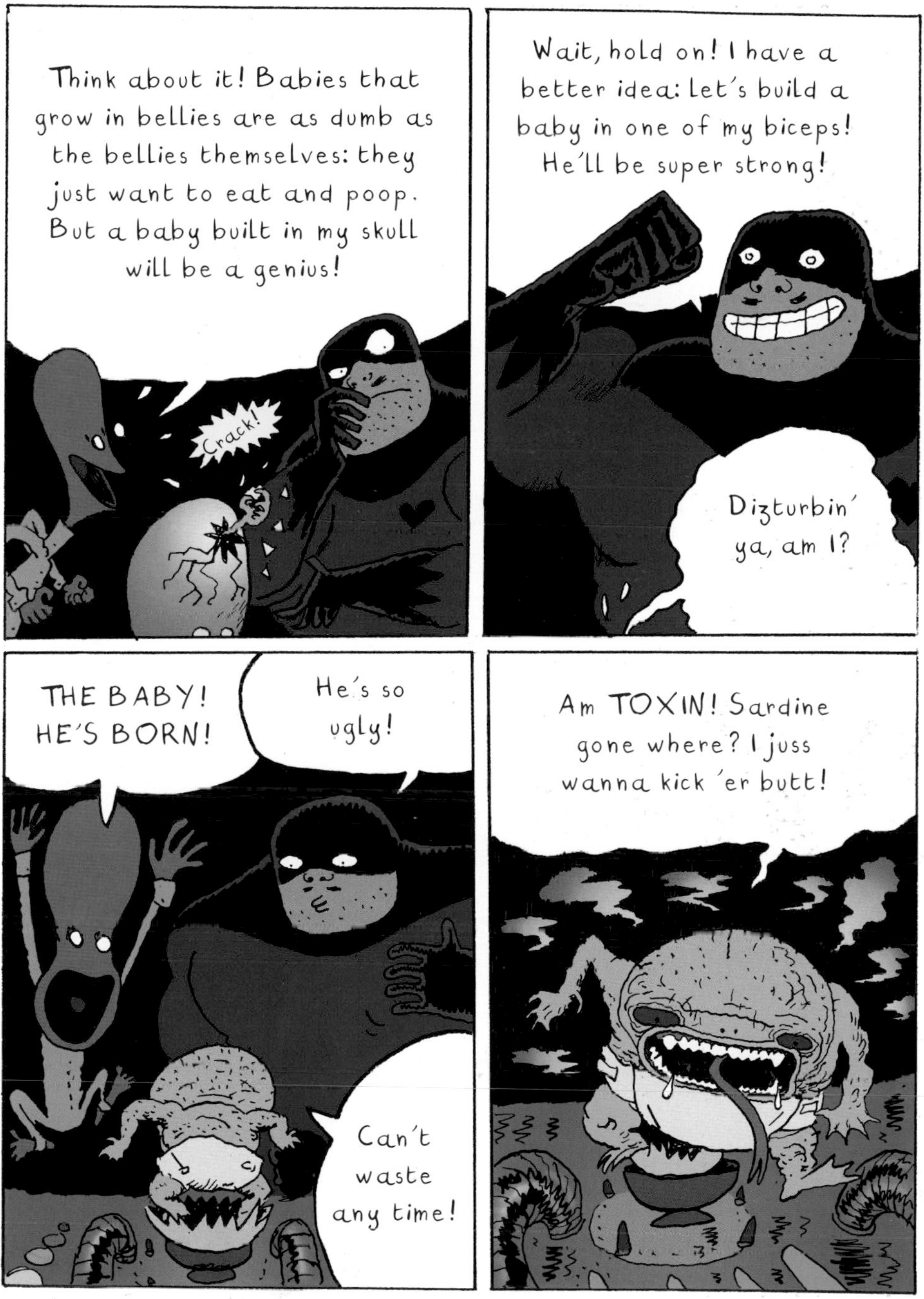
Think about it! Babies that grow in bellies are as dumb as the bellies themselves: they just want to eat and poop. But a baby built in my skull will be a genius!
Crack!
Wait, hold on! I have a better idea: Let's build a baby in one of my biceps! He'll be super strong!
Dizturbin' ya, am I?
THE BABY! HE'S BORN!
He's so ugly!
Can't waste any time!
Am TOXIN! Sardine gone where? I juss wanna kick 'er butt!

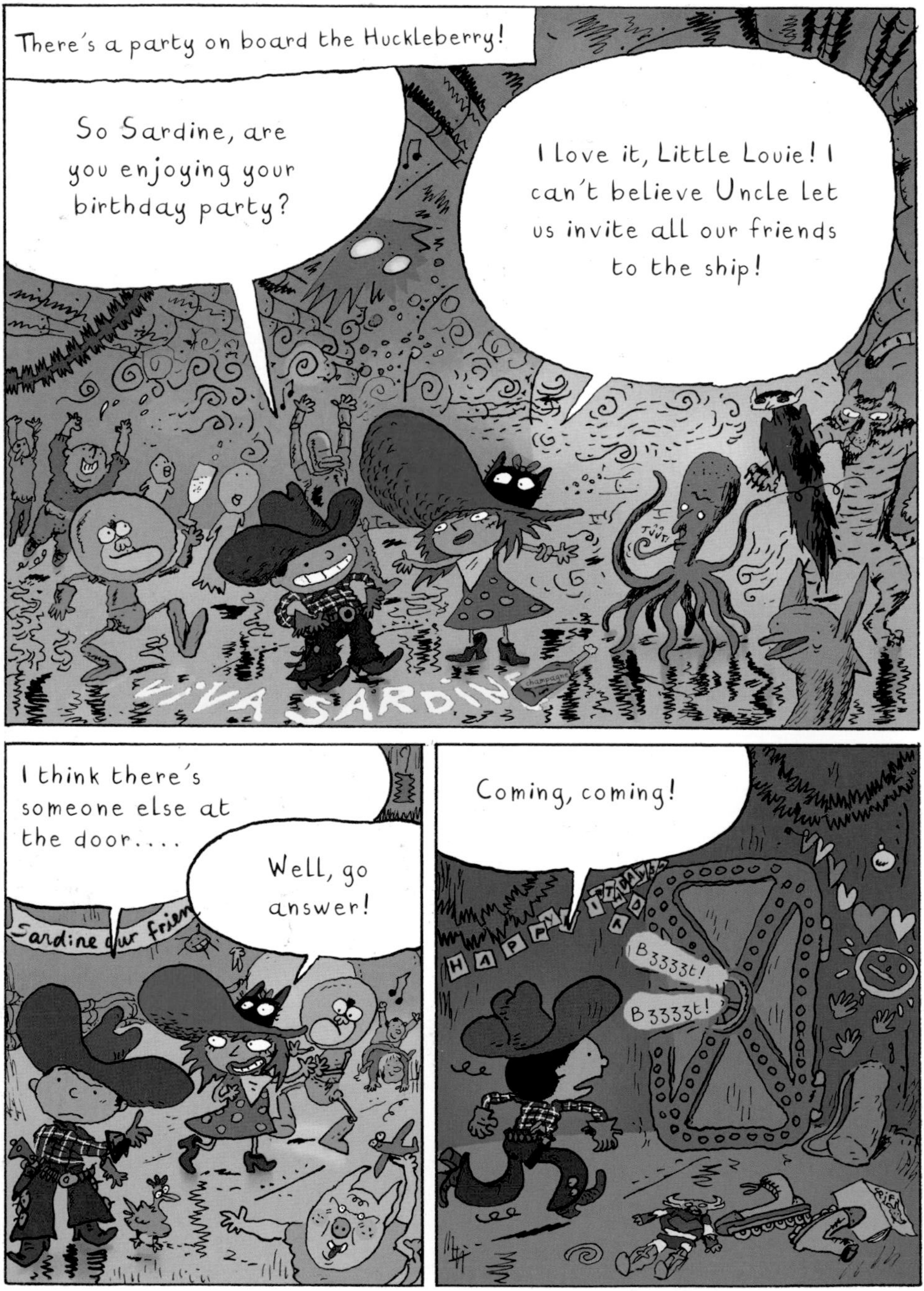
There's a party on board the Huckleberry!
So Sardine, are you enjoying your birthday party?
I love it, Little Louie! I can't believe Uncle let us invite all our friends to the ship!
I think there's someone else at the door....
Well, go answer!
Coming, coming!
HAPPY
B3333t!
B3333t!

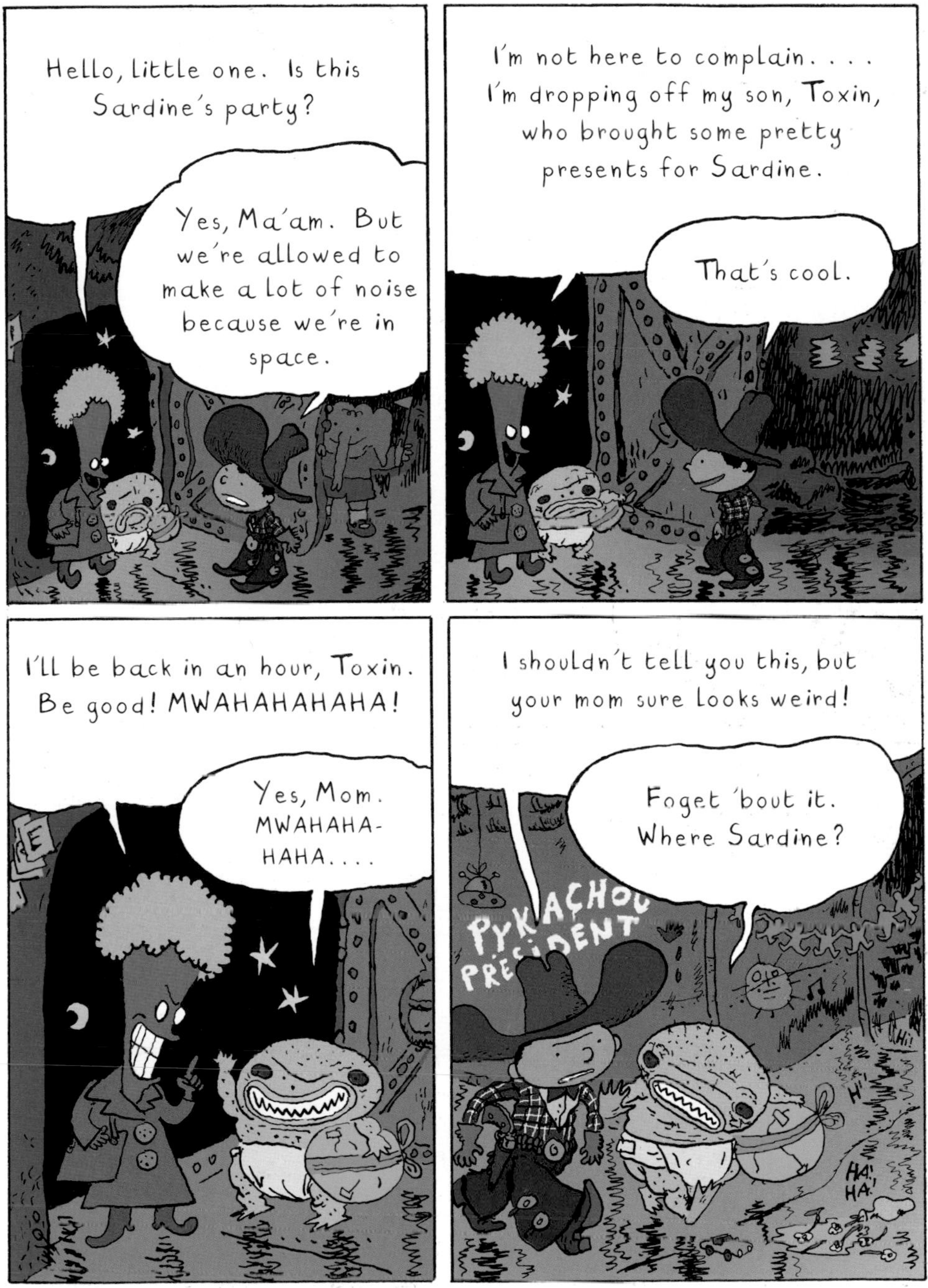
Hello, little one. Is this Sardine's party?
Yes, Ma'am. But we're allowed to make a lot of noise because we're in space.
I'm not here to complain. . . . I'm dropping off my son, Toxin, who brought some pretty presents for Sardine.
That's cool.
I'll be back in an hour, Toxin. Be good! MWAHAHAHAHA!
Yes, Mom. MWAHAHA-HAHA. . . .
I shouldn't tell you this, but your mom sure looks weird!
Foget 'bout it. Where Sardine?
PYKAÇHOU
HA! HA!

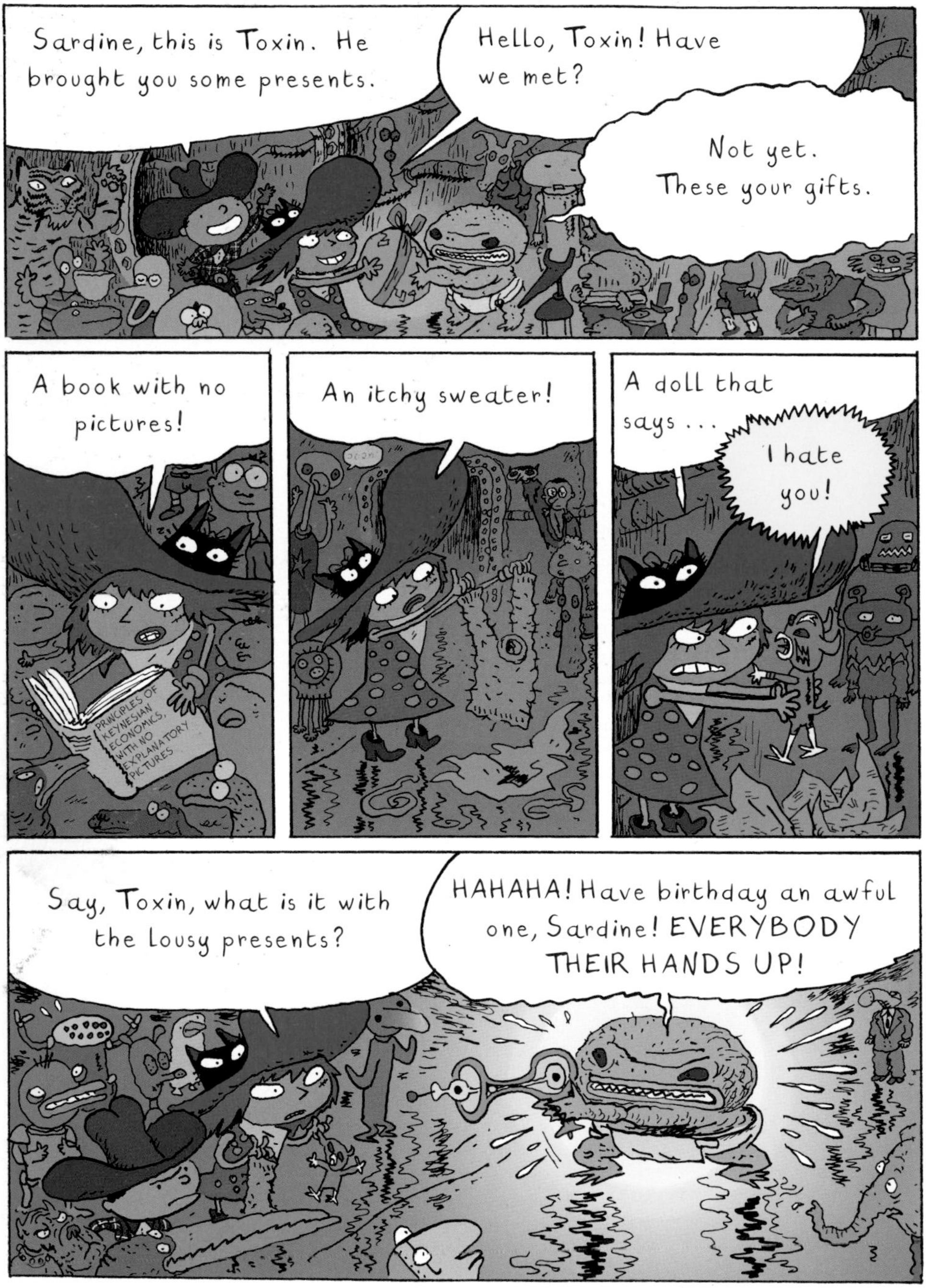
Sardine, this is Toxin. He brought you some presents.
Hello, Toxin! Have we met?
Not yet. These your gifts.
A book with no pictures!
PRINCIPLES OF KEYNESIAN ECONOMICS, WITH NO EXPLANATORY PICTURES
An itchy sweater!
A doll that says . . .
I hate you!
Say, Toxin, what is it with the lousy presents?
HAHAHA! Have birthday an awful one, Sardine! EVERYBODY THEIR HANDS UP!

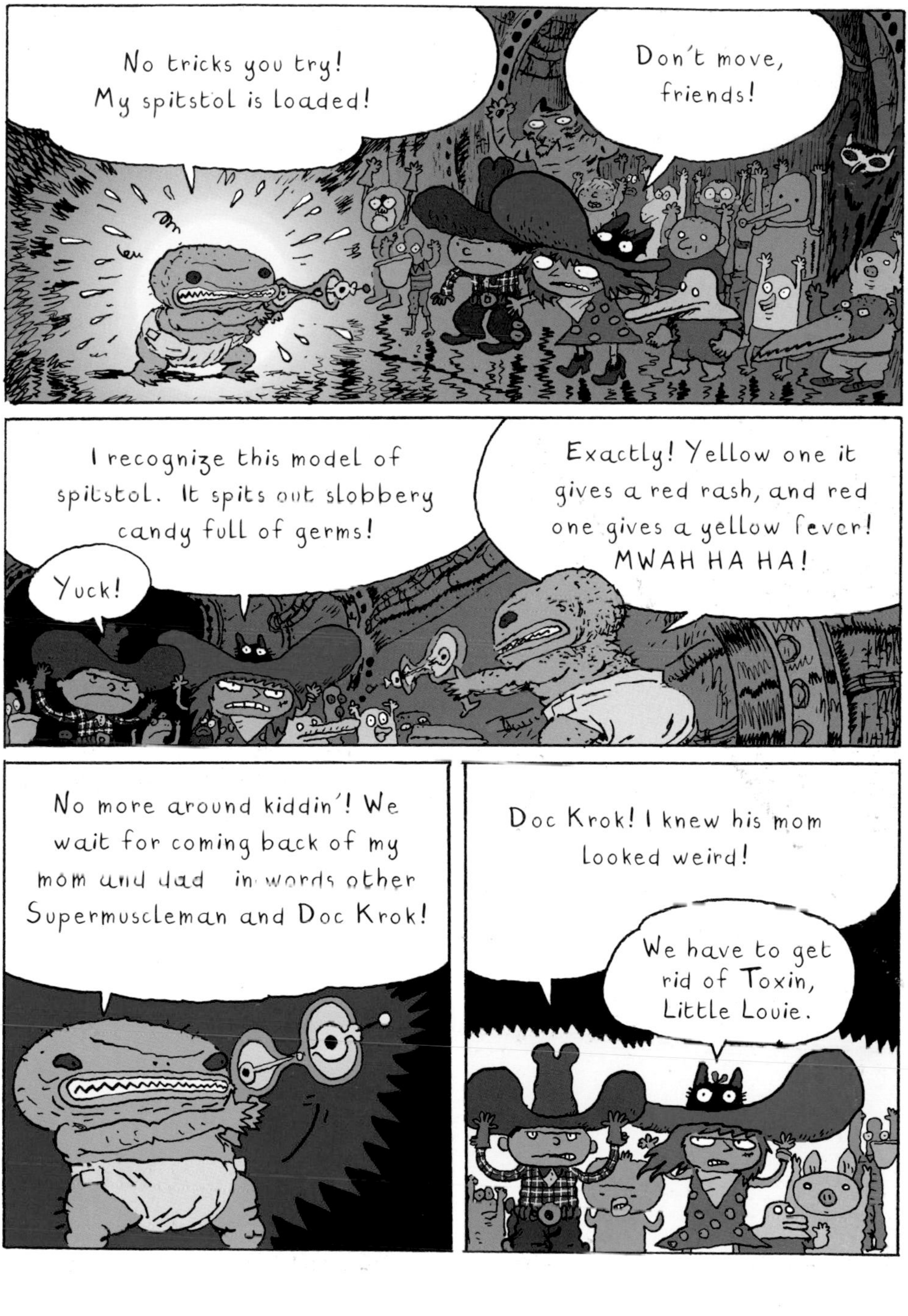
No tricks you try! My spitstol is loaded!
Don't move, friends!
I recognize this model of spitstol. It spits out slobbery candy full of germs!
Yuck!
Exactly! Yellow one it gives a red rash, and red one gives a yellow fever! MWAH HA HA!
No more around kiddin'! We wait for coming back of my mom and dad in words other Supermuscleman and Doc Krok!
Doc Krok! I knew his mom looked weird!
We have to get rid of Toxin, Little Louie.

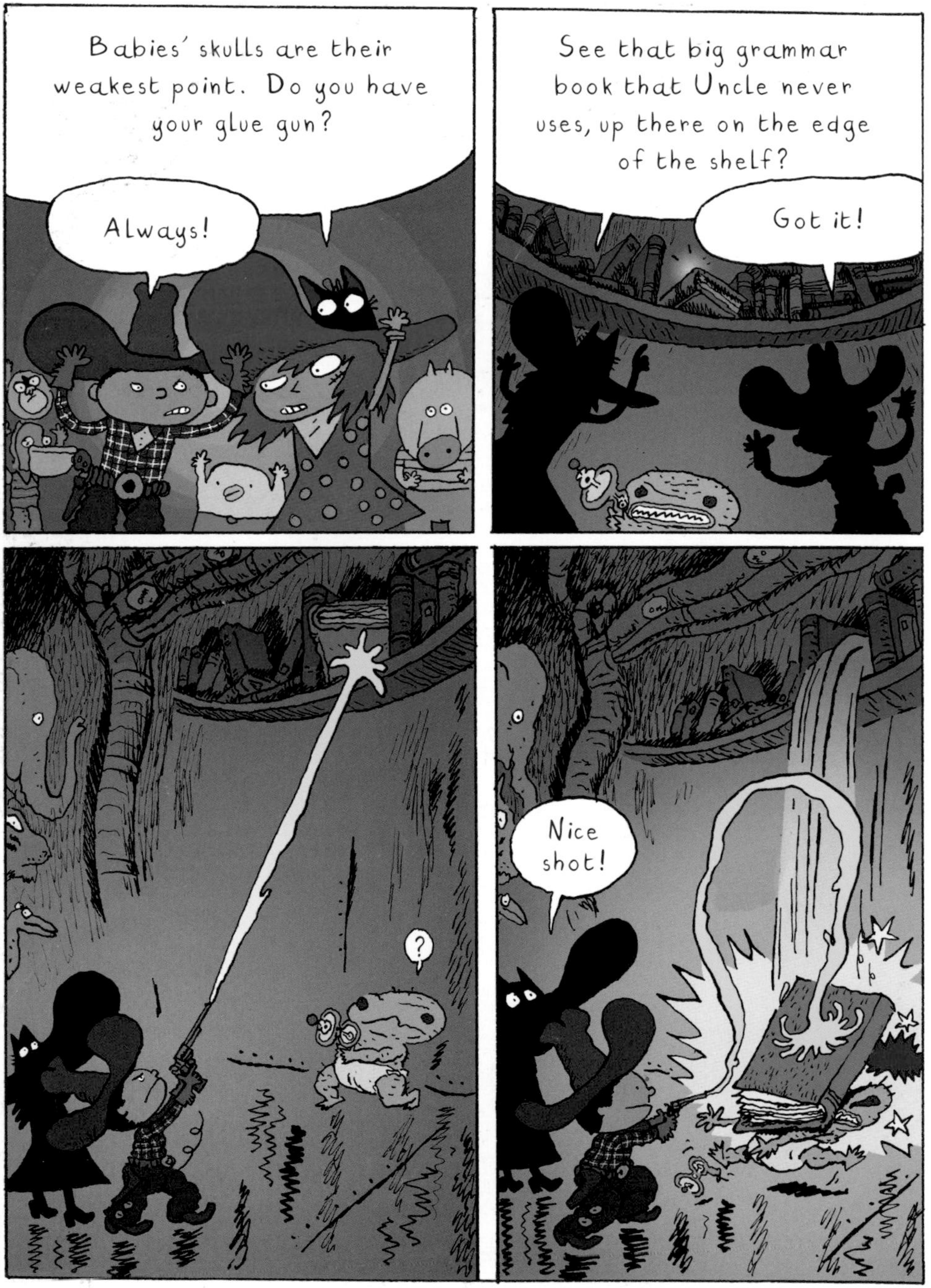
Babies' skulls are their weakest point. Do you have your glue gun?
Always!
See that big grammar book that Uncle never uses, up there on the edge of the shelf?
Got it!
?
Nice shot!

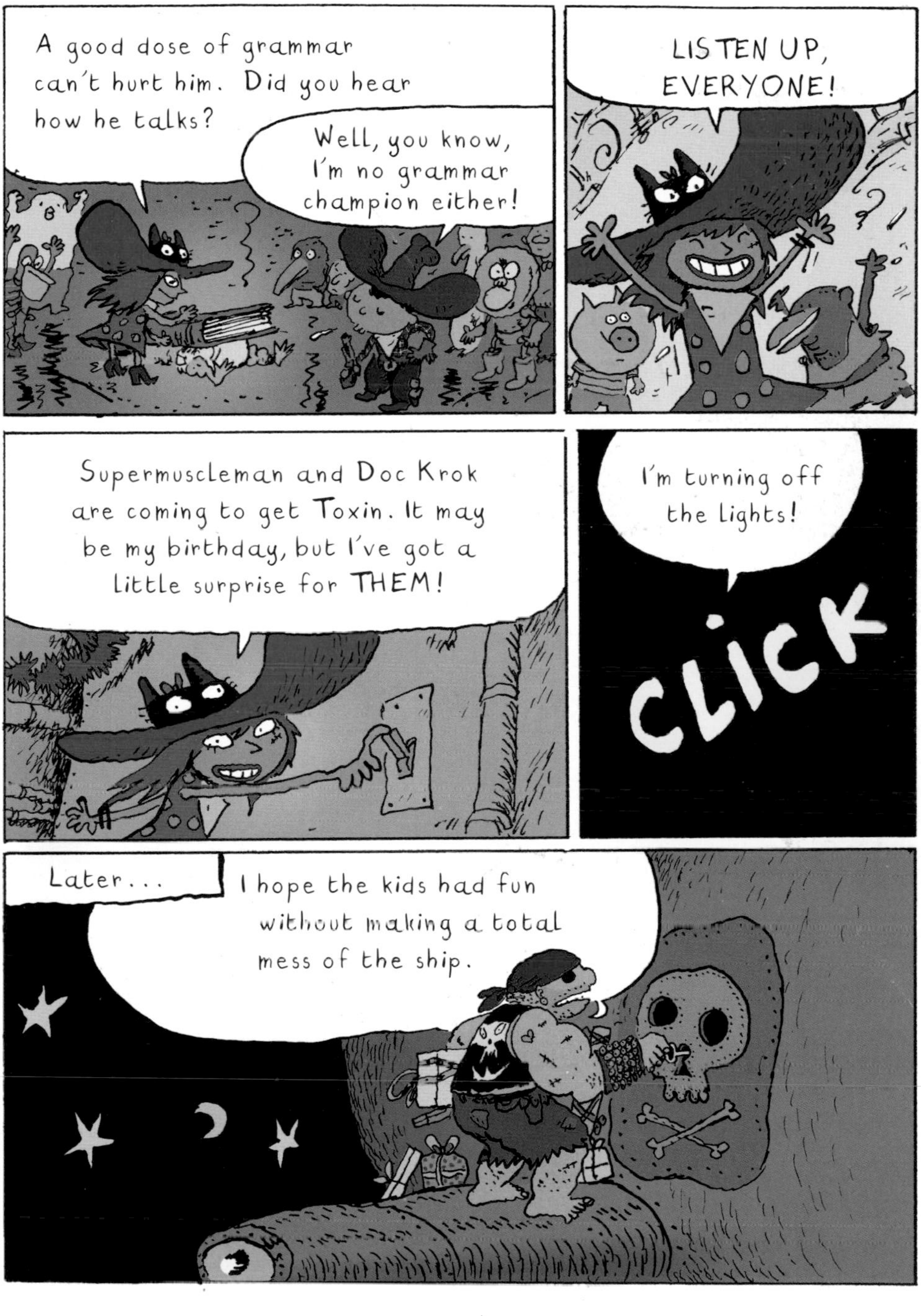
A good dose of grammar can't hurt him. Did you hear how he talks?
Well, you know, I'm no grammar champion either!
LISTEN UP, EVERYONE!
Supermuscleman and Doc Krok are coming to get Toxin. It may be my birthday, but I've got a little surprise for THEM!
I'm turning off the lights!
CLICK
Later...
I hope the kids had fun without making a total mess of the ship.

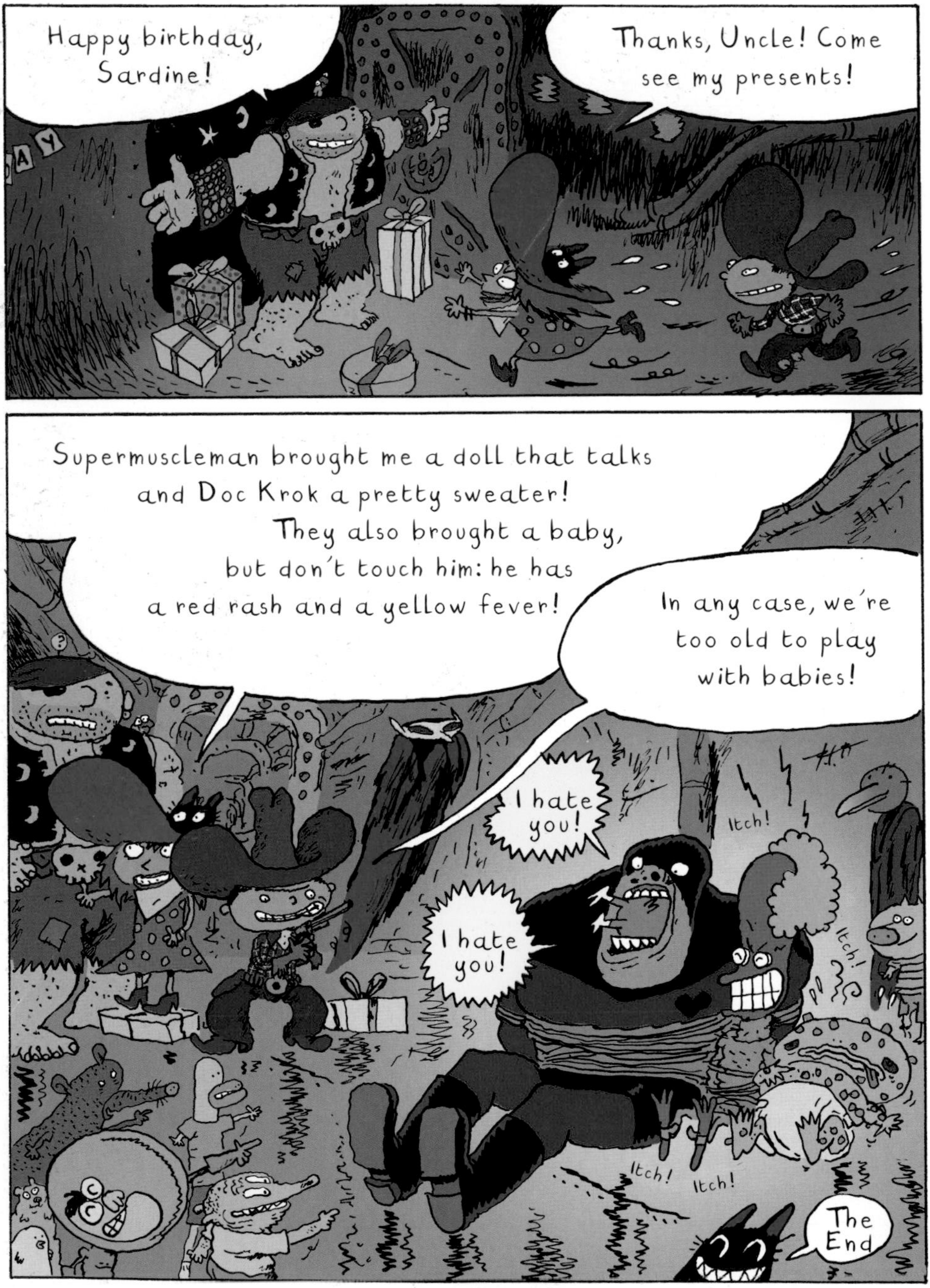
Happy birthday, Sardine!
Thanks, Uncle! Come see my presents!
Supermuscleman brought me a doll that talks and Doc Krok a pretty sweater! They also brought a baby, but don't touch him: he has a red rash and a yellow fever!
In any case, we're too old to play with babies!
I hate you!
I hate you!
Itch!
Itch!
Itch!
Itch!
The End

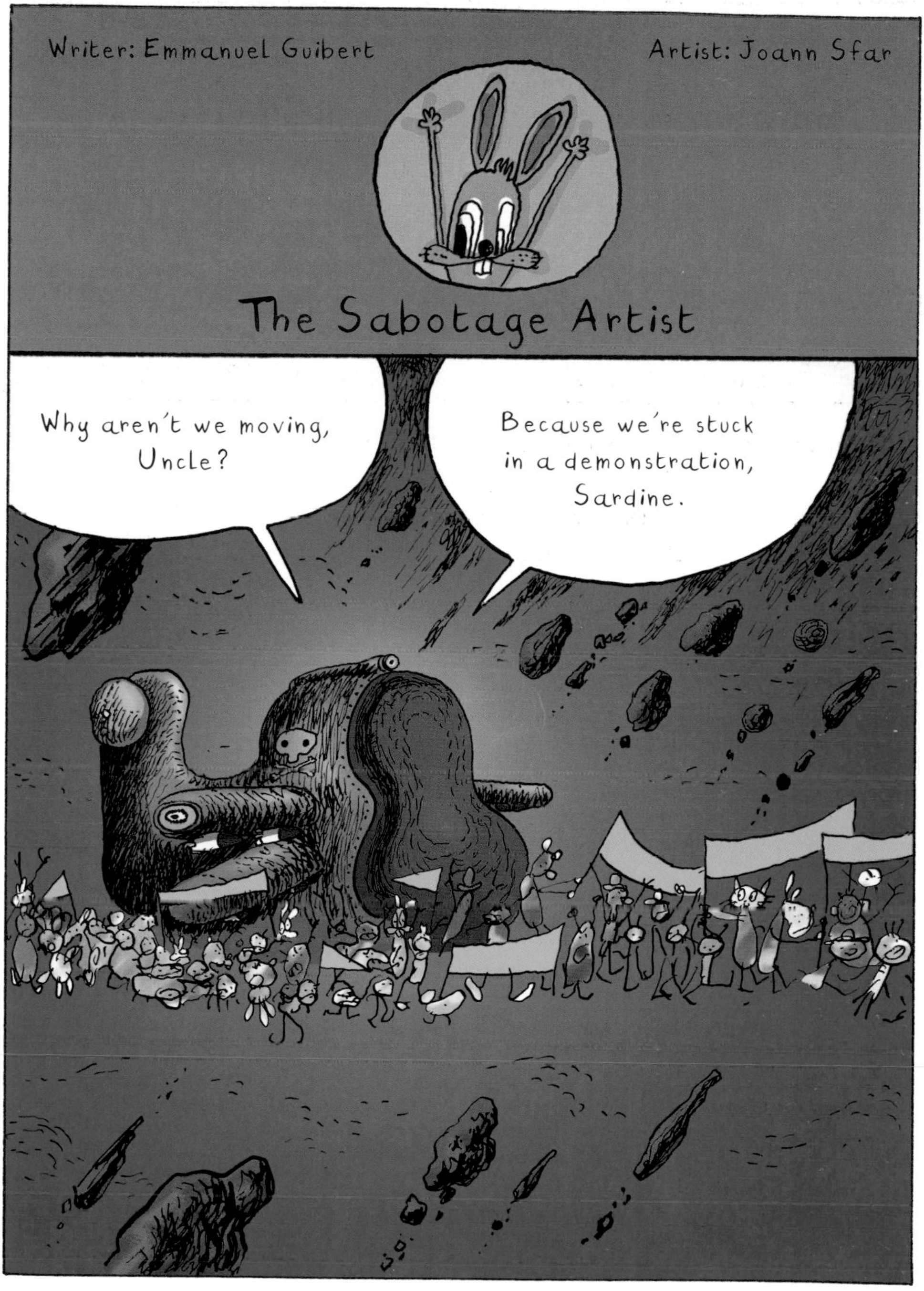
Writer: Emmanuel Guibert
Artist: Joann Sfar
The Sabotage Artist
Why aren't we moving, Uncle?
Because we're stuck in a demonstration, Sardine.

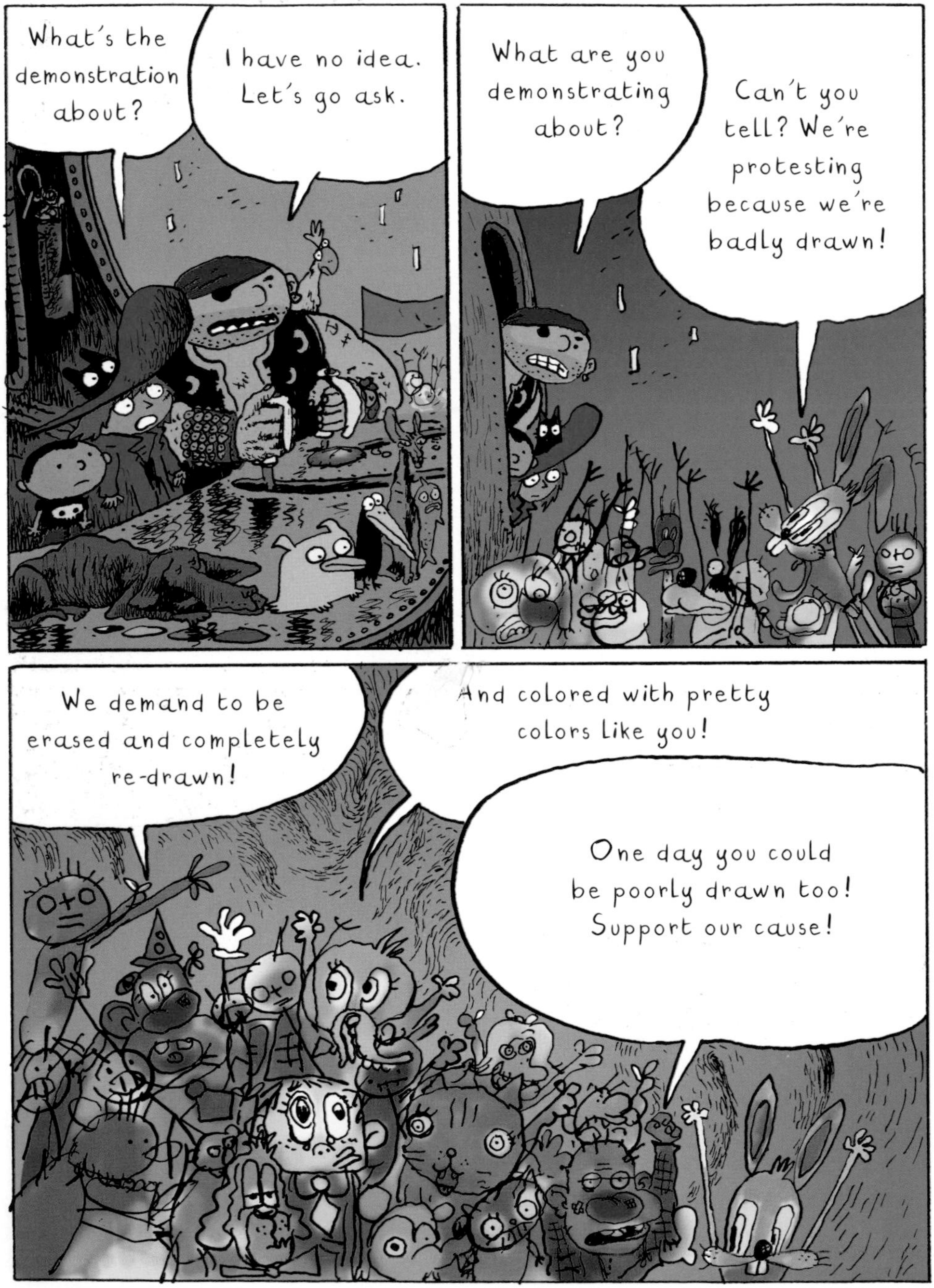
What's the demonstration about?
I have no idea. Let's go ask.
What are you demonstrating about?
Can't you tell? We're protesting because we're badly drawn!
We demand to be erased and completely re-drawn!
And colored with pretty colors like you!
One day you could be poorly drawn too! Support our cause!

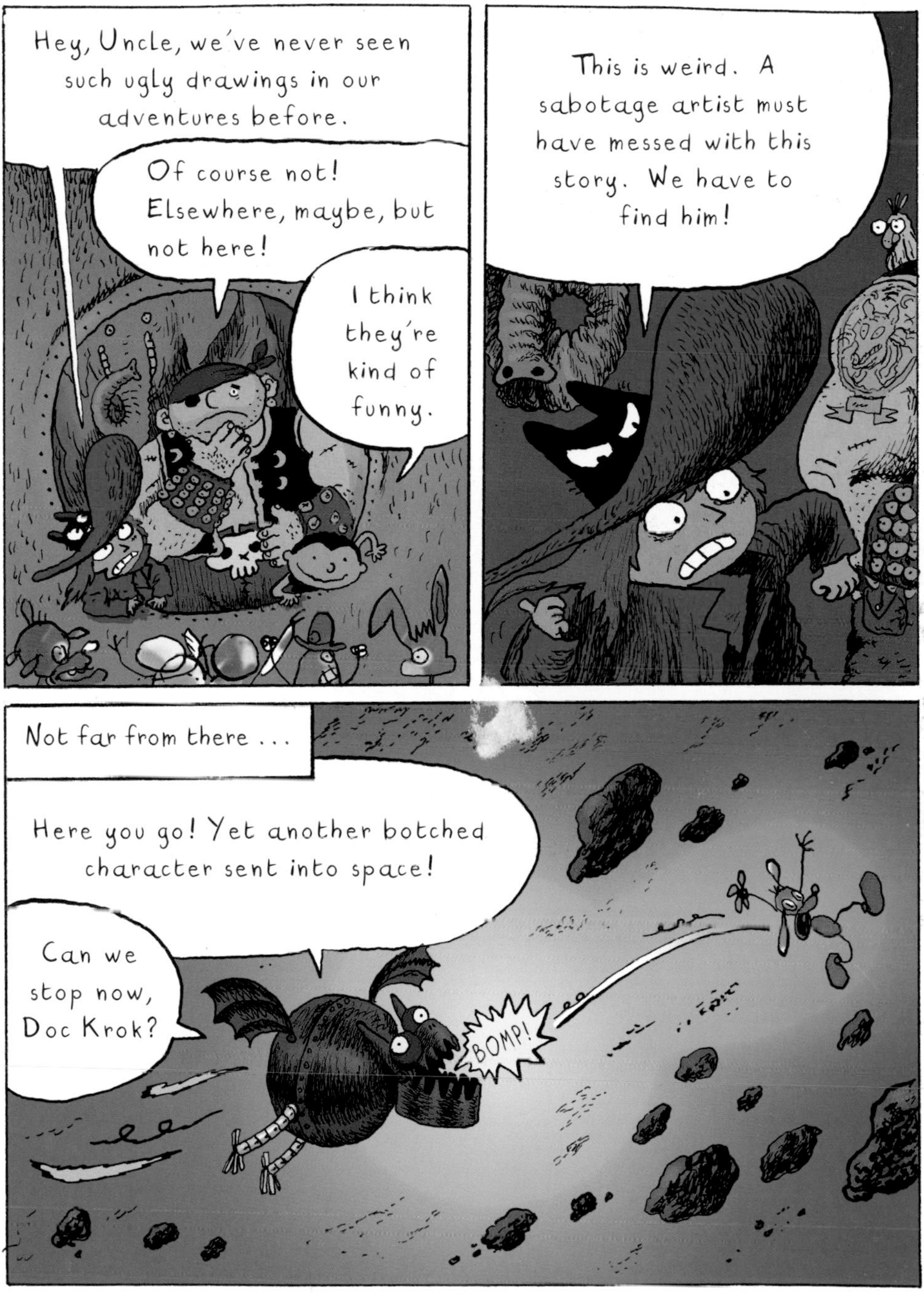
Hey, Uncle, we've never seen such ugly drawings in our adventures before.
Of course not! Elsewhere, maybe, but not here!
I think they're kind of funny.
This is weird. A sabotage artist must have messed with this story. We have to find him!
Not far from there . . .
Here you go! Yet another botched character sent into space!
Can we stop now, Doc Krok?
BOMP!

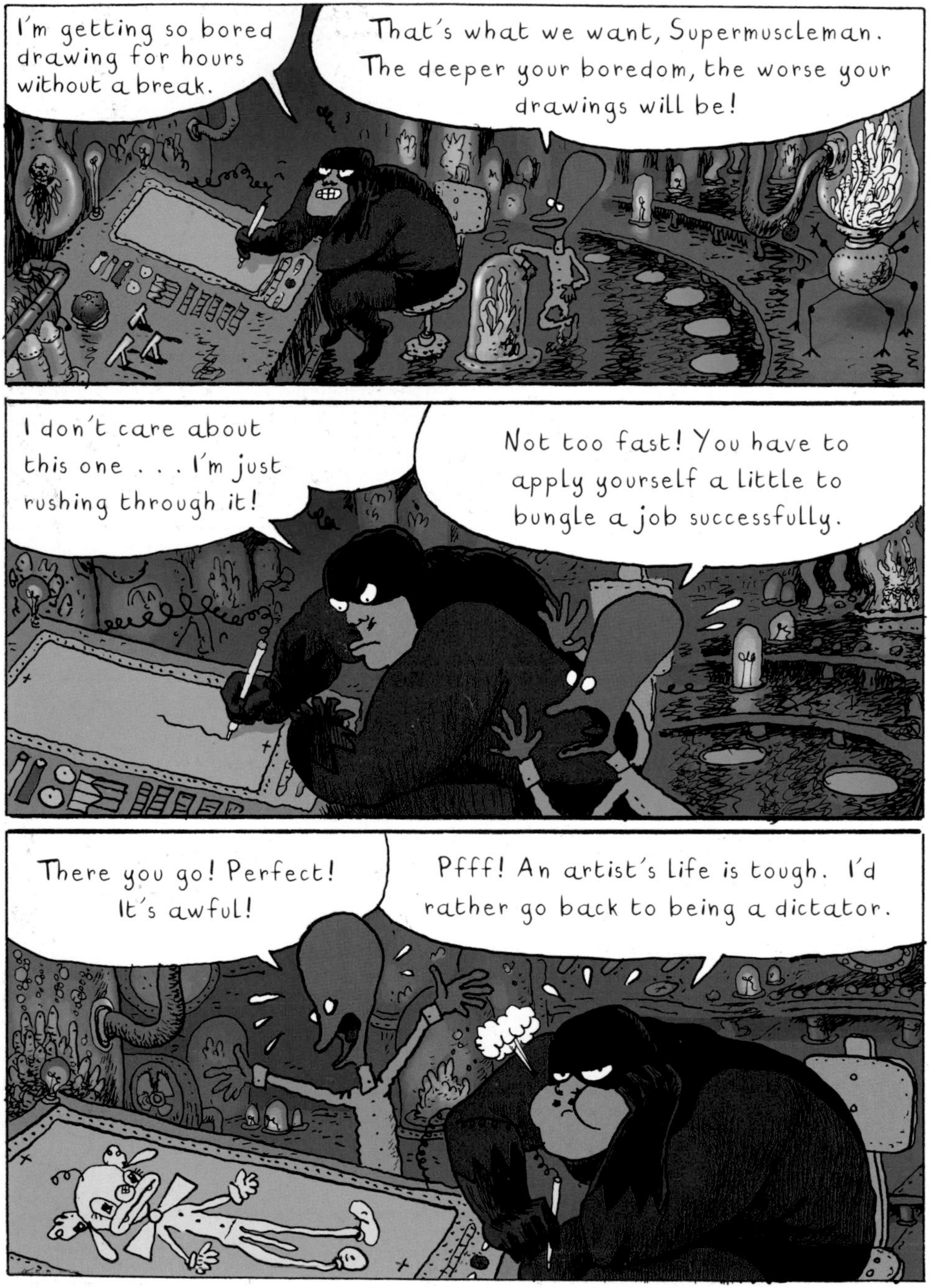
I'm getting so bored drawing for hours without a break.
That's what we want, Supermuscleman. The deeper your boredom, the worse your drawings will be!
I don't care about this one . . . I'm just rushing through it!
Not too fast! You have to apply yourself a little to bungle a job successfully.
There you go! Perfect! It's awful!
Pfff! An artist's life is tough. I'd rather go back to being a dictator.

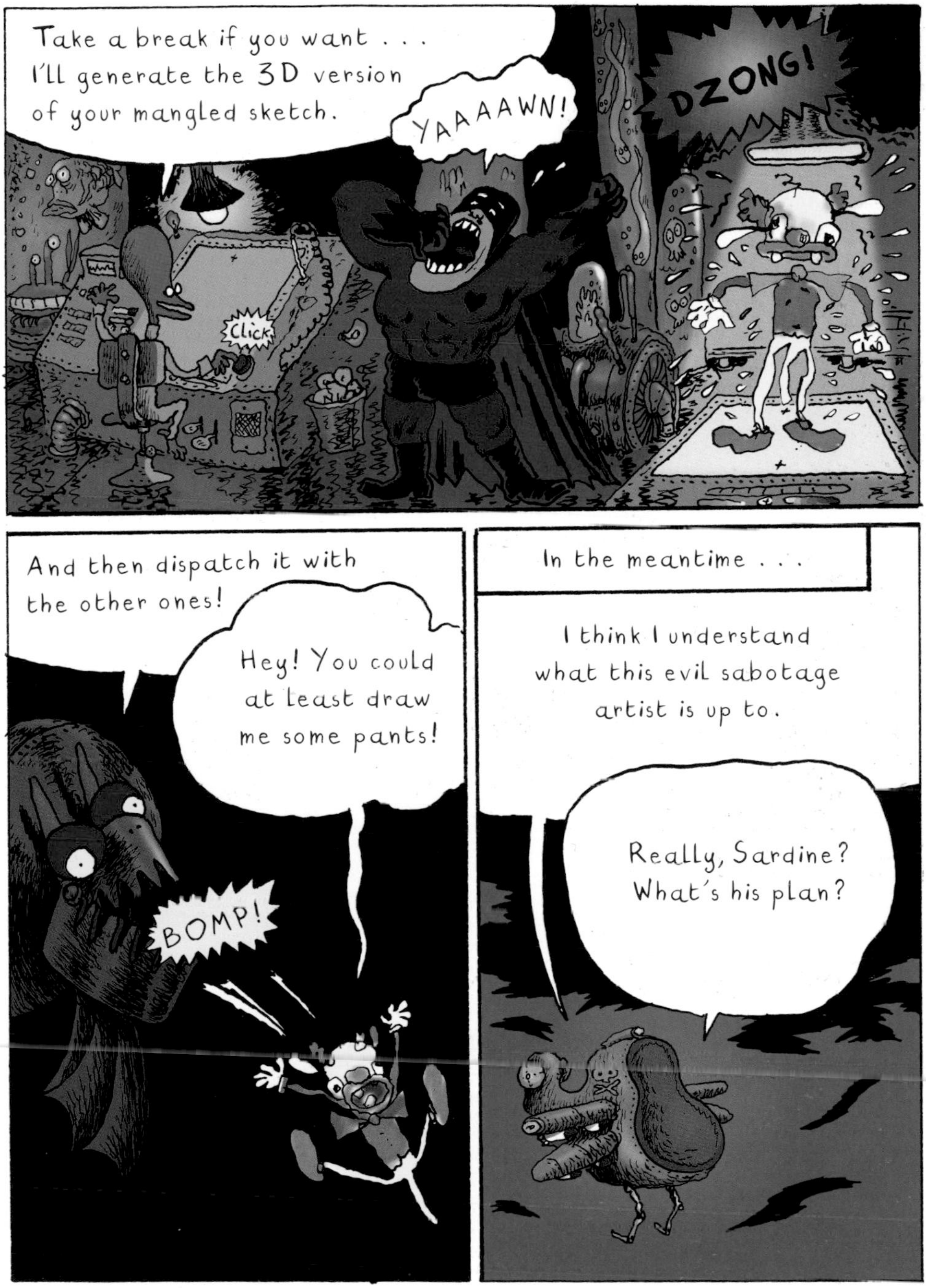
Take a break if you want . . . I'll generate the 3D version of your mangled sketch.
YAAAAWN!
DZONG!
CLICK
And then dispatch it with the other ones!
Hey! You could at least draw me some pants!
BOMP!
In the meantime . . .
I think I understand what this evil sabotage artist is up to.
Really, Sardine? What's his plan?

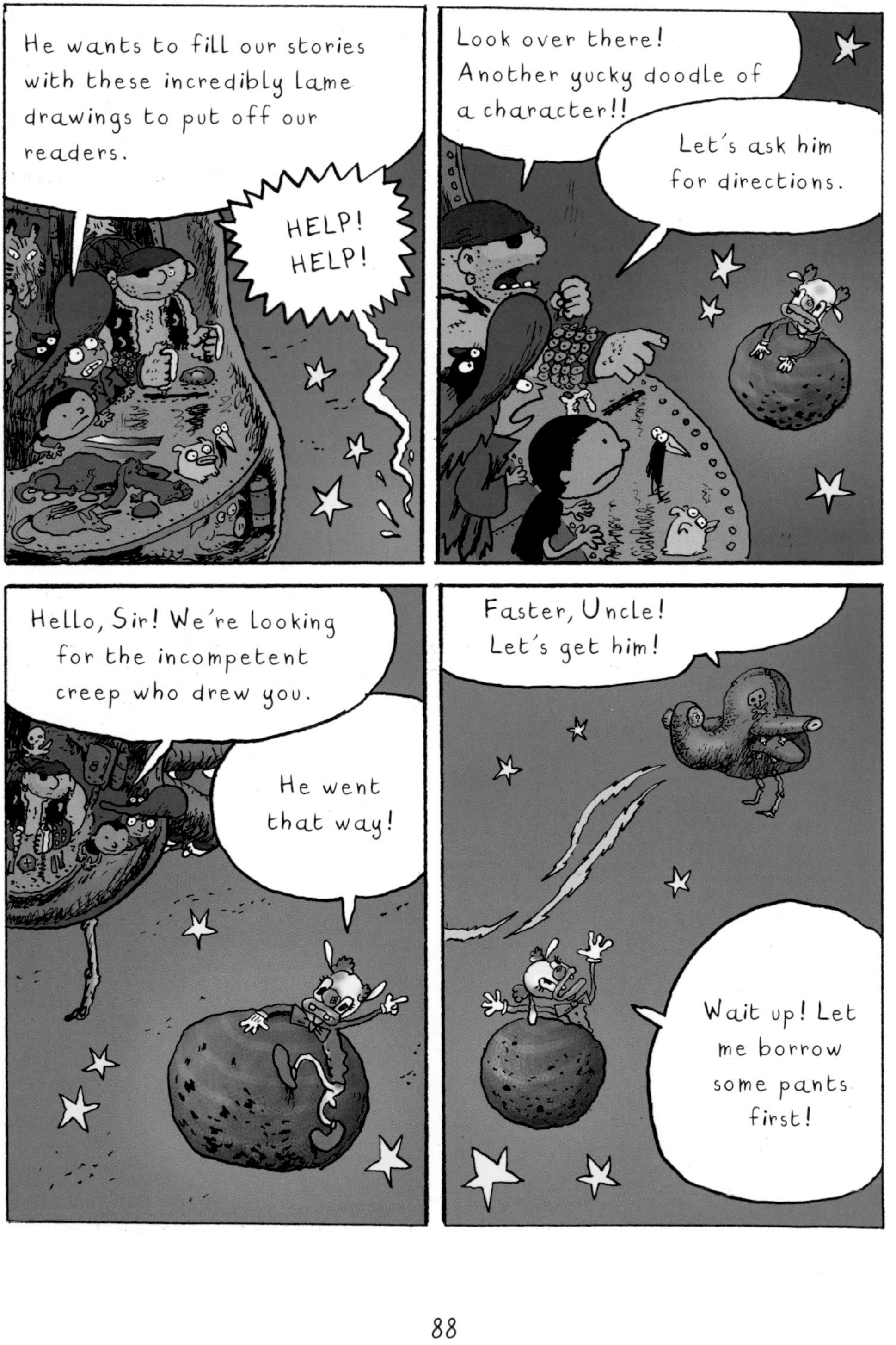
He wants to fill our stories with these incredibly lame drawings to put off our readers.
HELP! HELP!
Look over there! Another yucky doodle of a character!!
Let's ask him for directions.
Hello, Sir! We're looking for the incompetent creep who drew you.
He went that way!
Faster, Uncle! Let's get him!
Wait up! Let me borrow some pants first!

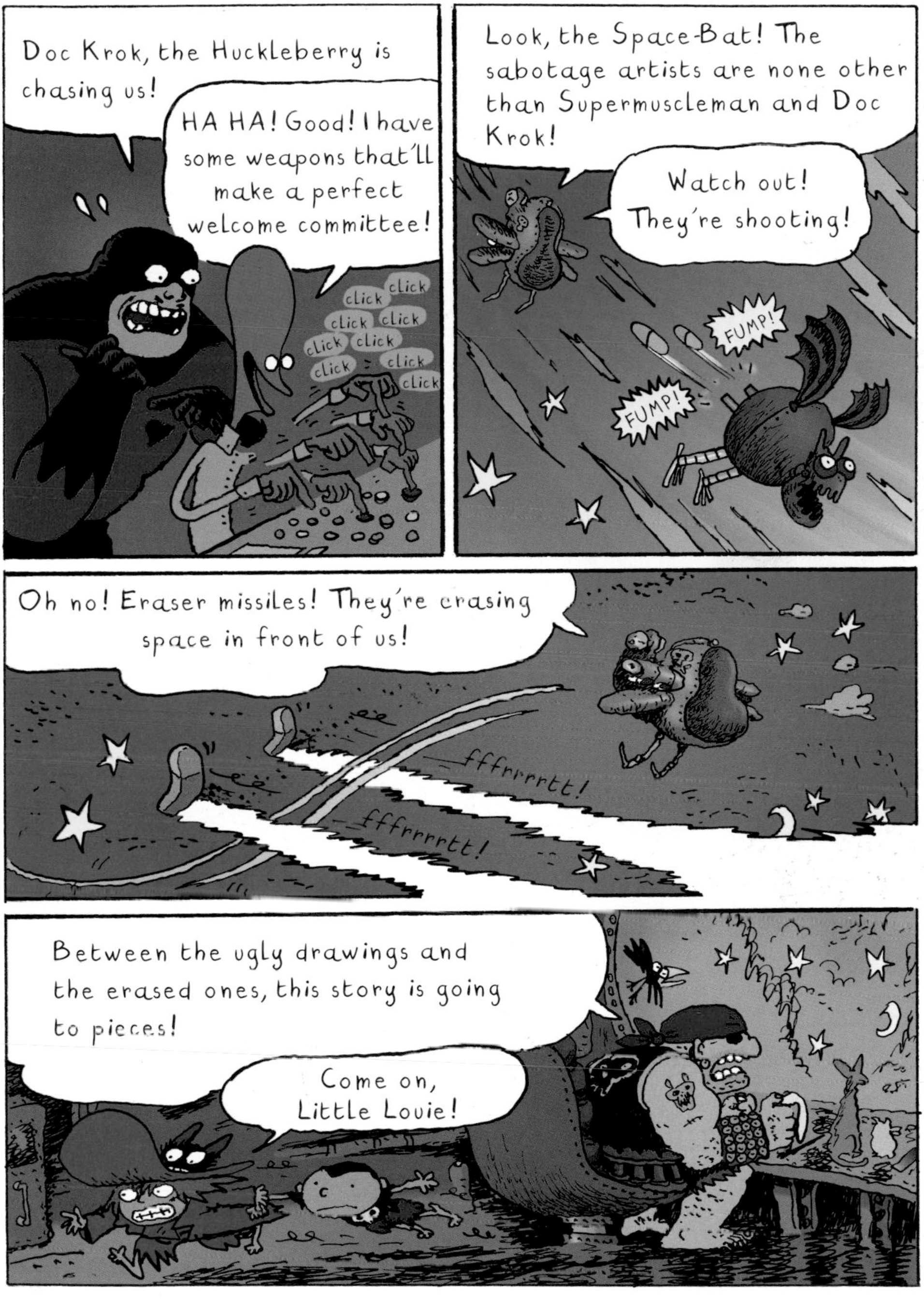
Doc Krok, the Huckleberry is chasing us!
HA HA! Good! I have some weapons that'll make a perfect welcome committee!
click click click click click click click click click
Look, the Space-Bat! The sabotage artists are none other than Supermuscleman and Doc Krok!
Watch out! They're shooting!
FUMP!
FUMP!
Oh no! Eraser missiles! They're erasing space in front of us!
fffrrrrtt!
fffrrrrtt!
Between the ugly drawings and the erased ones, this story is going to pieces!
Come on, Little Louie!

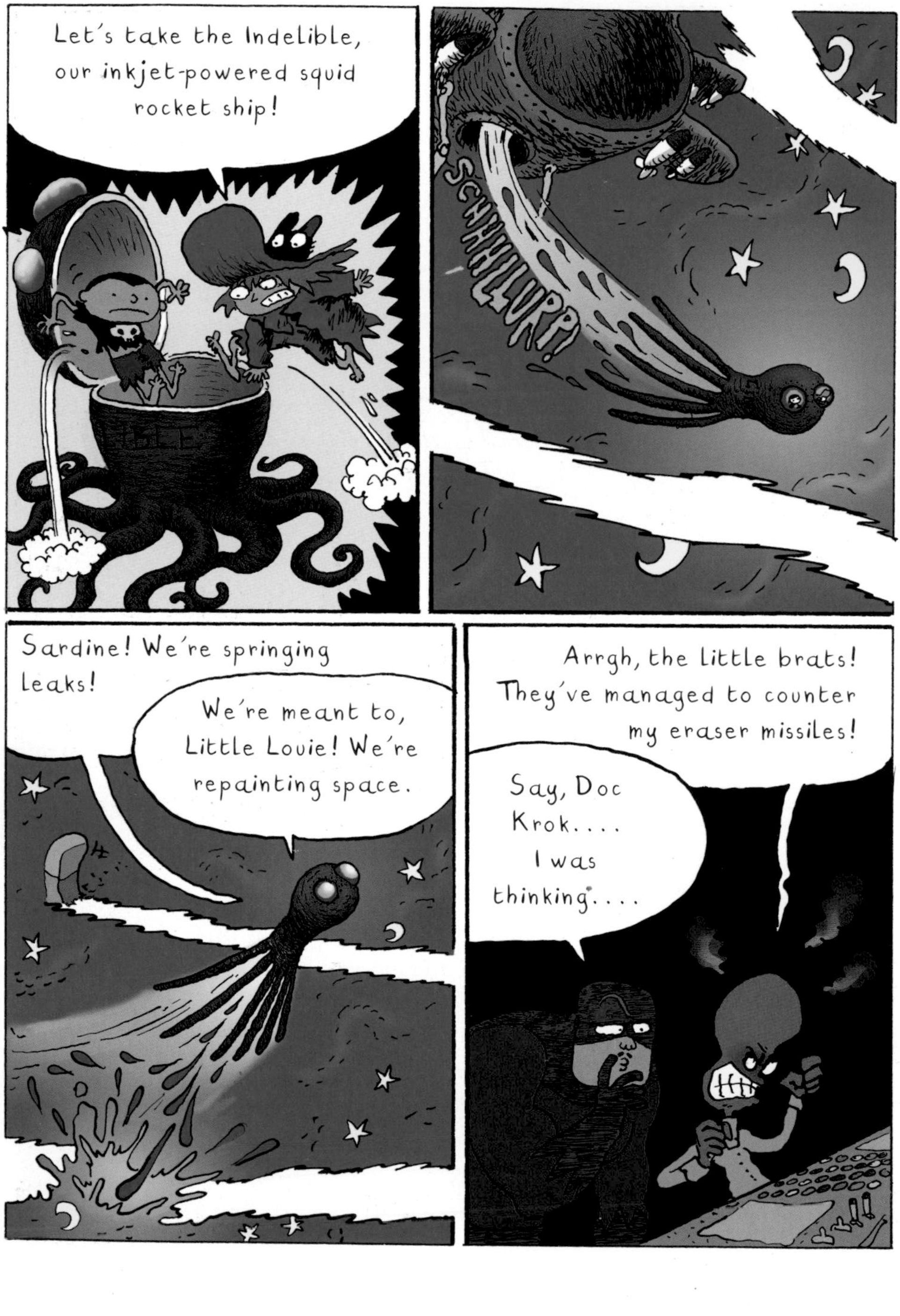
Let's take the Indelible, our inkjet-powered squid rocket ship!
SCHHLURPP!
Sardine! We're springing leaks!
We're meant to, Little Louie! We're repainting space.
Arrgh, the little brats! They've managed to counter my eraser missiles!
Say, Doc Krok.... I was thinking....

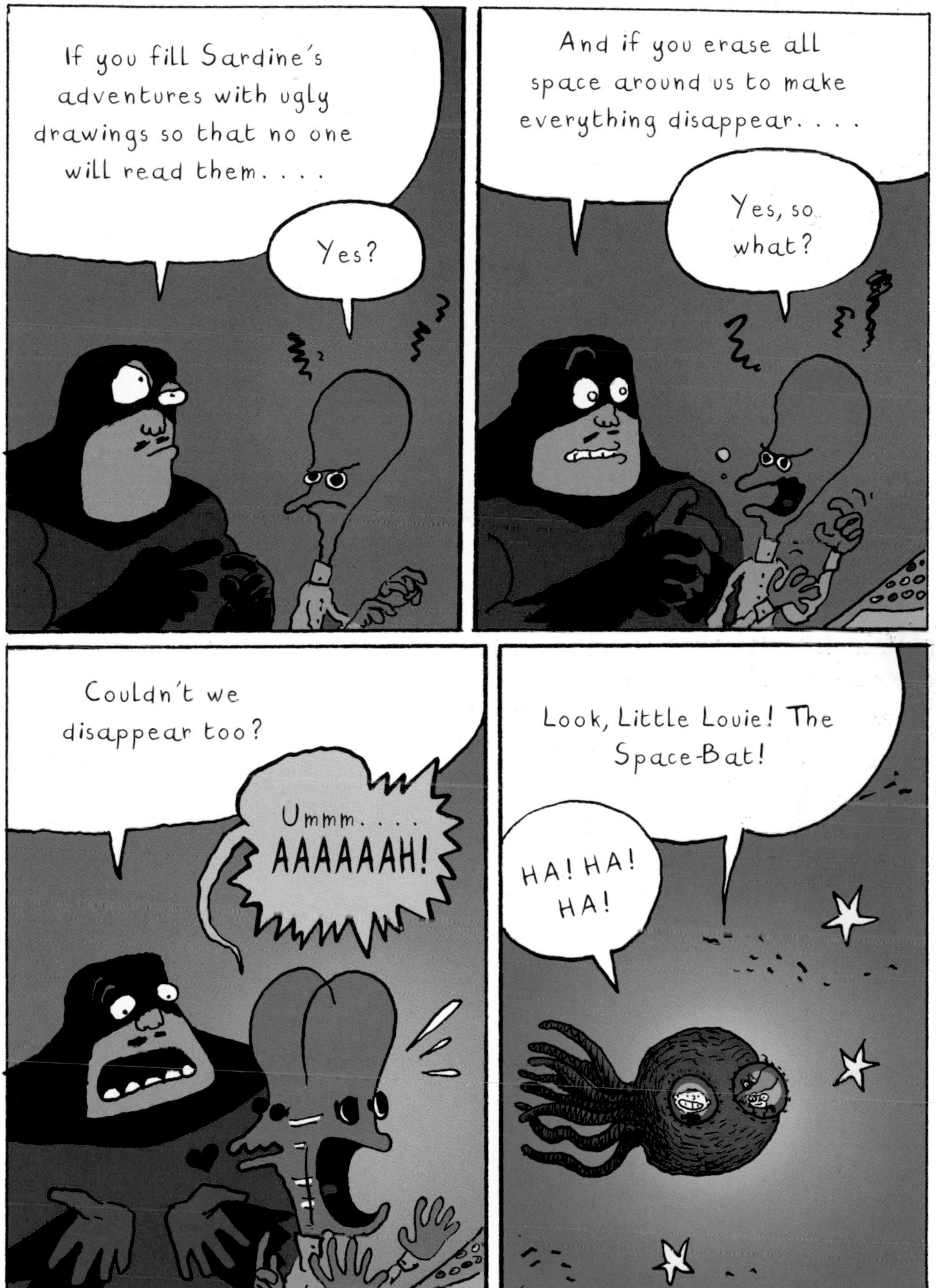
If you fill Sardine's adventures with ugly drawings so that no one will read them. . . .
Yes?
And if you erase all space around us to make everything disappear. . . .
Yes, so what?
Couldn't we disappear too?
Ummm. . . . AAAAAAH!
Look, Little Louie! The Space-Bat!
HA! HA! HA!

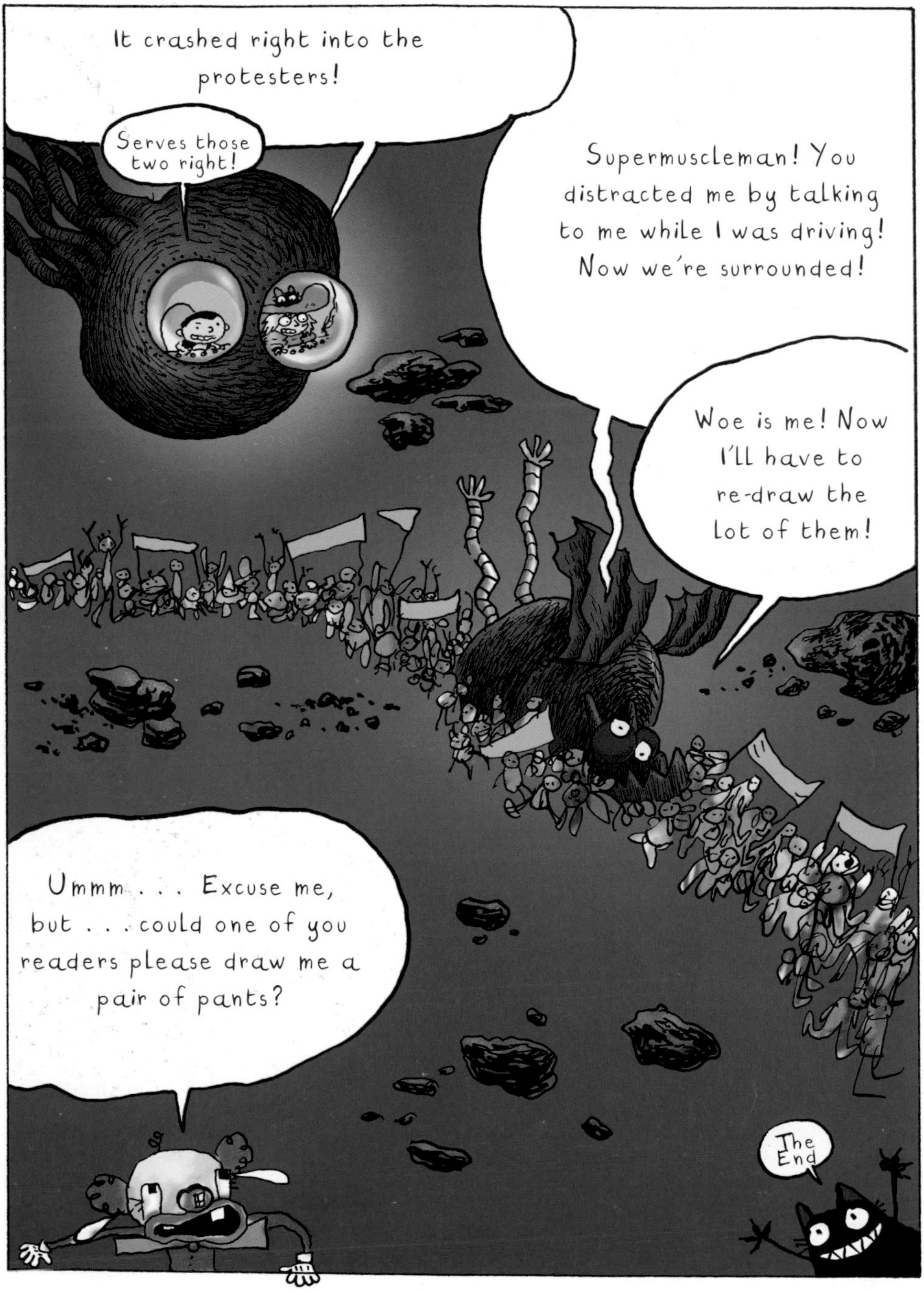
It crashed right into the protesters!
Serves those two right!
Supermuscleman! You distracted me by talking to me while I was driving! Now we're surrounded!
Woe is me! Now I'll have to re-draw the lot of them!
Ummm . . . Excuse me, but . . . could one of you readers please draw me a pair of pants?
The End

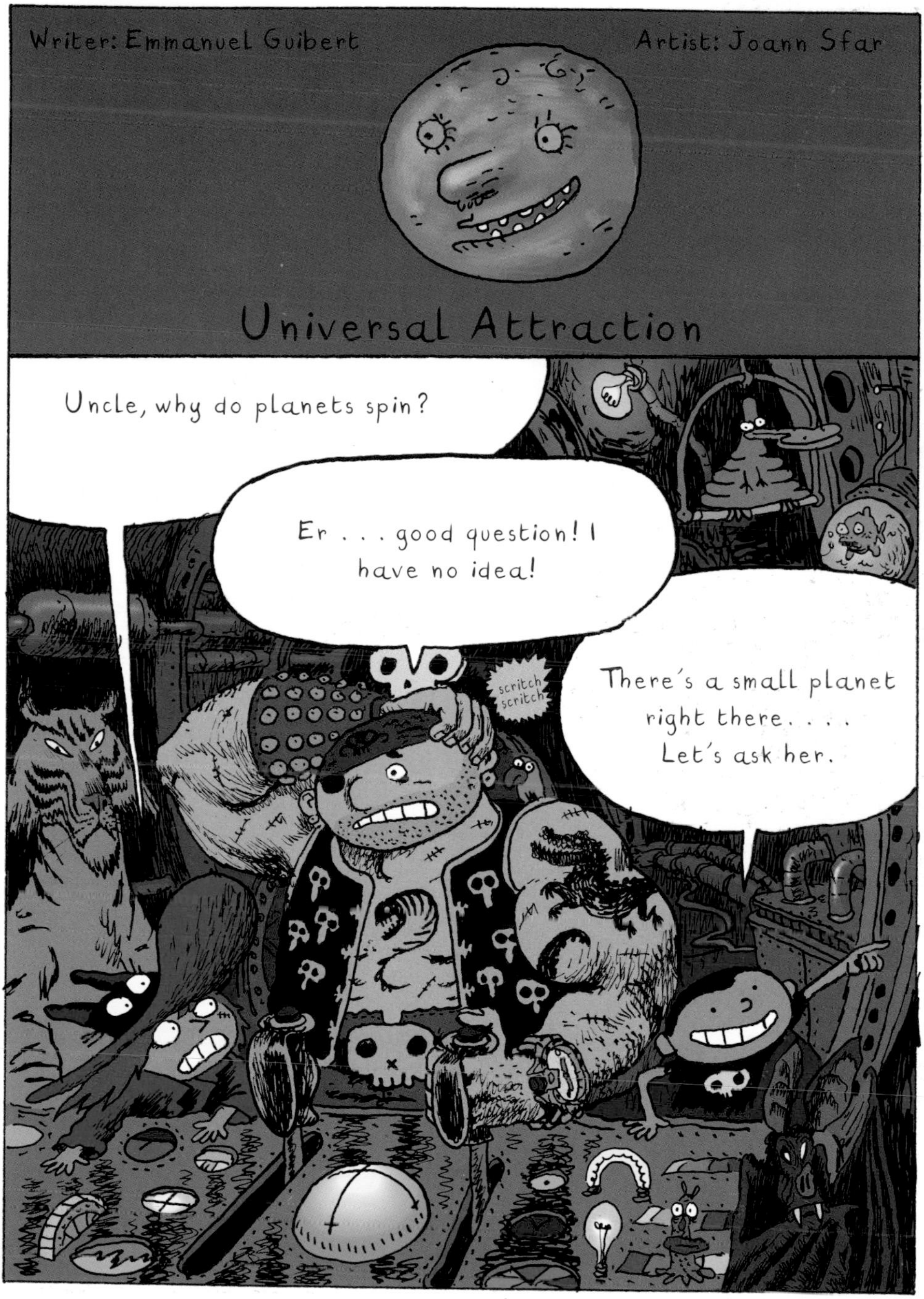
Writer: Emmanuel Guibert
Artist: Joann Sfar
Universal Attraction
Uncle, why do planets spin?
Er . . . good question! I have no idea!
scritch scritch
There's a small planet right there. . . . Let's ask her.

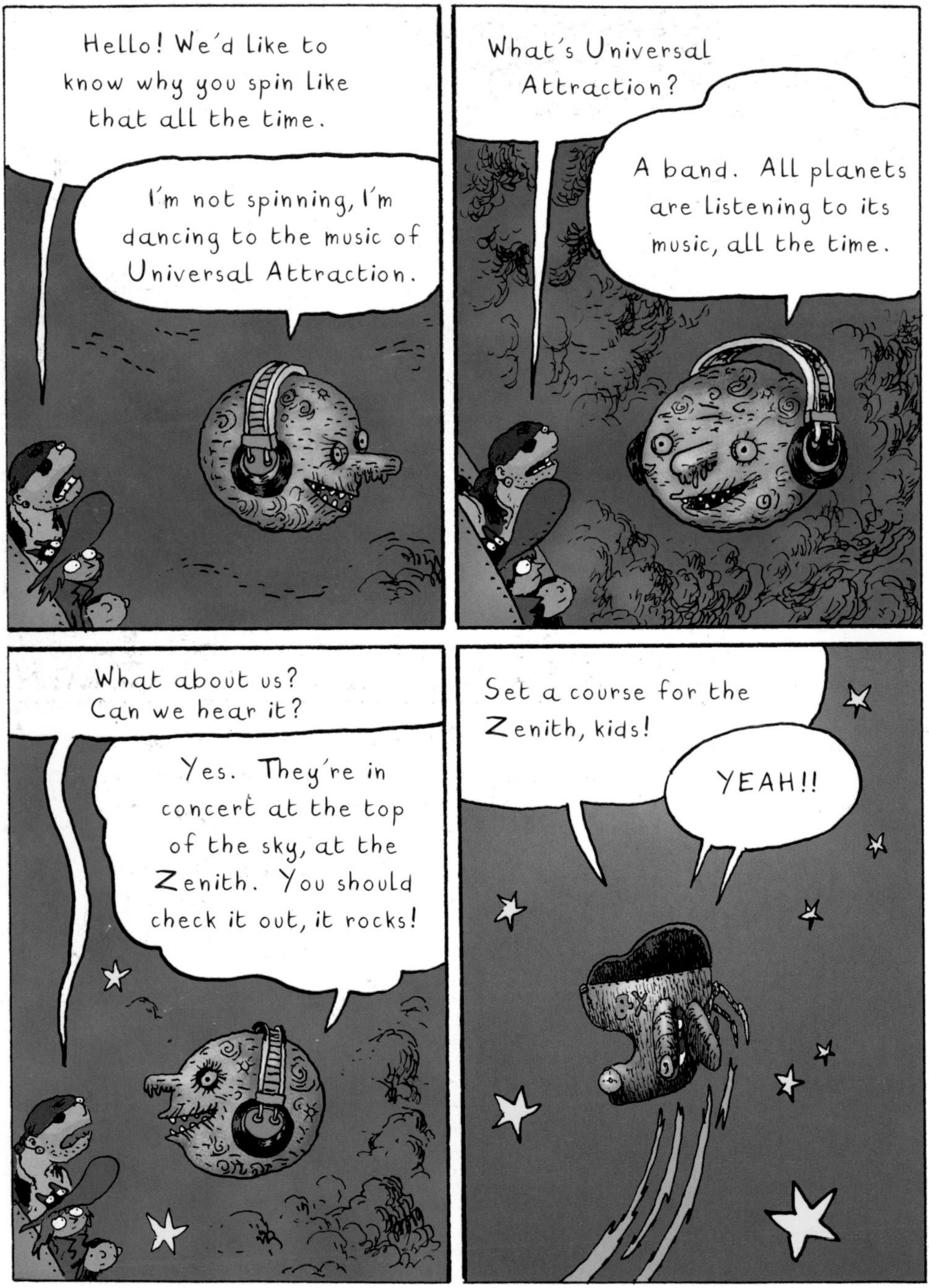
Hello! We'd like to know why you spin like that all the time.
I'm not spinning, I'm dancing to the music of Universal Attraction.
What's Universal Attraction?
A band. All planets are listening to its music, all the time.
What about us? Can we hear it?
Yes. They're in concert at the top of the sky, at the Zenith. You should check it out, it rocks!
Set a course for the Zenith, kids!
YEAH!!

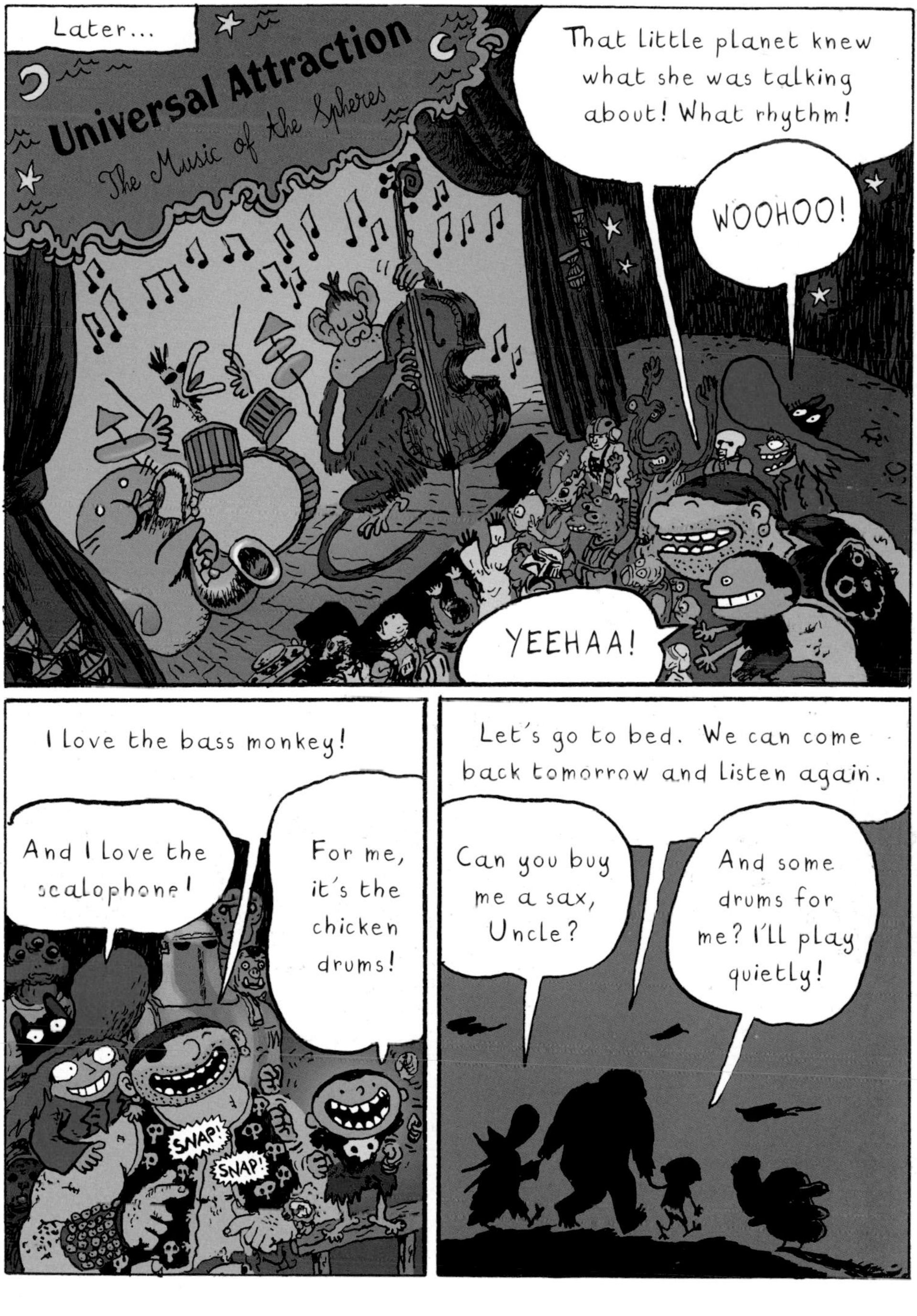
Later...
Universal Attraction
The Music of the Spheres
That little planet knew what she was talking about! What rhythm!
WOOHOO!
YEEHAA!
I love the bass monkey!
And I love the scalophone!
For me, it's the chicken drums!
SNAP!
SNAP!
Let's go to bed. We can come back tomorrow and listen again.
Can you buy me a sax, Uncle?
And some drums for me? I'll play quietly!

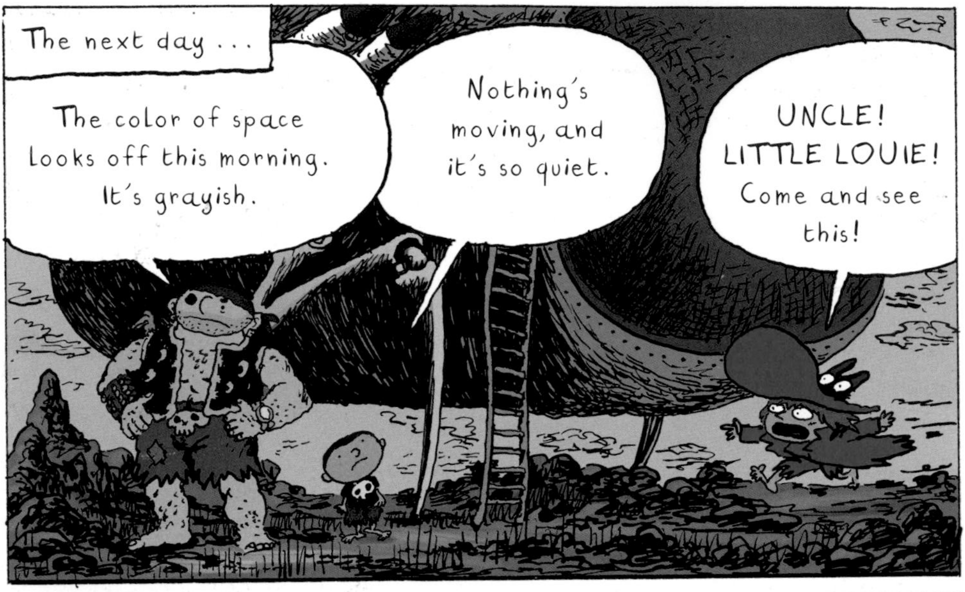
The next day . . .
The color of space looks off this morning. It's grayish.
Nothing's moving, and it's so quiet.
UNCLE! LITTLE LOUIE! Come and see this!

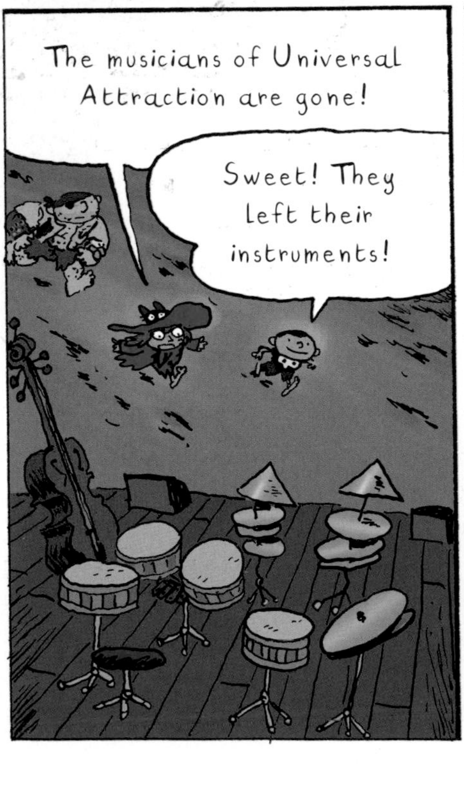
The musicians of Universal Attraction are gone!
Sweet! They left their instruments!

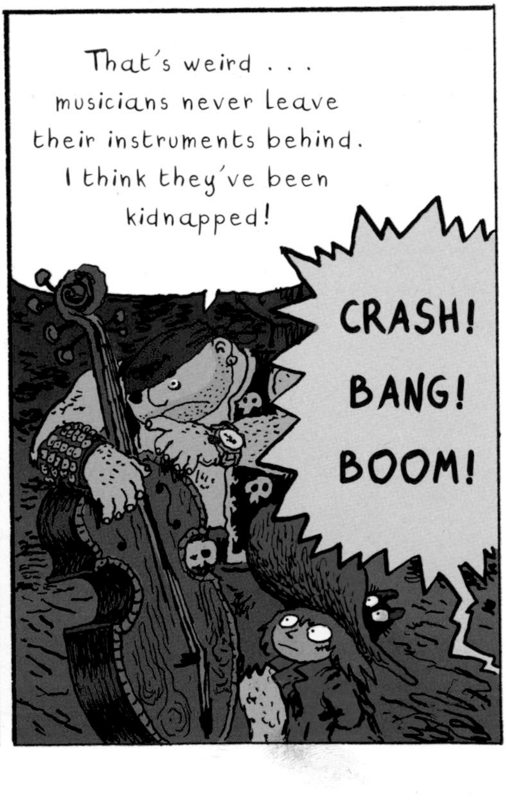
That's weird . . . musicians never leave their instruments behind. I think they've been kidnapped!
CRASH!
BANG!
BOOM!

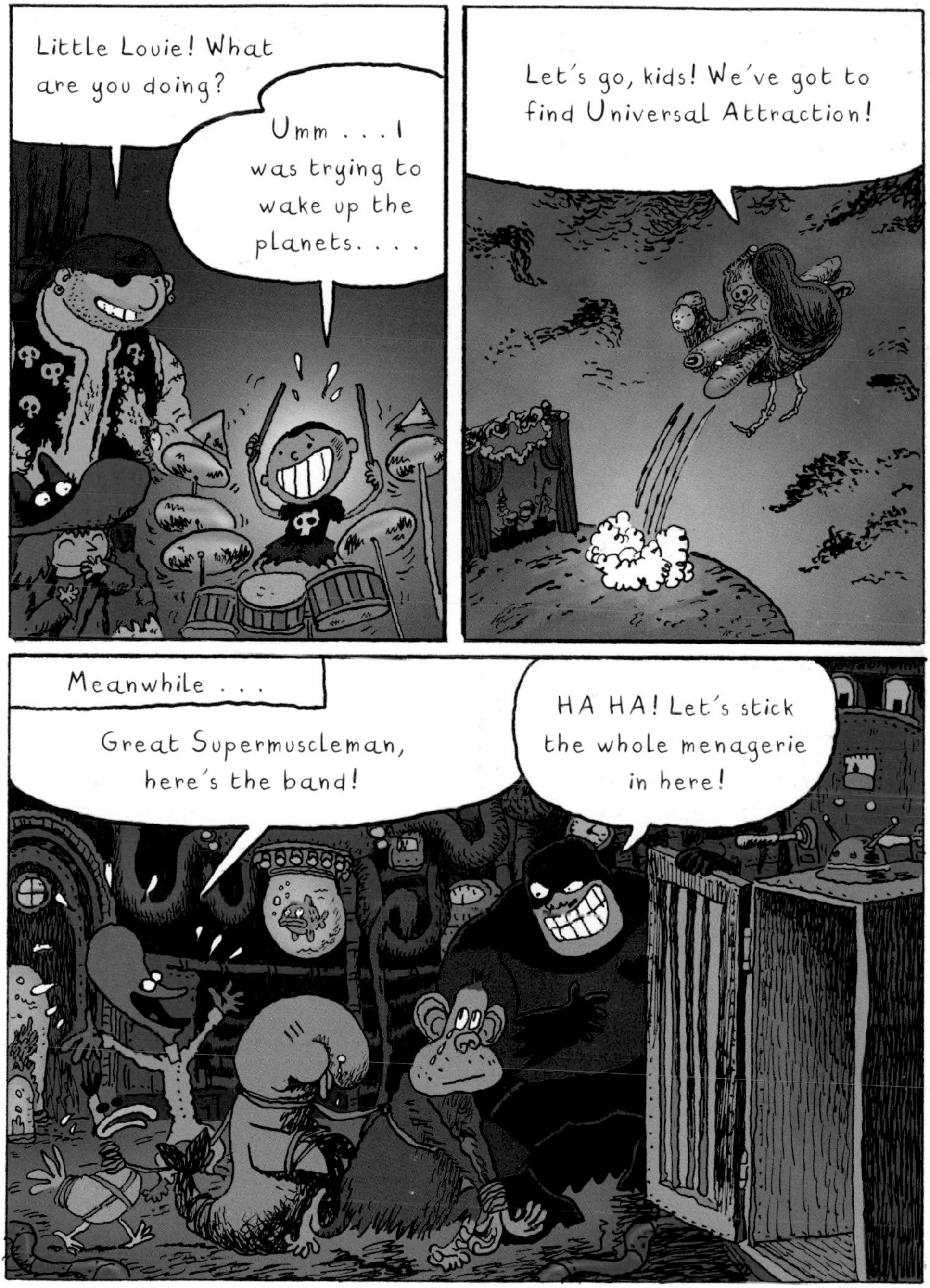
Little Louie! What are you doing?
Umm . . . I was trying to wake up the planets. . . .
Let's go, kids! We've got to find Universal Attraction!
Meanwhile . . .
Great Supermuscleman, here's the band!
HA HA! Let's stick the whole menagerie in here!

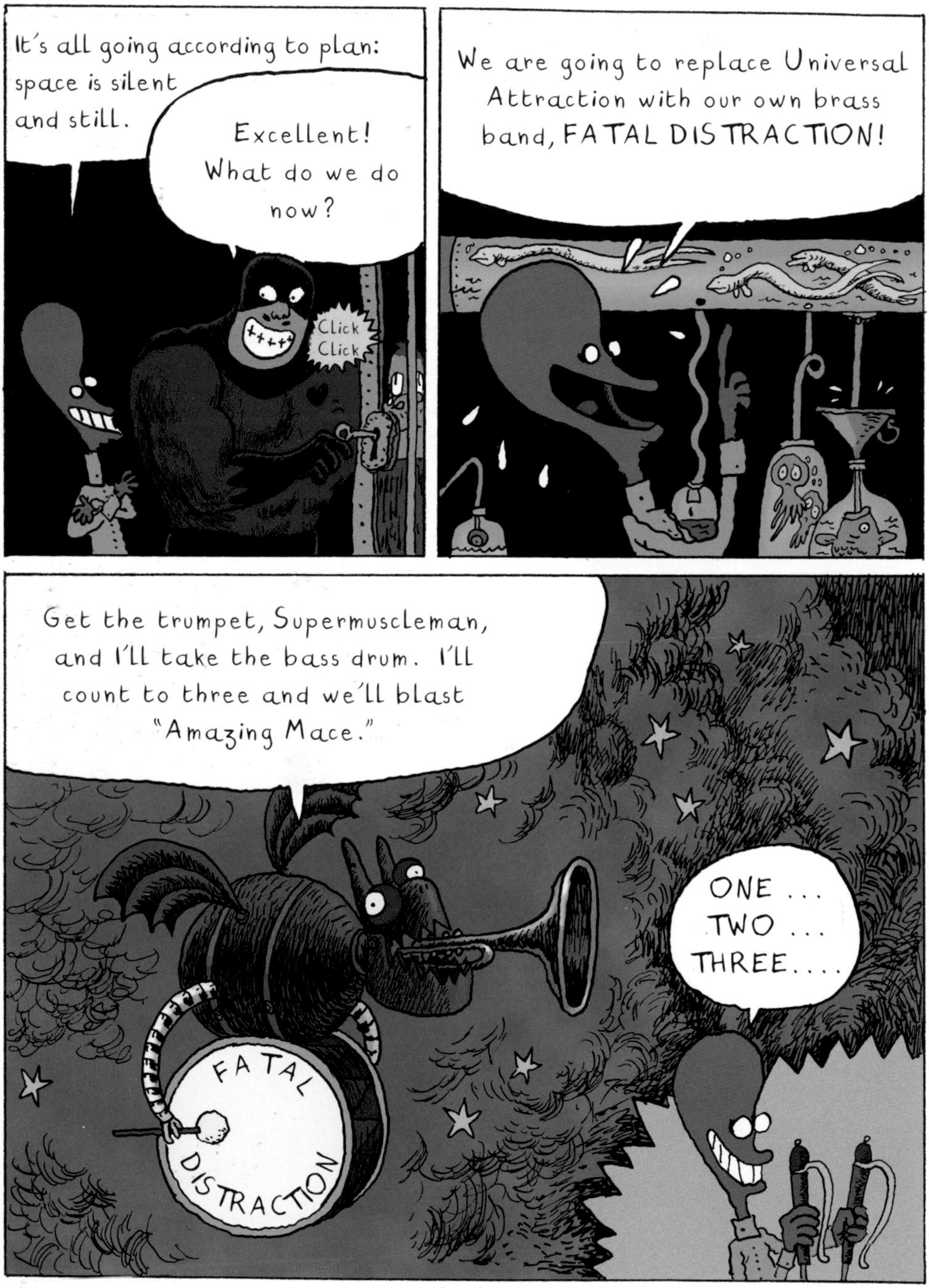
It's all going according to plan: space is silent and still.
Excellent! What do we do now?
Click Click
We are going to replace Universal Attraction with our own brass band, FATAL DISTRACTION!
Get the trumpet, Supermuscleman, and I'll take the bass drum. I'll count to three and we'll blast "Amazing Mace."
FATAL DISTRACTION
ONE ... TWO ... THREE....

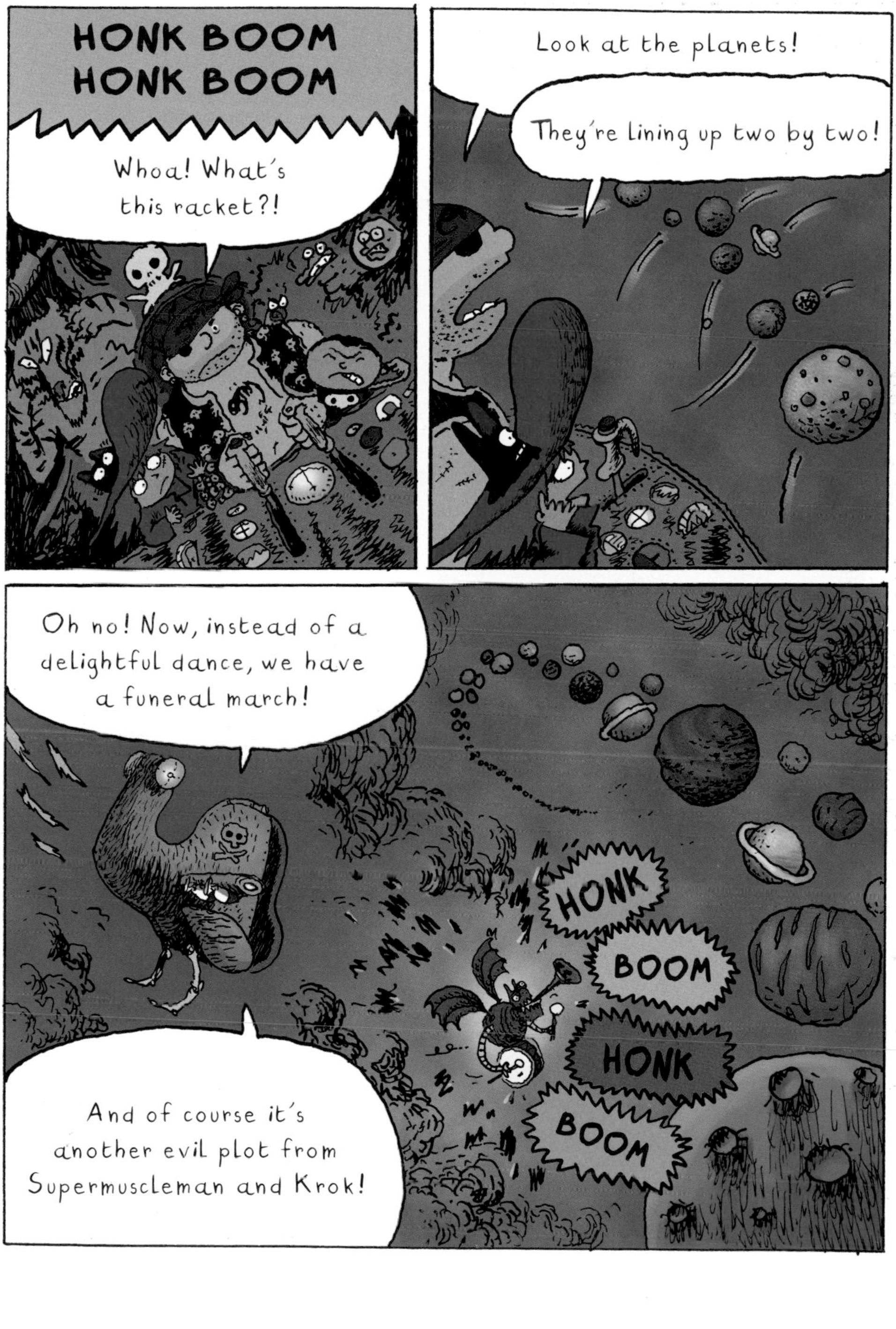
HONK BOOM HONK BOOM
Whoa! What's this racket?!
Look at the planets!
They're lining up two by two!
Oh no! Now, instead of a delightful dance, we have a funeral march!
HONK
BOOM
HONK
BOOM
And of course it's another evil plot from Supermuscleman and Krok!

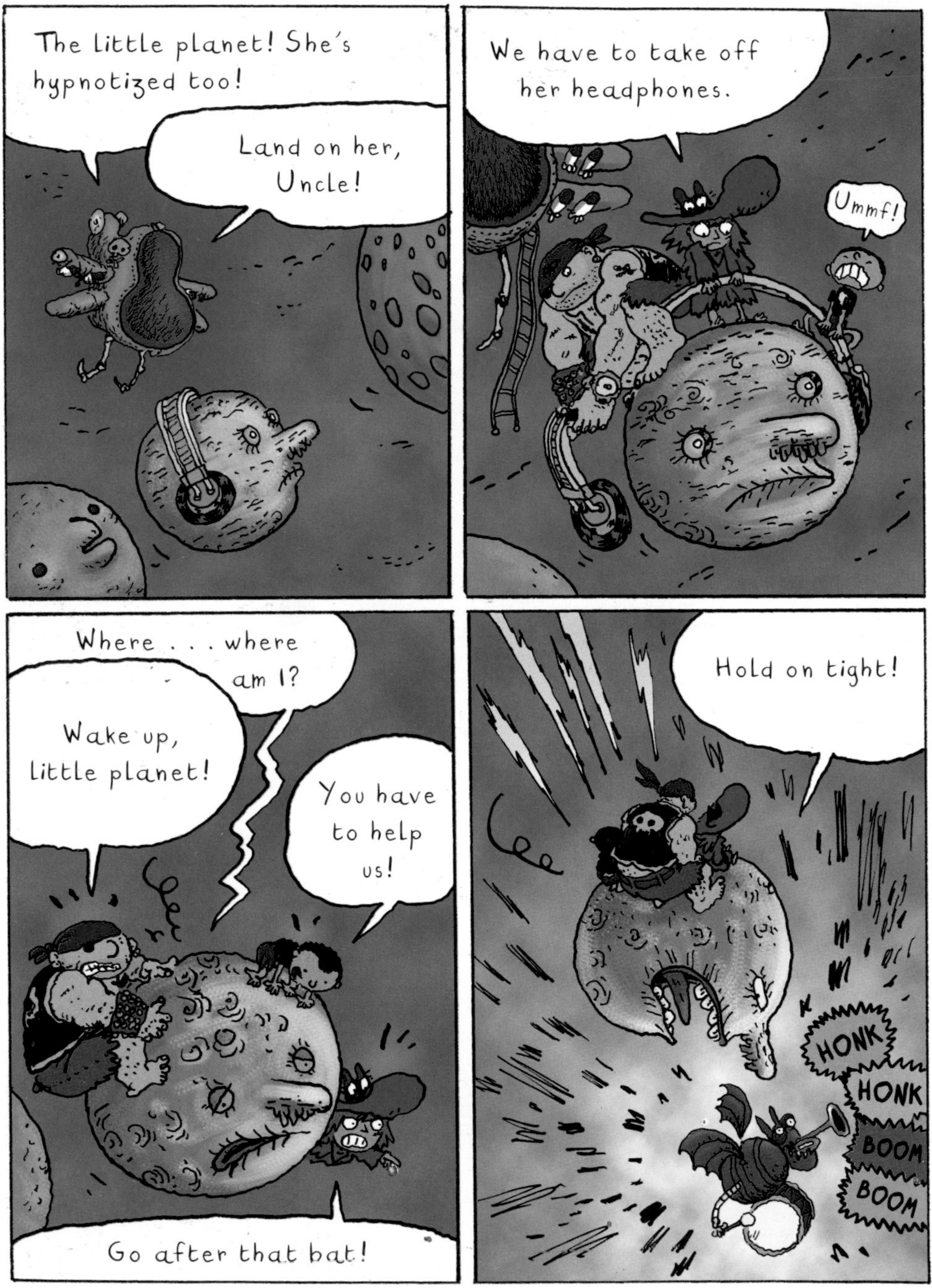
The little planet! She's hypnotized too!
Land on her, Uncle!
We have to take off her headphones.
Ummf!
Where . . . where am I?
Wake up, little planet!
You have to help us!
Go after that bat!
Hold on tight!
HONK
HONK
BOOM
BOOM

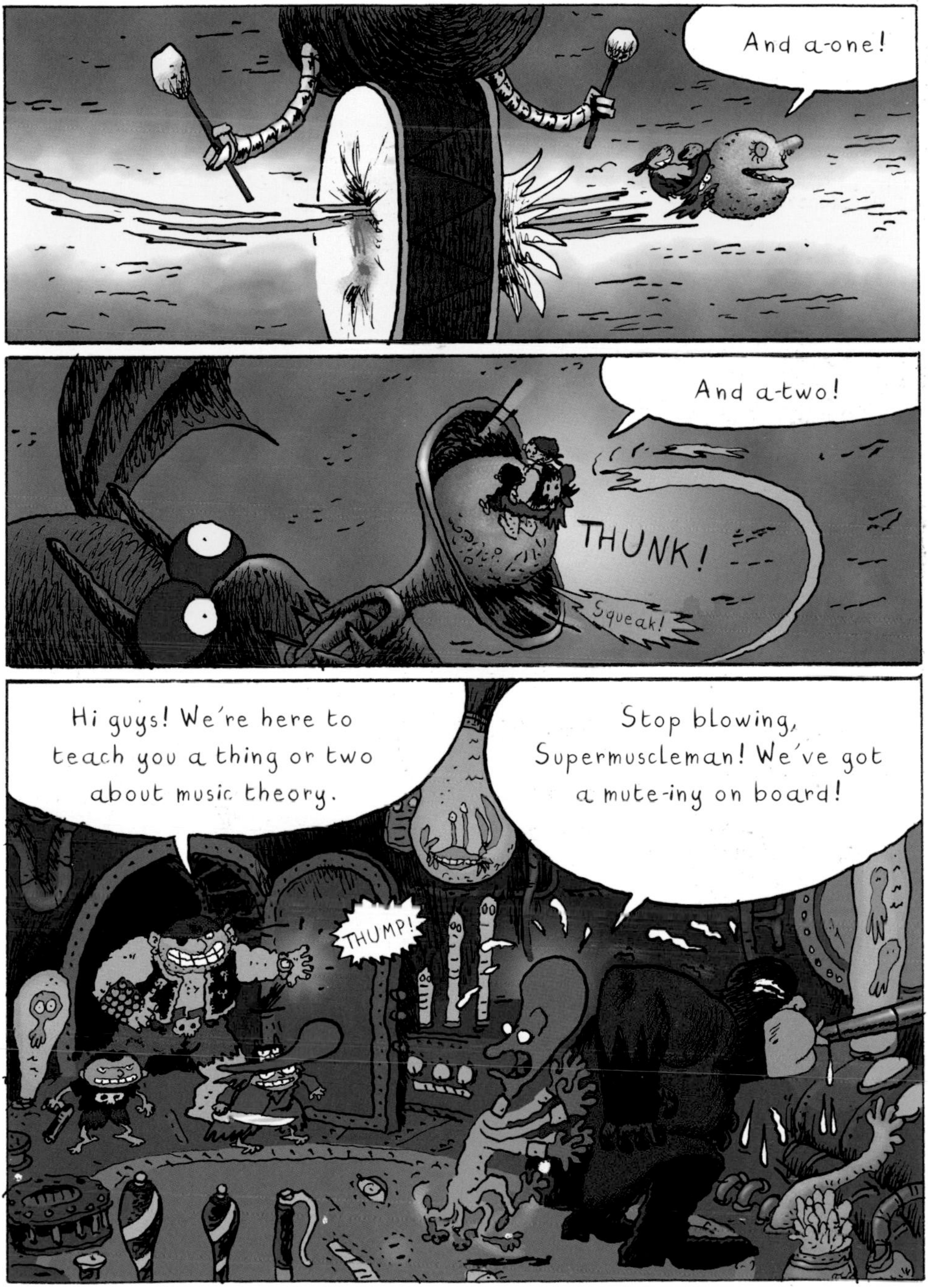
And a-one!
And a-two!
THUNK!
Squeak!
Hi guys! We're here to teach you a thing or two about music theory.
THUMP!
Stop blowing, Supermuscleman! We've got a mute-iny on board!

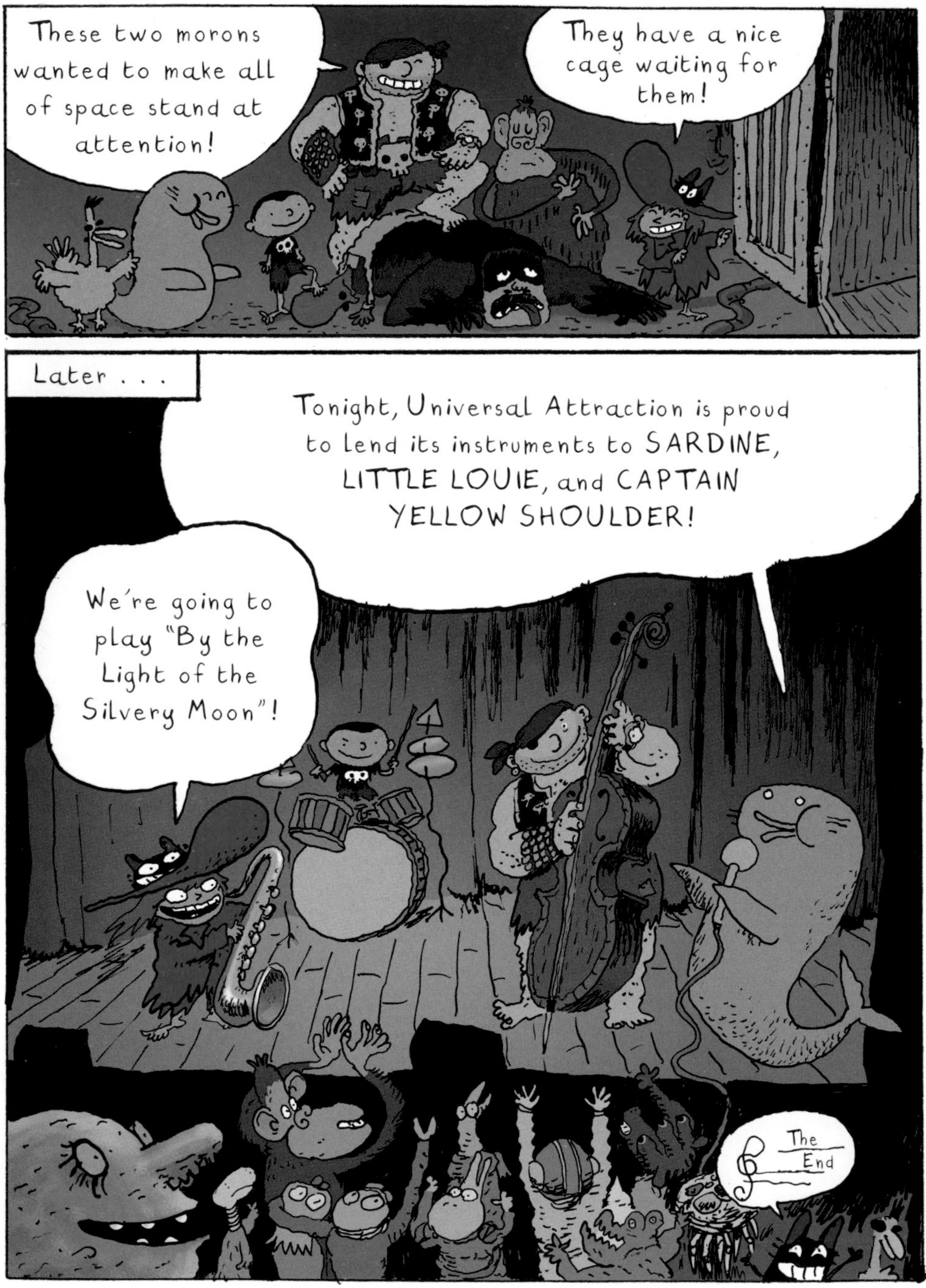
These two morons wanted to make all of space stand at attention!
They have a nice cage waiting for them!
Later . . .
Tonight, Universal Attraction is proud to lend its instruments to SARDINE, LITTLE LOUIE, and CAPTAIN YELLOW SHOULDER!
We're going to play "By the Light of the Silvery Moon"!
The End

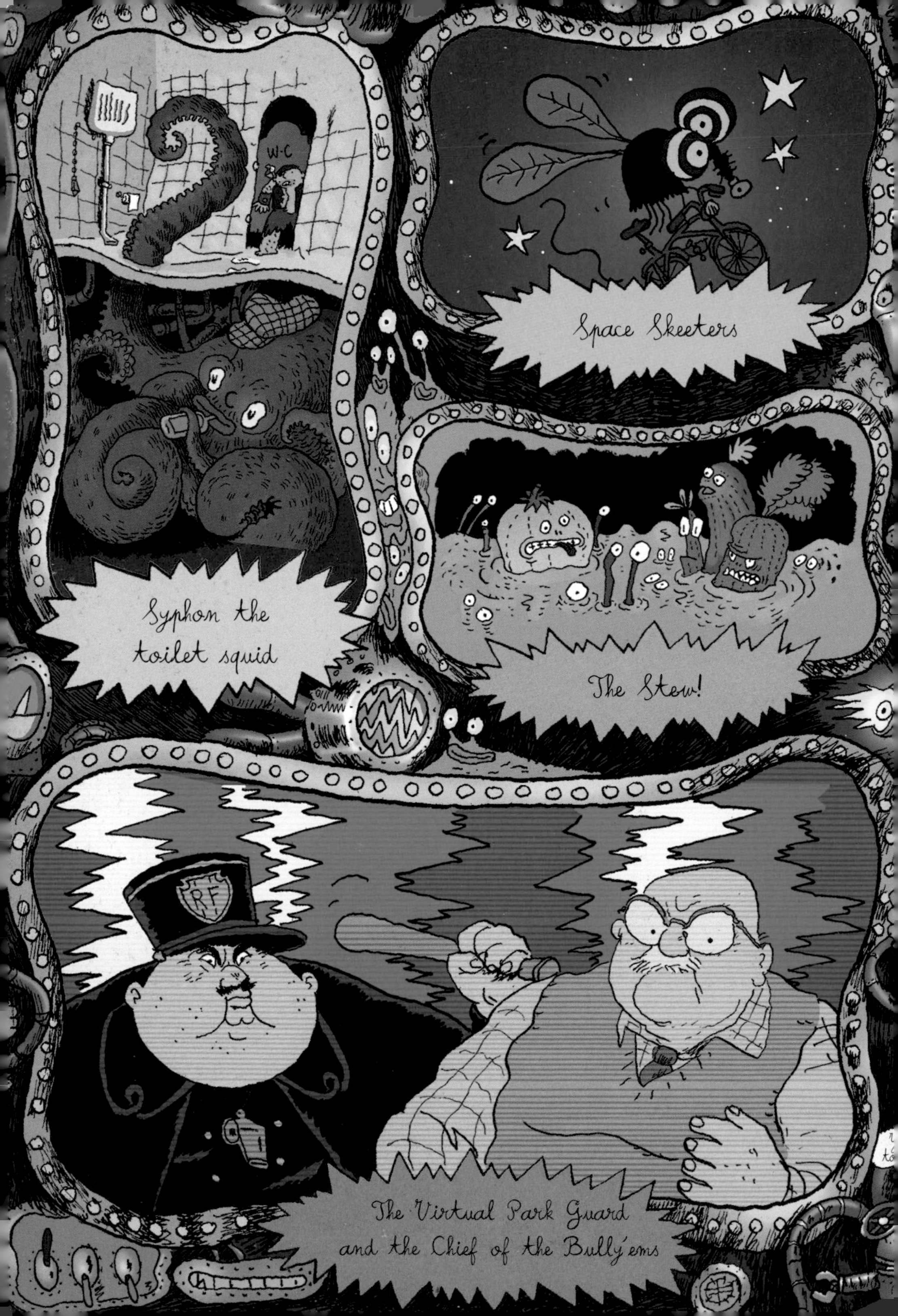
W·C
Syphon the toilet squid
Space Skeeters
The Stew!
RF
The Virtual Park Guard and the Chief of the Bully'ems

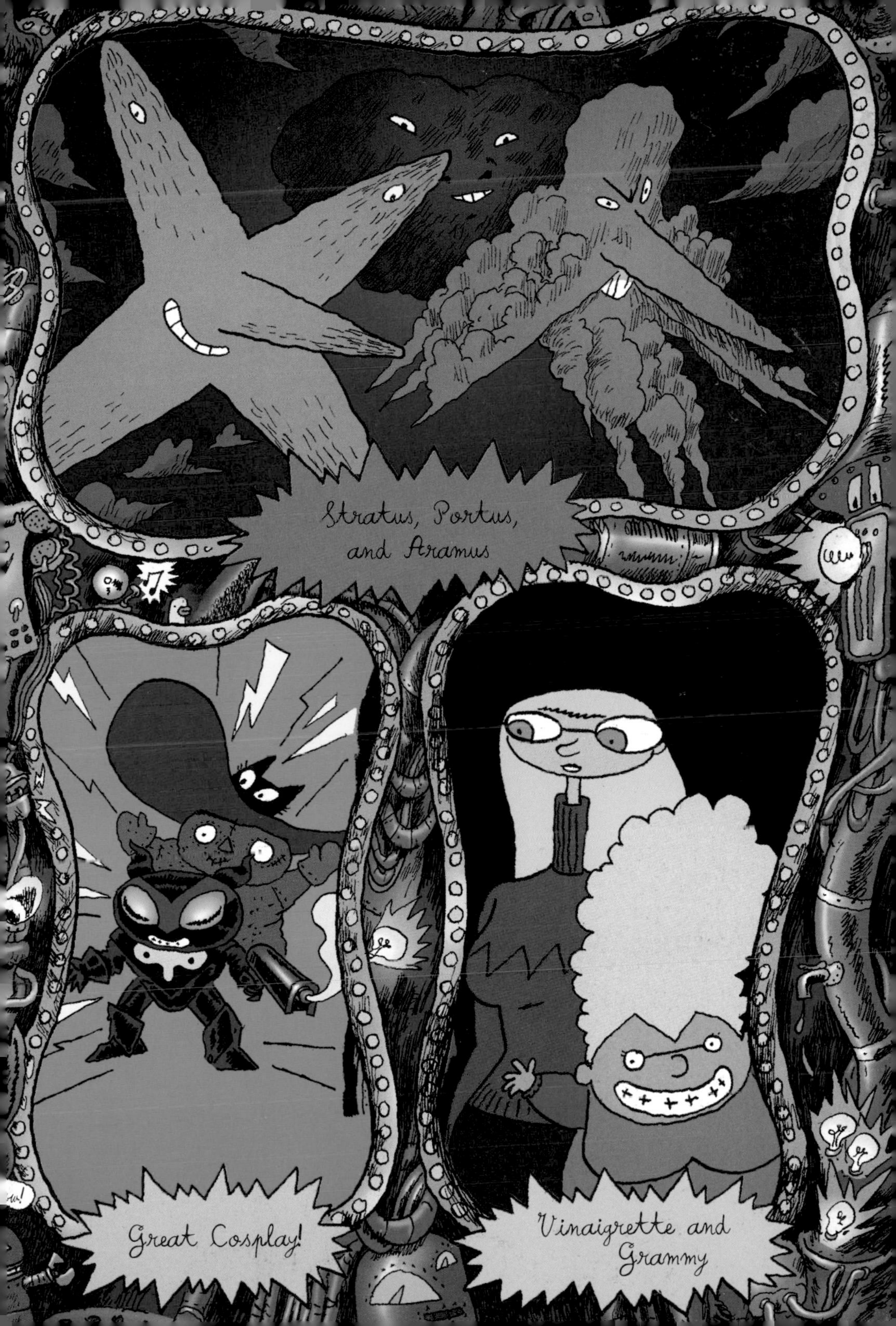

Stratus, Portus, and Aramus
Great Cosplay!
Vinaigrette and Grammy

First Second

New York & London

Copyright © 2002 by Bayard Éditions Jeunesse
English translation copyright © 2007 by First Second

Published by First Second
First Second is an imprint of Roaring Brook Press, a division of Holtzbrinck Publishing Holdings Limited
Partnership
175 Fifth Avenue, New York, NY 10010

Distributed in Canada by H. B. Fenn and Company Ltd.
Distributed in the United Kingdom by Macmillan Children's Books, a division of Pan Macmillan.

Originally published in France in 2002 under the titles *Le championnat de boxe* and *Le Capitaine Tout Rouge* by
Bayard Éditions Jeunesse, Paris.

Design by Danica Novgorodoff and Tanja Geis

Library of Congress Cataloging-in-Publication Data

Guibert, Emmanuel.
Sardine in outer space / Emmanuel Guibert and Joann Sfar ; translated by Sasha Watson ; colorist, Walter
Pezzali ; letterer, François Batet.-- 1st American ed.
p. cm.
Translations of stories originally published separately in French.
ISBN-13: 978-1-59643-128-7 (v. 3)
ISBN-10: 1-59643-128-8 (v. 3)

1. Graphic novels. I. Sfar, Joann. II. Title.
PN6747.G85A2 2006
741.5'944--dc22
2005021790

First Second books are available for special promotions and premiums.
For details, contact: Director of Special Markets, Holtzbrinck Publishers.

First American Edition April 2007

Printed in China

10 9 8 7 6 5 4 3 2 1

Some fine offerings from First Second for young readers of graphic novels...

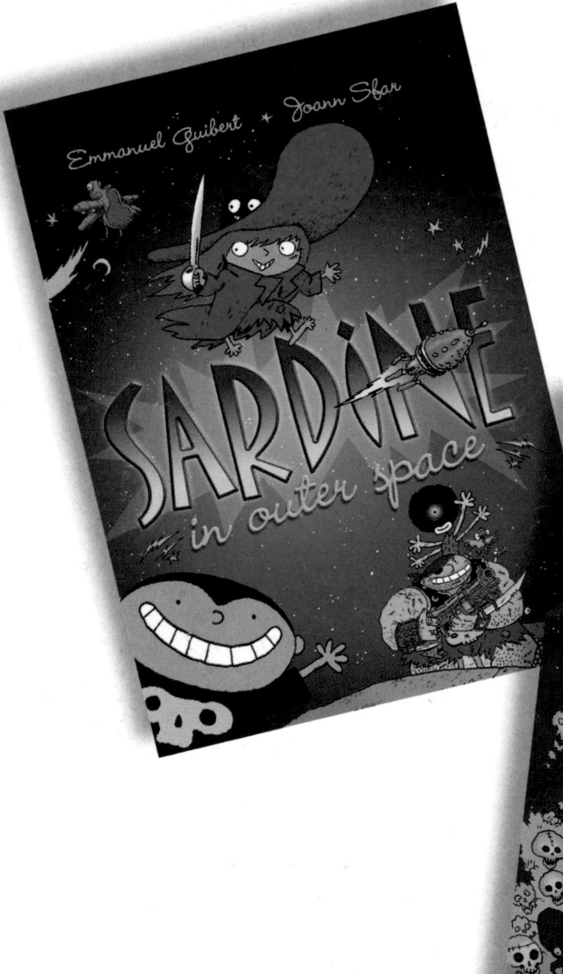
Emmanuel Guibert
Joann Sfar
SARDINE
in outer space

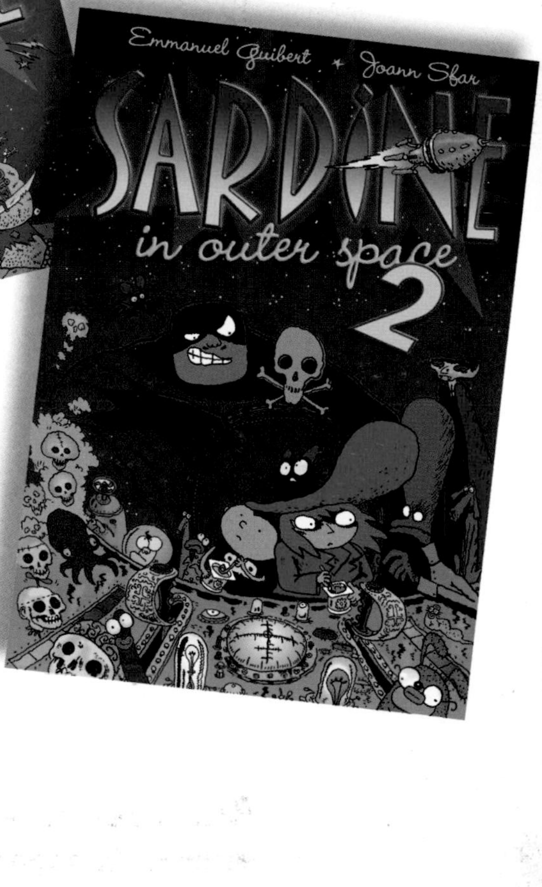
Emmanuel Guibert
Joann Sfar
SARDINE
in outer space
2

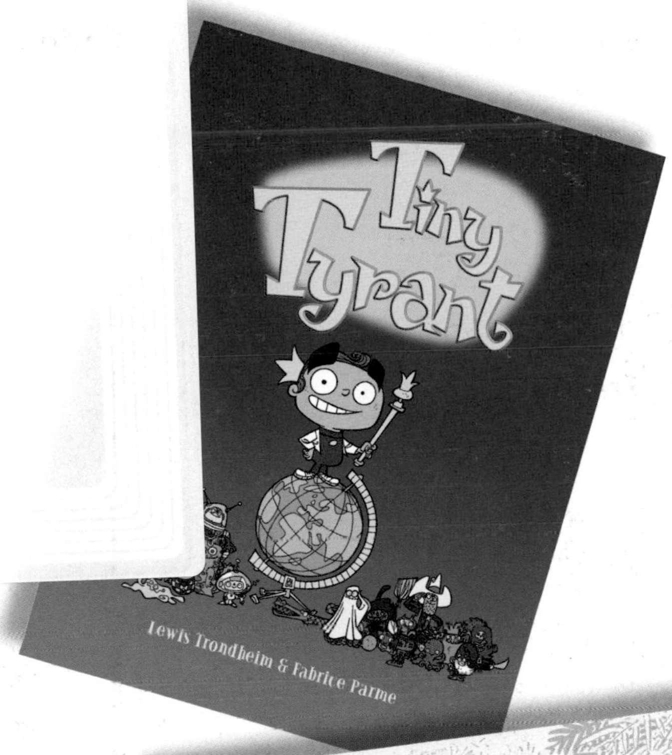
Tiny Tyrant
Lewis Trondheim & Fabrice Parme

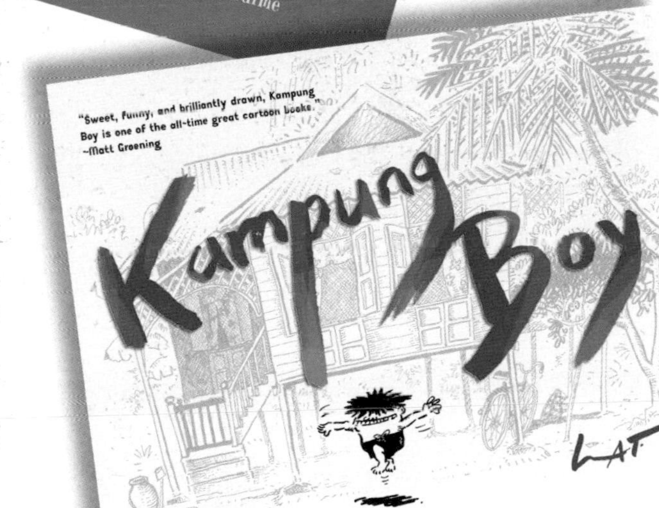
"Sweet, funny, and brilliantly drawn, Kampung Boy is one of the all-time great cartoon books."
~Matt Groening
Kampung Boy
LAT

And lots more to discover at

www.firstsecondbooks.com